Hound

Cerberus MC Book 7
Marie James

Copyright

Extras:

Cover design by: <u>Essen~tial Designs</u>

Synopsis:

My first job with the Cerberus MC was to grab a girl from a seedy bar. Easy money, right?

The moment I realized the blonde I was hunting wasn't around, I ended up captivated by a redhead dancing on the stage. With her striking features and sinful body, I knew she was trouble, but that didn't stop me from making her mine that night.

When I learned that she WAS the job, everything became clouded.

I was only looking for a one night stand, but when the dust settled and she ran, my only desire was to chase her.

Should I risk my job, and quite possibly my life, in order to have her?

Would she even stay if I caught her?

Acknowledgments

My amazing husband, you are first and foremost my biggest fan, and for that, I'm so incredibly blessed.

Laura Watson... my rock, my voice of reason, my cheerleader when I'm just not feeling up to it... thank you so much for supporting me!!

Brittney... thank you for *Hounding* me to write Cerberus 2.0.

Linda, thank you from the bottom of my dark soul for keeping my in line!!

Steph and MaRanda... you bitches are the best.

My amazing BETAS: Laura, Rachel B, Brenda, Sally, Angela, Shannon, Sadie thank you so much for your time looking over this manuscript!!

Mrs. Katie!! Thank you for the proofread!!

Michelle New, your teasers are amazing! Thanks for taking the time to work those up for me!

Foreword PR: both of you ladies are amazing! Thank you for being part of my team!

RRR PR: Welcome to the chaos!!

Shout out to Give Me Books. Kylie and the girls, you've helped me with almost every release, and I'm grateful for your support!

Bloggers. You keep the Indie world running smoothly, and I'm awed by the support you give each and every one of my books. If it weren't for you, no one would even know who Marie James is!

Readers!! ARC Team!! You amazing Stalkers!! Thank you for reading, sharing, and recommending! Thank you for reviewing and promoting! I appreciate each and every tag, like, and comment!

If you enjoy this book, please, leave a review and tell a friend. The book is loanable so send it to someone who's interested in reading! Discuss it.

Speak to one another about what you loved and what you hated, but more importantly, grab the next one!

Peace, love, and Southern sweet tea!

~Marie James

Chapter 1

Hound

"Best job ever," I mutter to myself as the topless waitress brings me another glass of whiskey.

Leaning in close, she runs her hand down my arm. "I don't normally offer private lap dances, but for you, I'll make an exception."

Acknowledging her with only a quick wave of my hand, I keep my focus on the stage. In front of me are the best pair of tits and abs tighter than I've ever seen on a woman before. I'm mesmerized by the red-headed seductress as she twirls around the pole in the center of the stage.

I toss back half of the whiskey in my glass but never take my eyes from the woman I plan to have before the sun comes up.

The girl I came here to find is nowhere to be seen. I did my job for the night, looking for the whiny kid who's giving her dad fits by not staying under his command. I search the front of the house as well as the back of the house where the girls are getting ready before taking it all off on the center stage. The brunette with bright blue eyes that I'm tasked with finding and removing is nowhere in the building. Determining that she must be off tonight, I let loose. Having a few drinks and watching the topless entertainment is only a perk of the mission. Of course, it's not recognizance, infiltration, and extraction, but there are benefits to this type of work as well.

The girls flitting around with bare tits and asses exposed by glittery thongs are nice to look at, but they each pale in comparison to the siren on the stage.

Hips rolling and long red hair following her like a smoky shadow dancing at her command, she's got the attention of every single man in the room, and I'm not immune to her charm. Hell, if all of my money wasn't tied up in savings accounts I'd write her a check for the entire sum just for the taste of her skin and the tight embrace of her cunt.

My mouth grows dry as I breathe heavily, short panting breaths taken in an attempt to keep my cock from busting through the seam of my suddenly too tight jeans.

Strippers are nothing new. Seventeen years in the Marine Corps traveling the world has led to more adventures with loose women than I can count, but there's something about this beauty that has me chomping at the bit to get her beneath me. The great thing about underpaid whores is that for the right amount, they'll let you do just about anything to them. I imagine this one will be no different.

Paying for sex used to make my skin crawl, but bedding a professional woman, who will have no expectations when the sun rises gained appeal as I got older. Leaving broken hearts in my wake is never my intention, and lying to a woman just to fuck her, I've decided, is more messed up than paying for a hole to plow for the night.

She hits her stride, the deep bass of the song ricocheting off the walls, the hoots and hollers becoming almost unbearable. Enthralled by the sway of her hips, just like every other man in here, I don't notice when the song ends, and she bends to gather the bills tossed at her feet.

Moving my eyes from the sway of her firm tits to look into her eyes, I'm met with a soulless, dead stare. She's definitely not one of the dancers who get off on dozens of men fawning over her naked body. I wish I could say I feel sorry for her, that seeing her misery so clear but ignored by every other guy in front of her will make me change my mind, but it doesn't. We all have demons we have to fight, and she's no different. Since I have my own shit to deal with and things to prepare for in the near future, I can't be bothered to concern myself with her issues. What I can do is make her come like a freight train and give her enough cash to make it easier to leave this life...if that's what she chooses.

When her eyes lock with mine, a tingle of anticipation rushes down my spine and straight to my cock. The swipe of her tongue over her full lips as she takes me in is enough to make the tip of my cock thicken and weep for her. I wink, pretending to be as unaffected as I can and mouth 'soon' to her. She's flushed from the exertion of her dance, but it doesn't stop her cheeks from pinking even more. She gives me a slight nod, acknowledging that our plans for the evening include each other before she stands and exits the stage with enough swing to her hips to keep every man in the building pining for her.

The DJ announces that "Orphan Annie" will be back at the top of the hour, forcing me to look down at my watch. Contemplating if I should find and fuck her now or wait for another show on the stage, I think about her odd choice of stage name. The little, redheaded girl with no family, as the story goes is, adopted by a mean woman who is never short of voicing her dislikes even after her husband, Daddy Warbucks comes into the picture.

I huff a small laugh, thinking about the storyline in today's age and why a woman no older than twenty-five would pick it. It makes me wonder if she was abused. Did *her* Daddy Warbucks take advantage and that was the real reason for the discord with the wife? Is she into older men?

That thought makes me smile considering I'm probably ten years her senior. Attraction to older men would benefit me in the persuasion part of the night. I shake my head. Honestly, it wouldn't matter. The wad of cash in my pocket ensures I'll be inside of her regardless.

Draining my whiskey, I wait for her next performance. Once again, as she makes her way on stage, I can't pull my eyes from the glistening skin of her body. The sweat dripping between her tits, rolling down the tight muscles of her stomach makes my mouth dry no matter how much amber liquid I pour down my throat. "Bad Girlfriend" by Theory of a Deadman blares from the surround sound as she keeps perfect tempo to the beat.

Her eyes find mine, holding them captive. Her emerald eyes bewitch me as I consider an attempt to access those savings accounts I thought about earlier in the night. Paid whore or not, I know one night with this temptress will never be enough.

She seems to be the headliner, the one woman who draws the men in, which means, from my past experience, her night is over. She's closing out the stage with one final dance as the waitress who's been serving me all night tells me it's last call.

Declining the offer for a final drink, I head to the door before she walks off of the stage. I wait in the shadows near the rear exit listening to the men grumble as they're escorted out the front and wait for my redheaded beauty to make an appearance.

The wait is so long that I question the interaction between us, question the sincerity I saw in her wide green eyes. She's the perfect tease, making me think she wants me just as I'm sure she does with every man who walks through the dingy front doors of The Minge Palace.

I'm near giving up, realizing that Orphan Annie is more trouble than she's worth when the back door opens and a flash of red exits the building before laughing at something someone inside says before it closes again. I step out of the shadows when she's less than a handful of feet in front of me. I expect her to startle, to clutch at her chest in an attempt to ease her pounding heart. Instead, she shocks me by staring directly at me as if I'm her puppet and waiting in the filthy alley is exactly what she expects. I clench my fists at the idea that she thinks she can have the upper hand.

"I've been waiting," I growl, loving the pink that returns to her cheeks.

"I searched for you out front," she whispers closing the distance between the two of us and running her small hands over my heaving chest.

"I figure you'd want the cloak of darkness even though your screams of orgasm will echo down the alleyway."

"So confident in your ability to please."

Her hands leave my chest and run across my back as she circles me. I'm her prey tonight, even more confident in her power than she displayed on the stage earlier. No matter how much I want to fight it, how much I want to prove to her that she'll be taking my cock as I see fit, I know without a doubt that Orphan Annie is going to use me and have me begging for more.

"Care to make a bet?" I offer as she stands in front of me once again.

Petite yet solid, she looks up at me as I imagine all the ways I can easily take her.

"No," she pants, her pupils so big in the moonlight I question the small halo of blue circling them.

Didn't she have green eyes on the stage?

I don't give it a second thought when her tiny hand covers but a fraction of my cock over my jeans.

"You want to stand out here making bets?" She gives me a squeeze tight enough to make me groan. "Or do you want to fuck?"

"Brazen little thing aren't you?"

I drop my hands to my sides as she fumbles with my belt and the zipper on my jeans. The relief is immediate as she pulls the denim back and my cock springs free.

"Mmm." The tiny noise from her mouth not only makes me jump in her hands but forces me to wonder what that noise will feel like if I push my cock down her throat.

"Another time," I hiss.

"What?" she asks confused just as I lift her and turn her with her back against the cold brick wall.

"Enough talk." The insistent ache in my cock doesn't leave much room for anything else.

Urging her legs around my hips, I can see the pain the stretch is causing as she tries to get them all the way around me. She doesn't have a hope of doing it though. I'm twice her size and ready to handle her, to position her any way I see fit.

Her skirt rides high exposing the glistening slit of her pink cunt.

"Dirty whore," I hiss as my fingers move the wetness up to lubricate the friction of my fingers on her clit. "You came out here prepared to fuck me?"

Her eyes slam shut, a tiny whimper escaping her lips as she rolls her hips against my hand trying to find her pleasure. Without warning, I slip two thick fingers inside of her, watching her face for the response I know she'll give. Eyes dashing open, hers find mine.

"So fucking tight," I praise. "If two fingers are all you can take, there's no hope my cock will fit inside of you."

Lips parting, she tilts her head to the side. "Give me more," she begs.

I withdraw and delve back in with three fingers, working them in and out, preparing her as best I can.

"Please," she whimpers, near the edge I refuse to let her fall over.

"I'm going to hurt you," I warn as I pull free from her tight pussy.

"Please," she repeats.

Against better judgment, I replace my fingers with the head of my cock and slam home.

She screams, half in pain, the other half in pleasure.

"Oh God."

"Fuck, Annie," I grunt as I pull back only to slam forward again.

"It's too much," she complains but relents when my thumb begins to strum over the tight bundle of nerves at the apex of her thighs.

"That's it," I urge.

I'm certain her back is going to have abrasions from shoulders to tailbone, but the consideration isn't something I have to give as she clamps on my cock, the tightest thing I've felt since I fucked a virgin in high school. The quick thought of that night, so many years ago, makes me realize my mistake, the same one I made then. However fucked-up and consequences be damned, I can't stop the ache of release already teasing my balls. My head flexes back, my orgasm becoming a living thing under my skin as I pulse inside of her. Bare. No condom.

When I'm done, I release my hold on her and stumble backward. I can't even look at her. I'm so disappointed in myself for the whiskey I drank that allowed the haze of my senses to make such a monumental mistake. I fumble with my jeans until I finally get them up and zipped, not even concerning myself with my belt.

"You said you'd make me come," she coos in front of me. "But you came too quickly for me to get mine. Want to go back to your place to finish what you started?"

"No," I hiss, keeping my eyes down as I shove my hand into my pocket and pull out a wad of cash.

She crosses her arms over her chest when I offer it to her.

"I'm not a whore," she growls, and it's then that I find her eyes.

"You just fucked me in a filthy alley after dancing for dozens of men on a stripper pole." I shove the money into her hands. "Believe me, Annie; you're as close to a whore as it comes."

"You motherfucker!"

"That," I say pointing at the cash she reluctantly holds in her hand, "is for the abortion if my stupid ass put that shit into motion, or for your bus ticket out of this fucking town, because so help me God if I caught something antibiotics won't get rid of from that filthy snatch of yours, I'll come back and kill you."

Her eyes narrow in challenge, and it gives me hope that a VD isn't going to be in my future.

Not giving her a second glance, I make my way out of the alley and stumble back to my shitty hotel room. I try to push her from my mind as I fall on the bed and pass out.

When morning comes, and the incessant chirping of text messages on my phone is frequent enough to drive me mad, she's still on my mind. I almost feel guilty about the blood on my cock, knowing I was too rough with her. I check each one of my piercings, knowing that one of the barbells must have cut her, but they're all intact.

The regret doesn't set in, however, until I check my messages and see the first one from Blade which was sent a mere two hours after I left Annie in that disgusting alley without concern as to whether or not she'd make it home safely.

Blade: I told you to find Georgia Anderson. Not fuck her like a whore in the alley.

So much for my new life. That redheaded woman from last night just fucked me harder than I fucked her last night.

Chapter 2

Gigi

"Shit," I hiss when I roll over in bed. My whole body aches, but the scratches on my back and the thrumming between my legs are my greatest concern.

The time on my cell phone may say ten after noon, indicating I've been in bed for no less than seven hours, but I feel like I haven't slept at all. I scrub at my eyes with the backs of my hands and twist my neck in both directions until the satisfying crack echoes around my shitty, one-room apartment.

Feeling dehydrated, as I always do after a night of dancing and cocaine, I reach for the half-empty water bottle on the coffee table in front of the crappy couch that doubles as my bed. I down it, wincing once again as I climb off of the couch and head to the sink to refill it.

Once the bottle is filled, I turn with my hips against the counter. The wad of cash that asshole gave me last night mocks me from the opposite counter. I could've tossed it back at him or thrown it to the damp, trash-riddled ground, but only a fool would do something as ridiculous as that.

Instead, I came home, feeling like the whore he suspects and counted it. Twice.

It's been a long time since I had access to that much money, and I couldn't help letting my mind wander to the next place I could go. I'm always moving, always planning for the next city, praying it's better than the last, but knowing better.

It doesn't have to be this way.

This thought makes my eyes shift from my ill-gotten gains to the empty cocaine baggie sitting beside it.

I'm a social user. That's the lie I tell myself right before I inhale the poison and take the stage at the club. I allow myself to believe it most days because I don't use on my nights off. Those are spent curled in a ball, feeling like total shit, while thinking of nothing but the better life I walked away from. It's in those moments that home doesn't seem so bad. It's those moments that the controlling hand of my father and his expectations don't seem like a reason to run at all.

I squeeze my eyes shut, letting the water soothe my sore throat and try not to once again feel bitter for turning into the twin that no one can love. I envy Ivy and her perfect grades. She's always been the one they can be proud of, while I remain the constant thorn in their side and the disappointment of all of the Cerberus kids.

The alarm on my phone chimes, telling me whether I want to or not, I have to get to work. At least tonight I'll get off at a decent hour since I'm covering another girl's shift. Working my off days as often as possible ensures I can move on quicker. Although not my intention when I walked up to the stranger in the alley, the money he gave me gets me a lot closer to my next city than I could get working at The Minge Palace in two weeks. I cringe at the name and head to the shower.

After my shower, I towel off and dress. With the red wig in place, I leave my apartment and walk down the street to the club so filthy even the low lights can't disguise how disgusting it is.

My throat, still dry from the cocaine and cigarette smoke from last night, only grows even more irritated as I make my way to the small corner I share with ten other women. The owner's office is ten times this big, but he expects us to walk on top of each other to get ready for the stage, going so far as to bitch and yell when we're late because we're waiting for others to get ready. I've been dancing here for two months. In two weeks I should have enough to leave. Dallas isn't my ideal geographical location, but I hope to make it to Austin soon. Sixth Street, or somewhere near there would at least bring younger, hotter guys; not the geriatric fucks that have made The Minge Palace their home away from home.

I hate the way the dull lights on the vanity make my skin look almost green. I hate the amount of makeup the owner requires us to wear so our faces stand out against the stage lights. As if the men are looking at our faces. They may glance at our mouths and wonder what it would be like to have our lips on their cocks, but our full faces aren't important to them.

I hate that I'm getting damned near naked on stage for money. But most of all I hate that I was running behind today and wasn't able to swing by Javi's place to grab another baggie of coke. Dancing sober is up there with a root canal or surgery without anesthesia. It's brutal and almost impossible to suffer through.

I look over at Dolly. The stage name was given to her in reference to her incredibly huge, albeit natural, breasts. The sneer she gives me tells me that asking for a bump would be fruitless, so I don't even bother.

I steel my spine and wait in the cluttered wing just off the stage. After shaking my hands out, a futile attempt to stop them from shaking, I tighten the knot on the front of my shirt. I mean, if you can call a sequined bikini top with Velcro at the neck and back a shirt.

I don't bother to lotion myself up at this club. The owner keeps it so damn hot in here it's a wonder I can control my movements on the pole. His reasoning is that if the men are warm, they're also thirsty. He makes money on the liquor and cover charge. He reminds us constantly just how gracious he is to let us keep our tips.

I roll my neck, but the soreness from my lack of sleep prevails. I hate myself for taking this extra shift even if it's nice to go to work while the sun is still out.

Peaches makes her way off stage, giving me the same sneer Dolly did just moments ago. Every one of the other dancers hates me. I usually find at least one woman at the club I'm working in that's friendly. The only person who pays me any attention in this shit hole is the owner, who talks to my tits more than he talks to my face and Gerardo who's creepy and makes me think he's picturing himself peeling my skin layer by layer when he looks at me.

The intro to Pour Some Sugar on Me is my cue to hit my knees and crawl out on the stage toward the pole. Mom and Dad always played this kind of music while we were growing up. As much as I love this song, I know I strip to it as a silent slap in the face to them.

Look at me now, Dad. And you thought you could dictate my life.

The men in the audience sit straighter, and I realize that this is the exact reason the other girls hate me. These guys here pay attention to me. They want the attention, the salivating mouths, catcalls, and horrendous suggestions of what I could be doing to them. I despise it. Dancing, stripper pole or not, is a means to an end. The only problem is, I'm so far from the end, considering I have no idea what my long-term goals are, that there's no conclusion to the degradation in the near future.

I tried waitressing. The money is shit, and even with clothes on, the men in the seedy diners I was able to gain employment and be paid under the table are just as vulgar as the men here.

When Def Leppard sings "loosen up" my top comes off. "Squeeze a little more" has my hands fondling my own breasts. I get way more tips when I touch myself. I trail my fingers from my lips, trying not to cringe when an awful taste fills my mouth, between my breasts and over the soreness left by the stranger last night. I revel in the discomfort, turning myself on for the first time since I first wrapped my legs around a stripper pole.

By the time I'm two-thirds of the way through the song and swinging around the pole, I'm turned on to the point the heat in the room actually cools my damp skin. When the final hard beats of the song ring out through the room, I'm on my knees barely able to catch my breath. I shouldn't be concerned about my breathing because it stops completely when I meet the dark, angry as hell eyes of the stranger from last night.

Before I can push myself up to stand and collect the wads of cash on the stage, he reaches in and jerks me off of my feet.

"The fuck are you doing, psycho?" Tossed over his shoulder, the ineffectual hits of my small fists against his muscled back don't even faze him.

"The hell, man?"

Gerardo. Thank goodness, I think but remember just how creepy he is. I'm torn, leaning more toward going with the stranger than owing the creepy ass bartender any favors.

"Move, dick face." My captor's words echo against my own body.

"Chad left me in charge tonight," Gerardo says as if it means anything to this big bastard.

Gerardo is shoved to the side, and I push against my stranger's ass with my hands to look up at him as we walk away.

"He's going to be pissed, Annie."

"Tell him I had a stomach ache. I'll be back tomorrow night."

"Like fuck you will," my jailer says with a swift, sharp slap to my bare ass.

I should be scared when a man I don't know, a man who treated me like shit last night, carries me out of The Minge Palace. I should be terrified when he slides me off of his shoulder and into a darkly tinted car smelling faintly of his cologne and stale cigarettes.

I may have made horrible grades in school, but my instincts have always been spot on. I knew the second I looked in this man's eyes last night, even with the clear intent that he wanted to fuck me written all over his face, that he isn't the type of man to hurt a woman.

Questioning my gut, I try to unbuckle the seat belt he pulls around me and snaps into place. The low growl in his throat is warning enough, and for some fucked-up reason, it turns me on. It's the same sound he made last night when he shoved me against the wall and slammed balls deep inside of me.

"Put this on," he hisses as he climbs into the driver's seat and tosses me a button-up shirt.

I unsnap the seatbelt as he pulls out of the parking lot, raising an eyebrow as I shrug it on. The fire in his eyes says he'd love for me to challenge him.

I question him. Ask him where we're going, just who the fuck does he think he is, and what his plans are, but I'm met with utter silence until we pull up outside of a hotel that isn't but a few degrees better than my apartment.

"Am I going to have to carry you inside?"

I narrow my eyes at him, trying to gauge exactly what the fuck is going on and spending more time than I should actually considering doing it without argument.

"Are you going to hurt me?"

A sinister smile turns his plush lips up until the corners disappear in his well-groomed beard.

"Only if you beg."

The arousal I'd thought had abated during the short drive once again flares to life. I anticipate another suggestive innuendo from him, but instead, he tosses my small clutch that I'd left locked in the back room into my lap.

"You look nothing like your driver's license photo, Georgia Leigh Anderson. Want to tell me what you're doing so far from home?"

I glare at him, pissed that he went through my things, but at the same time terrified for what it means for my family back in New Mexico. I want to get away from them, not rain down hell on them. I start to shake, wondering if this is the first step in sex trade abductions.

"You said you won't hurt me."

He frowns as if the notation is absurd.

"That means my family, too?"

He recoils, head snapping back.

"Surprised my head would go that way? You threatened to kill me last night."

He shakes his head, jaw flexing to the point I hear his back teeth grind together.

"Not one of my finer moments. Last night was more about fucking up than fucking you. What is a twenty-year-old girl from New Mexico doing stripping *illegally* in Dallas, Texas?"

How the fuck does he know where I'm from?

"What is some former Marine doing in Dallas fucking young girls in the alleyway," I challenge.

It's his turn to narrow his eyes.

"You see more than you let on."

I ignore his words. "Why am I here?"

"Do I have to carry you in or can you walk on your own?"

Call me curious, but the appeal to join him inside, to figure him out is too strong to do anything but climb out and wait for him to lead me to the door of his outside entry room.

Chapter 3

Hound

"Why am I here?" she asks, not for the first time.

I tilt up the bottle of whiskey I left on the particle board dresser earlier to my lips. I don't even notice the burn as it travels its way down my throat. She sits on my bed like she owns that place the second we step into the room.

"Why do you think you're here?"

It's crazy how quickly your maturity drops in the face of young people. I huff, and she gives me a questioning look.

"I imagine you enjoyed yourself so much last night that one time inside of me wasn't enough." She tilts her head, red hair flowing over her shoulder and touching her bare thigh. My shirt swamps her, but she knows exactly what she's doing showing that hint of bare flesh.

I tilt the bottle up again as a means to fortify myself when I know it will do nothing but lower my inhibitions.

She. Is. Work.

No matter how many times I repeat that fact over and over in my head, my body still craves her. My memories from last night drive me to touch her, to taste her.

I shake my head. That along with the whiskey have no effect on the need I have for her skin against mine.

"You need to stop being a little fucking tease. I don't have time for that shit."

She smirks, and I want to do nothing more than kiss that look off her damn face.

I shake my head again. No, not kiss. Kissing is the last thing I need to do. I have to convince her to head back to New Mexico with me and find a way to do that without her telling her father I fucked her in a filthy alleyway.

I was diverted from my very first day with the Cerberus MC in New Mexico to Dallas. Blade, the IT man behind the MC gave me specific orders to get Georgia "Gigi" Anderson out of the strip club she was dancing in and get her home safely. I fucked myself out of a job by literally fucking an MC princess. I've heard the stories of Kincaid, Dominic, and the others in New Mexico. They're fair, but nothing short of murder is headed my way unless Gigi and Blade both get onboard to not breathe a word of this to Kincaid.

"It's not teasing," she says pulling me from my frantic thoughts, "if it's what I want."

She spreads her legs, the thin sliver of glittery fabric the only thing between me and the tightest cunt I've ever slid inside of.

"I fucked you raw last night. A second round of my cock is the last thing you can handle right now." I mean it as a warning, but it comes across as a challenge instead.

"My pussy is sore but far from raw."

Those filthy words coming from her mouth may be the sexiest thing I've ever heard.

"I woke up this morning with my cock covered in blood. Don't tell me it isn't raw."

She grins, the light reflecting in her green eyes. Green? Blue last night? She has to be wearing contacts.

She rolls her lip between teeth too straight and perfect to belong to your everyday stripper. Girls like that are dancing in much better establishments than the one I pulled her out of tonight. It's a fact I should've realized last night before I let the sway of her hips and the tightness of her stomach distract me.

"That's what happens the first time," she reveals causing my blood to run cold and the bottle of whiskey to fall from my hand.

It hits the dingy carpet with a soft thud, and I watch her, frozen in place as she unfolds from my bed and reaches down to get it. The luscious curves of her breasts are visible as the shirt gapes open at the neck.

"You're twenty," I argue.

"You're forty," she counters.

"Thirty-four," I hiss letting her sassy ass attitude get the better of me.

If I thought I was screwed by fucking the Prez's daughter, add taking her virginity in a depraved way, and I know the police will never find my damned body.

She places the whiskey bottle on the dresser at my back, making sure to lean her lithe body against mine in the process.

"I promise I'm not too sore."

She trails her finger over me exactly the way she did last night. I imagine her doing exactly this to the men who spend the cash to get private dances, and it pisses me off more than it should. I try to convince myself that I'm angry for her father. Angry that she's someone's little girl who's dancing half-naked on stage, and not because I loathe anyone she's touched before.

You fucked her first. That's something she can never give to another man.

I shake my head again. Thoughts like that will get me killed, but I can't help but consider keeping her happy until I can convince her to go along with the lies I have to tell Cerberus.

I grip her wrist, remembering from last night that she liked it rough, liked it when I commanded her body.

"I owe you one," I remind her.

"True," she coos.

I shove her on the bed, and her eyes widen when her back hits the hard mattress. Her wet pink tongue swipes across her lower lip when I shift the erection in my jeans to a better position.

"Better make it two," she whispers when my knees hit the bed, and my lips begin to trail up the soft skin of her calf. "Call it interest."

I nip at the delicate skin behind her knee, fully expecting her to pull away or slam her thighs together. She surprises me when they open further on a moan.

I fucked her bare last night. Came inside of her like she was mine to do so. Tonight, under her spell again, I don't even question lowering my mouth to her heated flesh, pulling the thin strip of fabric to the side, and sucking her clit into my mouth.

She whimpers, unable to form words I assume, as I give her over eighteen years of pussy licking experience. I don't hold back. I want her liquid, pliable, willing to do what I say when the time comes to face her father.

She writhes under my attention, gripping the sheets and coming as her hands tug at the fabric in her grasp. By the time she's ruining the bed with her second orgasm, I've almost convinced myself that licking her into submission is not only the best course of action; it's absolute bliss for me as well.

Why I push her through a third release until she's begging me to stop is beyond me. I'm just as confused by my reluctance as she looks, lying on the bed satiated with a flushed glow on her skin.

Before I question myself, I'm pulling a condom from my wallet, the same one that was in there last night and releasing the buckle on my belt. I'm rolling the latex down my shaft when my phone buzzes on the dresser at my back.

Like a bucket of ice water being tossed on me, my hands still, pausing mid-stroke of my aching cock.

There are only two people in the world who have that number: one I've devoted my life to, and the other, a man I have to convince not to betray a lifelong friend.

Blade I can possibly get to understand the sin of giving into temptation; Isabella, on the other hand, would hold it against me forever. I've fucked up enough in the last twenty-four hours for a lifetime.

"Where are you going?" Gigi asks when I slide off the bed.

"Shower," I grunt as I pull my t-shirt off and lock myself in the bathroom.

With rough hands, I rip the unused rubber off my dick and toss it in the trash. The cold water does nothing to cool my heated skin. I grip my cock, stroking it from base to tip, knowing if I go back out there without coming I'm only asking for trouble.

I have no damn clue what my next step is. I don't know much about her, but I know a couple of orgasms aren't enough to convince her to go home and lie for me.

"Motherfucker," I hiss as my strokes grow harder.

Resting my forearm against the shower wall, I hunch over, giving into the sensation in my nuts as my orgasm begins to build. I'm disgusted with myself as I paint the wall in cum to the thoughts of the young girl in my shitty hotel bed.

I take my time drying off before pulling a clean pair of boxers from the small suitcase in the corner. I can't focus with her in the other room. I can't think of ways to make this work. Every idea ends exactly the same. My new job is gone, and my only other option puts me even further from Isabella, doing work I know I'll hate.

"Listen," I say when I pull the bathroom door open.

I don't say another thing, my words caught in my throat at the sight of her half-naked body asleep on the bed.

Relief washes over me at not having to deal with this shit tonight. Exhausted, I drop down on the other side of the bed and pray that I find some clarity, in the form of a solution, comes to me in my dreams.

Chapter 4

Gigi

Waking up to the sun streaming through the threadbare curtains without a cocaine headache almost makes me want to never use again. Dancing on stage last night sober to the thoughts of my dark stranger seems to have awakened something in me, something that makes me believe that there's a future for me after all.

Thoughts of last night encourage me to turn my head, looking at the sleeping man on the other side of the bed. I have no hopes of a relationship with him, but I'll be forever grateful for whatever fire he has sparked back into my life.

As quietly as I can manage, I climb out of bed in an attempt to not wake him. As much as I enjoyed our evening together, he's too much like my father to continue what has started between us.

I slide my heels on, unsure of when he even took them off, and tug my bikini top back on. The walk of shame in such little clothing is going to suck, but I get naked for money and became shameless long ago. With one last look at his sleeping form, I leave him sleeping in a bed rumpled by my orgasms, and not his.

Despair always hits me in the chest when I open the front door to my crappy apartment, and today is no different. I look at my clean but dismal surroundings. The worn sofa and scarred coffee table are the only furnishings. Only a handful of dishes fill the cabinets in the kitchen, and limited food takes up space in the small fridge. Looking at my life from a bird's eye view, going home almost seems better, but in doing so, I allow my parents to make decisions about my life. It's a sacrifice I'm not willing to make anymore now than I was several years ago.

My options were the military or college, neither of which interested me then, and they sure as hell aren't on my radar now. If I live at home, those are my choices. I asked my father last year at Thanksgiving to let me work at Jake's Bar. I'd be happy there. I know I would. My mother worked there when she and my dad got together, so I know he doesn't have an issue with Jake. It's the thought of his daughter working as a barmaid that leaves him less than thrilled. He forbade me, dismissed the idea in a second flat. That same night I walked away from the Cerberus MC knowing it would be my last time to walk away from it.

"Pity party, table for one," I mumble as I close my apartment door and kick off my heels.

Checking the calendar for tonight's schedule, I determine that I can nap for a couple of hours before I have to head to work. Unfortunately, I only toss and turn for what seems like an endless amount of time before my cell chirps an alert to get ready.

I'm shocked when I arrive at work and my stranger isn't waiting for me. Seems he got me out of his system even after his machismo act last night. Realizing I lost my virginity to a man whose name I still don't know sends a chill down my spine. It's reminiscent of the discomfort I felt after my first line of coke.

"I figured Chad would've fired your ass," Peaches huffs as she all but shoves me out of the way to get in front of the dimly lit vanity.

"I guess he's not ready to get rid of his top earner just yet," I snip with a quick shoulder jab to regain my space in front of the mirror.

"You'll be back at the bottom soon enough," Dolly says interrupting our conversation. "I've been here eight years. Featured more times than I can even count."

I huff a humorless laugh. "Seems like your good years are behind you."

"Hardly," she counters.

I cock an eyebrow at her. "Really? Your tits are nearly to your bellybutton, and you can't even swing yourself a foot off the floor on the pole."

Her eyes narrow, filling with a fire I hope I have in eight years after having to do God knows what in the future to survive.

"I have tendinitis in both elbows, you little bitch," she sneers.

"Get over yourself," Peaches says in a bored tone. "You know you'll have to hang it up sooner or later."

No one at this damn club has alliances. We're all each woman for ourselves.

Peaches fluffs her hair in the mirror, taking over the space that Dolly vacated.

"We all will eventually," she mutters taking stock of her own dim future.

I sigh and step back, guilty of my own self-doubt. It's still on my mind after I change out of my t-shirt and yoga pants and put on another gaudy, barely-there bikini. My nerves, as I stand just off the stage, are nothing like they were the first time, but they're still there.

I consider Vegas and the possibility of performing in some manner on Fremont Street. I have several months before I'm twenty-one and

Vegas, other than the seediest parts, is known for being sticklers on the rules.

A new girl I've never seen before exits the stage and I can tell by the fresh look on her face that Chad has once again hired a teenager. She's years away from twenty-one, but that doesn't stop him from paying her under the table until she's of age. He does the exact same thing for me.

The intro to Thunderstruck by AC/DC pulls me from worrying about *her* future and forces me out onto the stage. I have three dances on the stage tonight and then private dances if there are paying customers, which there always are. The lights seem brighter this evening, but I do my best not to squint and cover my eyes with my forearm.

I make it through more than half of my shift, and I hate that I'm disappointed that the guy from the last two days hasn't shown. He heard me tell Gerardo last night that I'd be at work today.

"You make me so hot," I lie as I grind down on a younger looking guy in the shadowed back booth of the club.

His hands clench on the cheap leather, unlike most guys who pay for private dances he keeps his hands to himself through the entire dance.

"I have lots of money," he pants against my ear as my back and ass rub against his front. "Name your price beautiful, and I'll gladly pay it."

I get no less than half a dozen offers just like this a night, but tonight it stings more than usual. Forty-eight hours ago, I'd just blow it off and tell the truth that I don't do that sort of thing. I'd give him the names of the girls that are always willing to go the extra mile for cash. Tonight, two days after I accepted cash for a quick fuck in the alley, I feel dirty. Not enough to give in, but shame hits me for the first time in over a year.

The song ends, and I pull away from him.

"Use it to buy your wife something nice," I tell him with a quick look down at his left hand.

The sparkle from his gold wedding band caught my eye more than once during the two dances he's paid for.

He clutches his left hand to his chest, coveting it and covering it with his right.

Shaking his head, I'm confused to see pain in his eyes, as if I'm going to search her out and tell her about his indiscretions.

"I'm not." He shakes his head again, more violently than the first time. "She's gone."

And I'm a huge asshole.

I give him a sympathetic smile. "There are several girls here who work after hours."

"No," he rushes out. "It has to be you. You look like her."

This poor sad bastard.

"Sorry," I tell him shrugging back into my top. "I don't do that sort of thing."

I try not to think about the pitiful man who's looking for nothing more than a connection to his wife after she's gone. It's difficult to comprehend that type of love for myself. My parents have it. I don't know that either one of them would survive the loss of the other, but I'm beyond certain that type of love isn't something I'll find in this lifetime.

Chapter 5

Hound

"That slippery bitch." I punch the empty spot beside me on the bed.

I never sleep through someone moving around in a room. I never let my guard down. Doing so is a disaster in the making in my line of work. It rankles that a tiny, twenty-year-old girl was able to sneak out of this shitty hotel room without me knowing it.

I can't let it bother me for long. Getting out of this room is all I can focus on. I've ignored Blade's texts and calls for two solid days, and I know the damn cavalry is coming, and there's no way to prepare for it other than having Gigi accessible when her father arrives.

I spend my day walking around the shitty town on the off chance that I catch her going to work, but give up after several hours and go back to the room. I'm ready to leave, whether it be to New Mexico or California. The security job in Cali is what I know I'll end up with. There's no way the Cerberus Prez is going to forgive a failed mission, especially one as simple as extracting his daughter from a strip club. Especially not after I fucked her.

I shower and head to the club just as night is falling over Dallas. Even the bright outline of the Bank of America Plaza in the distance doesn't improve my disposition. I want nothing more than to bend her over and whip her ass for the trouble she caused me, but I gave up blaming others for my actions many years ago.

I order a whiskey the minute my ass hits the sticky chair near the back. I watch, waiting for my moment and nearly come out of my seat when I see a flash of her hair as she provides private dance services to some sad schmuck in the back. She gives the dance one hundred percent, but I can tell her heart isn't in it. The only thing that keeps my fist from meeting that fucker's face is the fact that he keeps his hands to himself and never attempts to touch her. Even that asshole has better control over himself than I do.

Downing the whiskey, I wave the waitress over for another. With her here tonight, I know she'll be the one to close down the club, the final dance on the stage. So I wait, keeping an eye on her. A glance at my watch lets me know she'll be up there soon.

With only a look, I'm able to force a man from his front row seat. It's as close as I can get without being up there with her. Another whiskey. Another half-hearted dance by a girl too young to be a high school graduate. I'm disgusted at her presence on the stage, so I keep my eyes down, staring into my glass of whiskey like it's the most interesting thing ever.

One song fades to the next and I know, just by the musical selection that my red-headed temptress is ready to perform.

The hard-hitting bass of Thunderstruck pounds in my ears, and it makes me wonder about her song choices. AC/DC and Def Leppard are barely within my musical range.

I'm struck stupid when Gigi appears, once again in the smallest scraps of clothing known to man. She might as well be naked, the fabric only covering the areolas of her nipples and that tiny, glorious seam of her pussy. I instantly hate every man in this room, contemplating killing each one of them and ripping their eyes out.

She doesn't bother looking into the crowd. She concentrates on her moves as she rolls with incredible ease up and down the pole. Every muscle in her body is utilized during her routine. They jump, flex, and respond to her actions. So much control. So much power. My cock, just as it always does when she's around, thickens and lengthens uncomfortably in my jeans.

When she does finally look out over the crowd, and her eyes meet mine, all I get from her is a sweet knowing smile. I wink, hold my nearly empty glass up to her in salute, and continue to watch her performance. Her back bows deeper, her moves become even more sensuous, and her breathing more labored, which I know from watching her prior to tonight that it has everything to do with me and not exhaustion from dancing. She could dance for days without growing tired. Her body was made for it.

I'm damn near bereft when the song ends, and she begins to gather the money on the stage, triple the amount the other girls before her earned.

Enthralled by the delicate sway of her tits, I come out of my seat when one of the patrons reaches up and squeezes her to the point that she cries out in pain. I get two hits right in the man's nose before he's cognizant enough to stumble away.

Exactly like last night, I sling her nearly naked body over my shoulder and head to the front door.

A different man than yesterday, this one somehow managing to look even sleazier, steps in front of me and blocks my path.

"Gerardo told me what happened last night, Annie."

I feel her tense across my back.

"You know that if your boyfriends can't handle you stripping, they're not allowed in my club," he continues, talking to her even though he can't see her face.

I don't even attempt to stop the growl that begins low in my stomach only gaining strength as it makes its way up my chest and out of my mouth.

"You don't see a problem with these disgusting fuckers grabbing your dancers?"

The asshole's sinister laugh bubbles up, angering me even more.

"She knows better than to step out of the green zone. She took that risk when she got greedy for the cash on the other side of the line."

"You're a piece of shit," I hiss.

"True," he agrees. "But I'm the piece of shit that owns this place. You're fired, Annie. Don't ever darken my door again."

"Like I would," she mutters to the backs of my thighs.

I carry her out, only allowing her to slide down my body once we reach my car. I buckle her in the second her ass hits the seat.

With my nose nearly touching hers, I speak to her for the first time since last night. "Didn't you learn your lesson last night when I pulled your naked ass from that filthy stage?"

I expect her to cringe, to shy away from the acrimony in my voice, but she just gives me that same sweet smile she gave me from the stage.

"I'm a whore and a stripper. I don't even know your name, and you think you can dictate my life? You've lost your fucking mind."

I pinch my bottom lip between my teeth so hard I expect to taste the coppery tinge of blood any second. I made her feel like a whore. That mindset is on me, and it makes my stomach turn.

"You bled on my pierced cock which proves you're not a whore," I remind her. "And your stripping days are over."

She cocks an eyebrow, challenging me.

I hang my head and sigh. How can I expect her to trust me, to lie for me if I give her nothing in return? "My name is Jameson Rawley."

She smiles wider and whispers, "Jamie."

"Jameson," I correct. "Never fucking Jamie."

The nickname is salt in old wounds created by my father when I was a small child that apparently have never healed.

She rolls her eyes at my insistence, but her gorgeous face still holds the smile that will live in infamy in my dreams for years to come.

"Where are you taking me?" she asks when I climb behind the wheel.

"Back to my hotel," I advise as I pull out of the parking lot. "Unless you'll be more comfortable back at your place. We have a lot to discuss."

Finding out where she lives would be ideal. She's not going to like what I have to ask of her, and I know she'll want to run again.

"Yours is ten times better than mine," she mutters.

So she's left a nice home in New Mexico to live in squalor and dance naked for money? It makes me wonder if her father and the Cerberus MC are as upstanding as they're rumored to be. I can't imagine a young girl wanting to leave the comfort of her childhood home without there being a reason.

"Are you hungry?" I ask before we get on the road to my hotel.

She nods, looking nervous.

"What?"

"I left all my money at home. I was in a rush this morning and even left my clutch." She pauses. "And I dropped everything from the stage when you tossed me over your damn shoulder."

My brow wrinkles in confusion.

"I can't buy anything," she says. "I don't want to owe you more than I already do."

"One," I begin without even looking in her direction. "You've been around the wrong fucking boys if you've been paying for your own meals. Two, it's a cheeseburger and fries, not dinner with dessert at Reunion Tower."

She sighs, and from the corner of my eye, I watch her turn her face toward the window.

"And you don't owe me a damn thing."

We order at a drive-thru, but other than giving me her selection she doesn't speak until we pull up outside of my hotel room.

"I need to give you back the cash. That's your money," she says sullenly. "Keeping it only makes me a paid whore."

I lick my lips and let my eyes close as I try to calm down. Without another word I grab the food and head inside, knowing she'll follow me.

I unlock the door and set the food on the small table just inside. When she closes it behind her, I move and press my body against hers.

"That's the second time you've called yourself a whore in front of me."

"You called me a whore more than once the other night."

My blood runs cold in my veins. I'm guilty of that. Guilty of letting the night get away with me and taking it out on her. I do the only thing I can. I ignore her comments and continue.

"A third time will guarantee I stripe your ass with my belt."

Her chest heaves up and down as she lets my words sink in.

"Do you understand me?"

Her green eyes find mine, and I'm once again lost to her.

"Yes, Sir." It comes out sarcastic and petulant, just like she intends, but it doesn't stop the chill that races over my skin and the blood from rushing to my cock.

"That money is yours, for no other reason than I want you to have it. Do you understand?"

I press harder against her, knowing she can feel my thickening cock against her bare stomach.

"Yes, Sir."

I groan at the words slipping from her mouth in a breathless whisper, this time with no hint of the contempt it carried before.

"We should eat," I tell her and take a step back.

She sags against the door at the loss of my body. "I recall you being very good at eating last night."

"Not happening again, Georgia. Don't even think about it."

"Gigi," she says. "No one but my mother, when she's angry, calls me Georgia."

"Gigi then." I smile at her over my shoulder as I begin to pull the food from the paper bags.

We're silent for a few short minutes as we begin to eat, but I can't let this night end without talking to her about her dad, Cerberus, and the consequences of what I've done.

"Tell me why you left New Mexico." I shoot for nonchalance, but this girl can read me like a damn book.

Seventeen years in the Marine Corps, expert training in infiltration and interrogation, and I forget it all in the face of a gorgeous twenty-year-old who has only recently become a woman.

Chapter 6

Gigi

"Tell me why you want to know," I counter.

"Just curious," he lies.

I can see it in the erratic change in his pupils, but the tapping of his foot and barely noticeable tremble in his hands are enough to give him away.

"You want to know all about me?"

"Just making conversation." Another lie.

"How about," I begin but throw my last fry in my mouth before standing, "I give you all the sordid details of my life back in New Mexico after."

I reach for his hand.

"After?"

I nod and scoop his free hand up. The last couple of bites of his burger hit the paper wrapper, but he stands when I tug on him.

"After we're basking in the afterglow of fucking, of course."

He stops suddenly and our hands separate. "Not gonna happen, Gigi."

The nervousness in his voice confuses me. Less than twenty minutes ago, he got hard instantly when I responded to him with 'yes, Sir.' Now he's shying away from a romp between the sheets? I question his mental health as I turn to look at him.

"You want information?" He nods so fast it makes me grin. "You have to work for it."

A devilish glint appears in his eye, and I know that I have him. He's so turned on around me, I knew the battle would be a short one.

There is something different about him. Has been since he ripped me off the stage yesterday. It's almost as if he's a changed man from the aggressive one who fucked me against the rough brick outside of the club two nights ago.

"Strip," he commands before I can sit on the bed.

I'm only in a bikini top and thong, but I love that he wants me completely naked.

"You don't have any dollar bills," I tease.

"Strip because you want to, Gigi. Not because you're getting paid."

"There's no music," I pout.

"You don't have to make a show of it, woman. Just get naked. I have plenty of thoughts of you dancing and taking your clothes off burned into my brain."

My top comes off first. I toss it to him, hoping it lands on top of his head, but he snatches it out of the air and drops it to the ground. I go slower with the thong, ignoring the wetness that cools when the air of the room rushes over my exposed skin.

"Your turn," I suggest. "I'd love you to do it to music."

He growls when I wink at him. Why does that sound so hot?

"Not gonna happen. Not today or ever."

"Too bad," I whisper. Another smart-assed remark is on my tongue, but I'm rendered mute when he pulls his shirt off. I saw his back last night when he went to take a shower and saw most of his front this morning as he slept in bed, but those memories provide no justice for the sight in front of me right now.

"Wow." My lips smack together as if he's a gourmet feast. "You must work out a lot."

"Occasionally," he mutters as his fingers work open his belt and then lowers his zipper

I stare in awe, waiting for the reveal. I only got a quick glance at him last night before he chickened out and left the room.

"Oh," I pant when his dick flexes up, and not only a single piercing but a row of barbells is revealed. "That had to have hurt."

He kicks off his cowboy boots and shakes his jeans free of his legs. No underwear, exactly what I'd expect from a guy like him. A grunt fills the room when his hand reaches and strokes down his erection.

"It wasn't the most comfortable situation. Every one after the first sucks because you know what you're facing then."

I can't take my eyes off of his working hand, and swallowing doesn't dislodge the lump in my throat.

"So why get so many?" I'm stalling, and when he chuckles, I know that he knows it too.

How in all things holy did that fit inside of me the other night? It's very possible that the blood from our union was from damage rather than just losing my virginity.

"Getting shot hurts more." He says it with a nonchalance that makes my eyes snap up to his.

It's something my dad or one of his men would say, as if getting shot or stabbed is just another day on the job.

He gives me a small grin before walking toward me. His hand never stops handling his shaft. "Get out of your head, Gigi. This is supposed to be fun."

"It's bigger than I remember." I take a step further away from him.

"And when I bend you over the bed and fuck you from behind those barbells are going to feel incredible." He leans in and licks at my ear before speaking again. "And that ring at the top is going to send you over the edge more times than you can count."

Harsh breaths rush past my lips, and I'll be damned if his promises don't ease my nerves and make me want to just turn around for him.

I reach for him, but with practiced ease, he takes a step back so I can't touch him. Please tell me he's not one of those weirdos that doesn't want a woman's hands on him.

"Condom," he mutters with an agitation that doesn't fit the current mood.

I almost call him out on it, but he's bending at the waist and reaching into the back pocket of his jeans.

Holy. Glorious. Ass.

"Your ass is amazing," I observe.

He's smiling when he turns back around, the wrapper to the condom already at his mouth and tearing open.

"That makes two of us I guess."

I smile. He clearly works out. My body is from pole workouts and practice. I burn so much energy at work that other than perfecting a routine, I hardly ever go to the gym.

"It doesn't look any older than twenty-five, twenty-seven tops."

His eyes narrow but there's a playfulness to the glare he's giving me right now.

"Definitely doesn't look like a forty-year-old ass."

He charges, all aggressive and asserting his power, but I don't miss the arm around my back or the other catching our combined weight as we hit the mattress.

Mouth close to mine, he looks down at me. His eyes jump between mine, taking me in as if he's trying to read social clues I'm not even trying to hide. God, I love the weight of his body on mine. The heat of his dick on my inner thigh. The clean, masculine scent of his skin. I'm consumed by him.

"Thirty. Four," he hisses.

"Thirty-four," I repeat.

"My cock is thirty-four also," he says with a roll of his hips.

I moan and grind against him.

"Do you have a problem with me fucking you with my old cock?"

"No." I whimper when, with expert precision, he presses the head of his cock against my throbbing clit.

"Good. Now, I'd love nothing more than slam inside of your tight cunt and ride you hard all night, but that wouldn't be very good for you."

"Fuck me hard," I beg. "I can handle it."

"I'm going to fuck you all night long, Gigi. We can do hard some other time."

I nod. All of it sounds amazing. Hard. Soft. In the bed. Against the wall. Missionary. Twisted into a pretzel. Sign me up for everything and summer school to boot.

"Are you ready for me?"

How do I tell him I've been wet since I spotted him in the crowd back at the club?

"So ready," I say instead.

With an expert shift of his hips, his cock and the attached barbells leave my clit and rest right against my entrance. Without conscious thought, I tense.

"You have to relax, or I'm going to hurt you more than I want to."

The thought of a little pain with my pleasure brings a riot of emotions to my head, but he begins short strokes. Only a tiny dip inside before he backs away and moves in just a hair deeper each time.

"You're so good at this," I praise as he teases me open.

"Lots of practice," he grunts with an even deeper jab.

"Nice," I mutter.

Here he is thirty-four and fucking a girl who's only done this once before. I should be proud that he's being gentle and taking my inexperience into consideration. I know a man my own age wouldn't be bothered with easing in and making sure I'm comfortable, but the thought of him with other women makes my skin crawl.

It's the pheromones.

"What?" His hips stop assisting his intrusion, and he stares down at me.

I shake my head, realizing I said that out loud. "Nothing."

I moan so loudly I wonder if the neighbors hear when he shifts again.

"Are you jealous?" He continues to move in and out of me, and the sensation is making me lose my mind. Holding any train of thought is impossible at this point.

"No."

"I was jealous. More like pissed each time I saw you dancing for another man earlier. It has to be the pheromones because there's no other explanation."

He drives forward, deeper than he ever got in the alleyway.

"Fuck you feel good."

His praise washes over me leaving goosebumps behind.

"Am I hurting you?"

Speech is not a skill I'm capable of right now, so I shake my head. At least, I think I shake my head because in the next second my back is arching up and I'm speaking in Tongues.

"That's it. Fuck, take it all." He repositions, and when I realize he's looking down where we're joined, I swear I nearly come. "You like that reverse prince? Best piercing of them all."

He's got so much metal in his dick I have no idea which one he's talking about, but they feel amazing.

He rolls and grinds, and I have no idea how sex with him can hurt and feel like the best thing in the world at the same time. He's an expert. Sex is a skill he's mastered beyond anything I could've imagined.

"Don't tighten up, Gigi, or you'll end this too soon."

"I-I ca-can't help it," I stutter as my core clamps down on him. The orgasm catches us both by surprise. Hissing, he pulls out, and before the haze can clear, I feel his hot breath on my pussy. His hot tongue hits me next. The sensations are too much, more than I'm capable of handling. With hands flat on the mattress I try to push away from him, but he doesn't allow it.

"It's too much."

He chuckles. "As it should be."

"Why are you down there? Did you come?"

"I just need a minute."

Now, it's my turn to laugh. "Who's the inexperienced one here?"

"It's your tight-as-fuck pussy that's the problem." He nips at my inner thigh, and just like that, I'm ready for more.

"It's been a minute," I complain rolling my hips, pussy right in his face. "Make me come again."

"Jesus, you're perfect." He crawls up my body, nipping and sucking at my exposed flesh. I imagine it's only to give him more time to settle, but eventually, he makes it back up. We're once again face to face, and when he enters me this time, he doesn't take the same care he did earlier.

He thrusts in one long drive. I whimper, loving both the pain and the pleasure. When he makes me come the second time, he follows me right over the edge, using the growl that makes me tingle all over.

I don't realize I've fallen asleep until I open my eyes. I'm turned on my side, and he's sliding into me from behind.

I clutch his forearm that's resting against my stomach and lift my leg allowing him to plunge deeper.

"So good," I pant.

"It's the barbells this time," he reminds me.

I shake my head as he pulls out to the tip and shoves back inside. "Your cock would feel amazing without all the metal."

"I can't wait for you to suck it," he hisses growing close to release.

"I can't wait," I promise just as his fingers reach down and work my clit.

We come together, and it doesn't go unnoticed that he's still inside of me, arm still wrapped around me when I fall asleep again.

Chapter 7

Hound

"Hey," I whisper in Gigi's ear and push gently on her shoulder.

She grumbles incoherently and rolls further away from me.

"Gigi," I say louder this time.

The only response I get is a soft rotation of her hips as she tries to wiggle even deeper into the bed. How she can sleep comfortably on this shitty bed is beyond me.

Pulling back the blankets in an attempt to wake her with the cool air over her skin serves to be fruitless as well, but the pull of her bare ass can't be ignored. I reach my hand back, readying to slap the supple cheek, but think better of it. Instead, I slide further down the bed and plant my mouth at the apex of her thighs. I lift her hips to achieve a better angle, but it isn't until I tongue inside of her that she responds.

"Who knew such a little thing could have such a dirty mouth," I tease after she screams expletives even a sailor would cringe hearing. "Are you awake now?"

Whimpering, she rolls her sweet cunt against my face. It isn't until she's coming that I pull away.

"Hop on," I say with a sharp slap to her ass and fall back on the mattress.

"What?" she asks finally pulling her face out of the pillow.

I give my condom covered dick a quick glance. "Ride me."

She rolls her lips between her teeth, and I notice the sleep lines on her face. She's young, gorgeous and wise beyond her years. More mature than she should be. A couple of years of hard life experiences will do that to a person. I had to grow up fast as well, so I recognize all of this in her.

I grip her hips, helping her get settled. I'd love to act like I'm in control, even from the bottom, but when she clasps her little hand around my cock and lines it up with that perfect slit between her legs, I'm a goner.

We both hiss when she slowly slides down my shaft. Her eyes flutter closed when she pulls up, abs flexing, so I let mine do the same. Every sensation is multiplied without sight. The skin of her hips is softer. The smell of sex and her faint perfume is stronger, like a blanket surrounding us. The taste of her pussy is sweeter on my tongue. The tiny moans that transition to grunts and screams of pleasure are the icing on the cake.

She's insisting on slow with her movements, but slow isn't something my cock can take. I'll come too quick feeling each and every one of her tiny internal muscles gripping at me.

"Faster," I urge holding her hip and flexing to ram inside of her. "God, that's not any better."

My eyes snap open when I feel the sting of her slap on my face.

"The fuck?"

"Why are you fucking me if you don't like it?"

As if by some miracle, my cock thickens even more at her insecurity.

Grabbing her and pulling her to my chest, I flip her over and ram inside of her harder.

"Slow was going to make me shoot my load too soon." I punctuate my statement with a deliberately slow rotation of my hips before speeding up and pounding into her. "Fast, I thought would be better. I'd last longer."

She moans, head thrown back, the soft skin of her neck exposed.

"I was wrong. The clench of your pussy is too much, no matter the tempo."

I bite and suck at her neck, ramming, sawing in and out of her like I'll never be inside of her again.

When the door crashes open at the first clasp of her orgasm, the first pulse of mine, I see it as a sign, an omen of things to come.

I couldn't stop coming if someone was holding a knife to my throat. I just signed my death warrant anyway, because when I look up, I'm staring right into the eyes of Diego "Kincaid" Anderson.

"Daddy!" Gigi yells, trying to wrap the tangled sheet at her side over her chest.

I tug it free and help cover her body, ready to fight all the men standing at Kincaid's side for seeing what they have. True to their reputation, the men turn, giving us their backs and Gigi the privacy she deserves.

"You could've knocked," she mumbles.

"Georgia Leigh Anderson," Kincaid hisses. "Get your ass dressed right now!"

I can feel the tremble in her body, and I want nothing more than to protect her, but four against one with these motherfuckers are horrible odds.

I tuck the sheet closer to Gigi before pulling out of her. If he wanted to hurt me before, Kincaid is likely imagining my dismembered body when I groan as I leave her body.

"Not helping," Gigi whispers as she crawls out from underneath me.

"I'll kill you," he sneers before turning his attention back to his sheet-wrapped daughter. "Go get dressed."

I expect her to defy him, to argue that all she has to wear is a thong and bikini top, but she scurries into the bathroom without a backward glance.

I see the fist coming. I have time to react, time to deflect the punch, but I let the hit land on my left cheek, right where Kincaid intends. I deserve every punch he lets fly at my face. I deserve the gruesome crack of my nose as it shatters under his angry fists.

"Enough," one of the other MC members says as he drags Kincaid off of my chest.

Wiping the blood from my face onto the sheet, I can't even look him in the eye. What argument would I have? There's nothing I can say to make what I did right. There's no way to explain away the reason I ended up in bed with the boss' daughter. Again. And again. Hell, I'd do what he did and more if I walked in on my daughter getting plowed by a man that was sent to protect her.

"This?" Kincaid hisses. I finally meet his eyes as he points at me. "This is who you recommend for my club. I can't trust him not to sleep with my daughter. How in the ever-loving fuck can I trust him with my men when things go to shit on a mission?"

The man that pulled him off of me, the one Kincaid is challenging, is his older brother Dominic.

"Dammit," I mumble looking over at the grey-haired man. He's massive, the silver color of his hair and small smile lines at the corners of his eyes are the only things that hints at his age.

"He comes highly recommended," Dominic says with doubt in his eyes.

And I do. My time in the Marine Corps and my FORECON training and experience, on paper, practically over-qualifies me to be a Cerberus member. But, Kincaid is right. Trust is more valuable than experience. Faith that I'll have the men's backs is paramount to success. I've lost it before I could even prove to them how valuable I can be by fucking a girl I never should've touched.

I can't blame her. I can't burden her with my choices. I had every intention of speaking with her last night, convincing her to see my side of things, but the temptation of her body was too much, irresistible by her mere nearness. It would've been all for nothing seeing as we were just busted in on in flagrante delicto.

Kincaid doesn't say another word. He merely glares at me, chest heaving and paying no attention to my blood marking his knuckles.

The bathroom door opens, and Gigi steps out. The gorgeous red hair that trailed behind her when she scurried in there earlier is now clasped in her hands in the form of a wig. My attraction to her had everything to do with that red hair, but I can easily admit, with long dark hair flowing over her shoulders, she's even more gorgeous. The sight of her timidly standing on the threshold, swallowed up by my t-shirt, a pair of my boxers peeking out at the bottom cause more problems for me. She's beautiful, and even with five angry bastards in the room, my cock doesn't seem to mind.

I grunt, twisting to the side of the bed, feet planted on the floor and cover my thickening cock with the thin blanket at my feet.

One of the men chuckles, and I look to see another guy, bearded like myself and maybe only a few years older. I'm not as inconspicuous as I thought. The laugh is odd though. Meeting his eyes, all I get is a smirk and a slight shake of his head before he walks over and reaches out a hand for her.

"Come on, Gigi. Let's head to your apartment and get you packed."

"I don't need an escort, Kid," she grumbles drawing my eyes back to her. "What are you going to do to him?"

I look over at her father when he begins to speak. "Hound is my problem now."

Her eyes widen, confusion drawing her brows together.

"Hound?" She shakes her head as she glares at me. "You know my dad?"

"Let's go," Kid says making me almost come off of the bed when he places his hand on the small of her back to guide her out of the room.

A man covered in tats and piercings follows them out, leaving myself, Kincaid, Dominic, and another bearded man alone in the room.

"You had the simplest job." Kincaid begins to pace back and forth on the worn carpet, the other two men giving him a wide berth. "Blade tried to hide the fact that she was dancing from me. Gave you the opportunity to extract her and bring her home. I can tell you, Hound, coming in here and watching you come inside of my daughter is ten times worse than coming to Dallas myself and pulling her naked from the stage."

"Topless," I correct. "They sell liquor, so they have to keep their pussies covered."

"Jesus. What's wrong with you?" the bearded man I don't know asks, speaking for the first time.

"He seems like an idiot, Shadow," Kincaid says. "Like a man who can't keep his mouth shut or his cock in his jeans."

I shake my head. "I didn't say it out of disrespect. I just don't want you to imagine her on stage completely naked."

"Like it makes any difference with the memory of seeing you fuck her!" He roars loud enough to make my head snap back.

The tattoos on his arms dance and ripple as he continues to pace, his hands clenching open and closed repeatedly.

"I won't touch her again," I vow. "It was a mistake. A lapse in judgment on my part."

"Biggest mistake of your life," Kincaid adds.

I look him straight in the eye. "Not even close."

Kincaid holds my gaze for a long silent moment, and I feel the relief of reprieve when he turns and walks out of the room. Shadow follows him, but Dominic stays behind. I wonder if it's his turn to throw a couple of punches. Gigi is his niece after all.

"Don't go anywhere," he instructs. "We haven't decided what we're going to do with you."

"Yes, Sir," I answer giving him the respect he deserves. From what I know of the Cerberus MC, Dominic is the only one who served longer than I did. He's the one with the most experience of the group. A man I'd hoped would mentor me while working for Cerberus. It's another thing I'll lose when they leave me behind because I couldn't keep my dick out of the Prez's daughter.

Chapter 8

Gigi

"They know each other?" I ask as Kid shuffles me into a dark-tinted SUV in the parking lot.

"It's club business, Gigi," Jaxon mutters before closing the door in his face.

When he opens the front passenger door and takes a seat, I've had enough of the unanswered questions. Enough of the dismissals I've been getting my whole life. They may think they protect us from danger, but they leave us open to manipulations and betrayal.

"I don't give a shit if it's club business, *Snatch*." He turns his head toward me, mirth on his face. His son Lawson, my childhood friend's fiancé, looks so much like him it's almost startling. Using his club name, the one we were never allowed to use as kids gets his attention. "How does he know my dad?"

"He *was* going to work for Cerberus," Kid answers as he snaps on his seatbelt.

"Was?" I shake my head. "It's not an option for him now?"

Why does the thought of Jameson, or Hound, whoever the hell he is, being back in New Mexico make me want to go back to my childhood home?

I find Kid's eyes in the rearview mirror. "What do you think, Gigi?"

"I think I'm a grown ass woman who can make her own decisions. Who I have sex with is none of his damn business. It's only another way for him to try to control me."

"It isn't about who *you* sleep with that concerns your father. Hound sleeping with you was a betrayal your dad probably won't be able to get past," Jaxon chimes in. "Where are we heading?"

I give Kid the address without a second thought. I have no job since I was fired last night. Staying in Dallas isn't an option now, and Farmington is closer to Vegas where I plan to head in a couple of months after my birthday. I'd be a fool to refuse a free plane ticket and a nice place to sleep for a while, but it doesn't mean I can't play the only card I have.

"Make sure you tell my dad that if he holds what Hound and I did against him, if he doesn't allow him to work for Cerberus because of me, I won't return to New Mexico."

"You're going home," Jaxon assures me.

I shake my head. "I may get on a plane and step foot on the property, but I'll be gone in days. If he wants me to stay for any period of time, Hound will be there, too."

Jaxon huffs, and I feel like a little girl all over again. It doesn't matter that I'm a grown woman; to these men, I'll always be a child.

"He'll never allow a relationship between you and one of his men," Kid says from the driver's seat.

"You're too young for him," Jaxon adds.

"I'm what? Three years older than Khloe when you first brought her to the clubhouse." I watch the pink coat Kid's cheeks.

I laugh when Kid chokes a little. "Yeah," he agrees.

"The age difference is too much," Jaxon amends.

"There's a fourteen year age difference between Uncle Dom and Aunt Mak."

Jaxon once again narrows his eyes at me. "You deserve more than being the fuck buddy of a biker."

I raise an eyebrow at him. "Didn't Aunt Misty get pregnant with Griffin when she was Shadow's fuck buddy?"

Jaxon doesn't have a leg to stand on or a rebuttal. Kid laughs from the front as I sit back further on the bench seat in the back and cross my arms over my chest.

"That's what I thought," I mutter. "If Hound doesn't go back, neither do I."

I try to ignore the tension in the SUV by looking out the window, but a red Dr. Pepper sign painted on the side of an old brick building reminds me of the blood staining Jameson's face. So I opt to stare at my hands instead. If I concentrate hard enough, I can still feel the flex of his muscles under them from last night and this morning.

Is his lie of omission a betrayal?

Is this exact situation what he wanted to talk to me about before I persuaded him to fuck me instead?

Was my father the reason he seemed nervous?

"And you definitely deserve better than this," Jaxon mutters as we pull up outside of the shitty apartment complex I've called home for the last two months.

I don't justify my living arrangements with a comment. Honestly, there's nothing I can say that can make this place look any better.

"I don't have much," I tell them as I open the door. "Give me twenty minutes."

Kid and Jaxon both push open their doors.

"We have a plane to catch in two hours," Kid says coming around to the front of the SUV. "We'll help, so it only takes five."

"You didn't bring the Cerberus jet?"

They rarely travel commercial.

"We did. But your dad, Uncle Dom, and Shadow will be sticking behind for a few days. They have business to take care of," Jaxon clarifies.

It turns out I only needed the five minutes on my own to pack my meager belongings. Taking stock of what little I do have is depressing each time I move on from one city to the next.

The trip to the airport is spent in silence just like the entire plane ride back to New Mexico. People stare and move out of our way wherever we go. Mainly because Jaxon looks like the scariest man that's walked the face of the Earth, but Kid has bulked up in recent years, becoming a force of his own. I feel safe, protected around them, even though I'm not one hundred percent here of my own free will.

***

When I step out of the SUV in front of the Cerberus clubhouse, my first instinct, just like every time I return home, is to run. Judgment, pity, and looks of disappointment mark the faces of the new generation of Cerberus members. I barely know any of them, so any of them thinking they can judge me only pisses me off.

"Boys," I say and wink at the small group gathered around a motorcycle.

Every one of them nods in acknowledgment but cringe away from the flirtatious greeting.

"Leave them alone," Jaxon mutters under his breath as he walks by. "You've caused enough problems for the club."

I huff an incredulous laugh. "Didn't realize I had to get club approval on the guys I decide to fuck."

"None of these Cerberus members will touch you, Gigi. Leave them be." Kid has now joined ranks with Jaxon and my dad.

The Cerberus guys have always been off-limits. It was easy for them when I was a teenager. Their standards were too high to mess around with a young girl. After adding in my father being their president and boss, we were untouchable.

"None of the ones here at least," I challenge as I walk past both of them and around the clubhouse to my parents' house.

I left my scant belongings in the SUV. They wouldn't let me carry them even if I offered, so I don't bother to waste my breath.

My mother, the amazing, beautiful woman that she is, waits for me to approach on the porch.

"I've missed you," she says with pain in her voice. I walk into her open arms. "I'm so glad you're home, Georgia."

I let her warmth wrap around me, let it seep into my bones, let it strengthen me because I know I'll need it when my dad gets home.

"I missed you, too, Mom."

She sniffles, and unlike the last time I was home and her tears pissed me off, today after the way I've lived my life the last couple of months, they almost make me cry along with her. Tears after coming home show weakness. I know I'm leaving again soon, and they would only be used as ammunition against me when it's time to go again.

"Are you hungry?" she asks not letting go of me.

I shake my head against her chest. "No, I ate at the airport."

When she releases me, she doesn't bother to wipe her tears away. She's the strong one, the one who holds the family together, the one who is often on my side, even when I'm fucking up.

"Ivy, Delilah, and Lawson are home for the next two weeks before they head back to Brown for their senior year."

"Mom," I groan and pull completely out of her grasp. "Please don't start in on the college thing before I even step inside of the house."

"I'm not," she vows with her hands held up in surrender. "I just wanted you to know that you have people to hang out with if you wanted."

"Thank you," I tell her, but I'm still suspicious of the information she's given me.

Maybe she thinks I'll take off within days, like last year. I was home for three days before my dad shut down my idea of sticking close to home and working at Jake's.

I follow her in the house, loving how it smells exactly like my childhood and hating it at the same time.

"I put fresh sheets on your bed and dusted. The windows are open to air it out some, so make sure you close them before you go to bed." She turns and smiles at me again. "Are you sure I can't fix you something to eat?"

"No, thank you."

Unsure of what to do next, I just stand there swinging my arms at my side, much the same way I did as a kid.

"Maybe a shower will perk you up?" A gentle suggestion, but I know she doesn't leave any room for an argument.

My parents aren't harsh. They don't often yell. They've never lain a disciplinary hand on us. I assume because mom was abused by her first husband. They weren't mean, but Ivy and I were raised in a very strict household. My dad runs his home the same way he runs his club, with military precision and no room for argument.

Chapter 9

Hound

"I'm like a fucking caged dog," I bitch to the empty room.

It's been nearly a solid day since Kincaid and his crew busted down the door. Three days since I made a mistake, that after thinking it through, seems less like a lapse in judgment and more like the only outcome.

I'm certain the draw I have to Georgia Anderson would still be there if I saw her on her dad's property in New Mexico. I know without a doubt that even if I'd known it was her that very first night, there's a massive chance the night would've ended the same way. The only positive is that I wasn't entrenched in the club when I saw her for the first time.

I'm sitting at the small table when the banging comes on the door. I debate whether I should answer it, but I know if I don't they'll just kick it open again. I only left once yesterday to grab food and Breathe Right strips because my nose is so swollen from Kincaid's fist I could hardly breathe.

When I open the door, the man I identified as Shadow is standing there.

"Nice sticker," he says with a chuckle, indicating the strip still on my nose.

His attitude suddenly pisses me off. Sitting in a room not sure of what's going to happen, but having enough respect for the club to face the consequences, has made my normally expansive patience a little thin.

"Want one to match," I growl.

He laughs again.

"Come on. We got shit to do."

When he turns and walks away, I just stare at his back for a second before grabbing my wallet and keys to the room.

"Where are we going?" I ask after hustling to catch up with him near an SUV with completely blacked-out windows.

"For a ride," he mutters. Pointing his finger, he all but commands me to get in on the back driver's side.

"Lovely," I say to myself and open the door.

Dominic is driving, and Kincaid is glaring at me from the passenger seat.

"Sir," I say to him with a nod. It doesn't thaw him in the slightest.

I don't ask where we're going again. I ride in silence, and they do the same.

Ten minutes later, we're pulling into the nearly empty parking lot of the strip club.

"The Minge Palace?" Shadow mumbles in disgust as he looks out the dark window.

Kincaid shakes his head, fists clenching against his thighs. Not for the first time, I imagine how I would act if a daughter of mine was involved in the things Gigi has been up to. I'd burn this place to the ground.

"The owner has girls younger than Gigi working here. Saw another girl that couldn't be over seventeen."

Dominic looks at me in the rearview mirror and Kincaid and Shadow turn their glares in my direction.

"Information Cerberus or Blade at a minimum could've used days ago," Dominic growls.

"You made me a promise," Kincaid says in an even voice that doesn't fit the mood inside of the SUV.

"Yes, Sir."

"If you go back with us to New Mexico, are you going to be able to keep it?"

I nod, praying I can, but knowing I just told my first lie to my new boss.

"Yes, Sir." I swallow roughly and hate the sweat that is popping up on my forehead.

The parking lot is suddenly filled with activity. Police cars, unmarked SUVs, and even one patrolman on a motorcycle circle our SUV.

"You get the security tapes," Dominic says to me. "We don't have time to cut Georgia out of them. Destroy every one but the one from last night. She won't be on that one."

I nod and climb out of the SUV the same time they do.

We fall in an arrow pattern with Kincaid leading the charge until a man in a Texas Alcoholic Beverage Commission jacket steps in his path. I wait for the guy to shut us down, but he reaches out his hand.

"Kincaid," the man says in greeting.

"Agent Mooreland," Kincaid returns.

"Thanks for the heads up on this. How did you hear about it?" Mooreland releases Kincaid's hand and turns to face the front of the building as the other men get ready to enter.

"My man Hound came in for a little peep show and noticed how young the girls were. Said half of them weren't only underage, but the owner was supplying them with alcohol and drugs."

I realize with the lie that he has no intention of letting any other person outside of Cerberus know that his daughter was one of the underage girls dancing here just a few nights ago.

"Good catch," Mooreland says.

The praise makes my stomach turn.

"We ready?" Kincaid asks to move things along. I know he doesn't want to spend a second longer here than absolutely necessary.

Entry is simple enough. The patrons are grouped together in one corner, girls in the other as the local agencies move in further looking for the owner. When Kincaid nods at me, I take it as my cue to head to the security office. The lock is easy enough to pick, and I make entry in less than twenty seconds.

For privacy for the felony I'm about to commit, I shut the door behind me. I ignore the cocaine, marijuana, and various bongs. They aren't the reason I'm here.

Surprisingly, the security cameras are top notch. Not surprising is the owner is so narcissistic he wouldn't think that anyone would get past that simple damn lock because he didn't even have the program password protected. Quickly I download the entire database to the jump drive I always carry on my keys.

I imagine being able to keep my promise to Kincaid will be much easier if I have Gigi on video, for those nights I'm alone and can't keep my mind off of her. It's sick and disgusting, but even knowing that doesn't keep me from doing it. I wipe the video feeds from the system, plant a virus in the computer, and pray the techs that run through it will be able to find the video from last night. I imagine the owner has enough trouble coming, but a little child pornography is always a good thing when a piece of shit is going down.

I scoop up the brick of pot and a bag of coke and leave the room.

"Whatcha got there?" Mooreland asks as I turn the corner from the hallway.

"Party favors," I tell him and toss them his direction. "Found them in the security office."

"Perfect," he says and begins talking into a handheld radio to, I assume, the DEA. "Got something you'll be interested in."

He nods and walks away.

"Let's bounce," Shadow says coming from out of nowhere.

I follow him, meeting Kincaid and Dominic near the front door.

"Find what you needed?" Kincaid asks when we close ourselves into the SUV.

"Yes, Sir," I answer. "Added a little photo gallery and fake web searches as well."

The small twitch at the corner of Kincaid's mouth gives me hope.

"Of what?" Shadow asks from beside me as Dominic pulls away from the shitty club.

"Kiddie porn and a little bestiality for good measure."

Shadow begins to laugh, and Dominic's and Kincaid's chuckles follow.

"Yeah," Dominic says. "You'll do just fine, Hound."

At least the tension is lifted some before we reach my hotel.

"How much time do you need?" Kincaid asks.

"Just have to run in and grab my go bag and suitcase."

He nods as I climb out. I lied to him again because I spend at least a full minute with Gigi's pillow to my nose, breathing her in and trying to memorize her scent.

If she's in New Mexico, I know staying away from her is going to be the hardest mission I've ever faced in my life. Even knowing that if I touch her again, Kincaid will make me wish I was dead may not be enough to keep my hands off of her when she's standing in front of me.

I toss the pillow down, clutch my keys in the pocket of my jeans to remind myself that at least I have something of her, and grab my bags and head back to the SUV.

Silence fills the inside of the SUV when I climb in, and the tension hanging in the air means they were discussing me. They don't tell me to get my ass out, so I settle in for whatever comes next.

"I'm going to keep you very busy," Kincaid says five minutes into our drive to God knows where.

"Yes, Sir," I respond.

"I can tell you to stay away from Georgia, and for your safety, I pray you can. But understand that stubborn girl doesn't listen to a word I say. In fact, she does exactly opposite of what I instruct. So even though I'll forbid her to speak to you, know in advance, she's going to do it anyway."

"Yes, Sir."

It's then that he turns to look at me.

"You can just give her up that easily?" I swallow the lump in my throat. "Pretend like nothing happened? Don't feel an urge to fight for her?"

I shake my head. "I don't know what you want me to say, Sir."

He continues to glare at me.

"I made a promise to you. I'll do my best not to break it."

"You'll try?" It's the calm in his eyes that makes my skin crawl.

"Yes, Sir." Another swallow.

"Yeah, Hound," he sneers. "I think you'll be very busy."

I feel like a million pounds have been lifted off my back when he turns to face the front. Just the scrutiny of his glare was weighing me down.

"You're fucked," Shadow whispers before turning his focus outside the window.

Chapter 10

Gigi

"I still don't understand," I tell my sister.

"What's not to understand?" Ivy says with her brows drawn tight. "After our senior year, Delilah, Lawson, and I are moving back to New Mexico. We want to be close to family."

Even though we're twins, Ivy and I couldn't be any more different from each other.

"Doesn't Lawson have that repair shop in Providence?" I thought I heard some mention of it at Thanksgiving last year.

"He's going to open another one here," Delilah says with a light squeeze to Lawson's thigh.

"But you left years ago to be near Drew," I remind Lawson.

He shrugs. "Drew graduated in May, and he plans to attend a year of college on the east coast and a year here in New Mexico before going through the police academy in Albuquerque."

"A cop?" I ask.

A wide, proud smile spreads on Lawson's face. "It's what he wants to do."

Even a kid as young as Drew has a plan for his life. I look around the empty clubhouse living room when Delilah and Ivy start talking about friends from college. My dad is expected back at any time, but most of the other members left on some mission to South Africa this morning. They aren't expected to be back for over a week. A few members are around, but they always hightail it out of the clubhouse when we show up, either to get away from us or preferring to be in the garage during daylight drinking hours.

"What do you think?" Delilah's question pulls me from my wandering thoughts.

"What? I'm sorry. I spaced."

All three of them placate me with smiles. Ivy has already said something about my loose t-shirt and sweats, and I have no idea if they know what my life has been like since the last time I saw them, but no one has asked.

"Do you want to go to Jake's this evening?" Delilah asks again.

"What's the point? He won't serve us." I shake my head, a second away from turning the offer down, but I know anything is better than being stuck here. "Sure."

I can always sneak a flask like I used to do in high school.

"What about that blue dress you brought?" Ivy asks.

I'm only catching bits and pieces of their conversation, but that's no different than it's always been.

When the front door opens and my dad, Shadow, and Uncle Dominic walk through, I wish we were already at the bar. I may have to pregame with that flask long before the sun sets if my afternoon goes the way I suspect it will.

I haven't said a word to my father since he busted in on Jameson and me back at the hotel in Dallas.

"Hey, Daddy." Ivy beams as Dad walks in our direction.

The front door closing with more force than necessary draws all of our attention. My blood heats at the sight of Jameson looking back at the door in confusion.

"Sorry," he murmurs, refusing to make eye contact with me.

"He's trouble," Lawson whispers to Delilah.

"Everyone," Uncle Dom says walking a few feet closer. "This is Jameson 'Hound' Rawley, the newest Cerberus member."

"I'll show you to your room," Shadow says and turns toward the long hallway off of the kitchen.

I watch his muscled back until he disappears, and then I meet my father's eyes. Per usual, I can't read his face. He's a master at calm and cool passivity, but I'll take this over the anger and violence I saw in Dallas.

"Hey, sweetheart," Dad says accepting Ivy's hug.

Dad shakes Lawson's hand, and they do that weird manly back slap thing as if he and Law are old friends. It's weird, especially when I consider how little time they've had to get to know each other.

"Georgia," Dad says after he's done with greeting Delilah. "I'd like to speak with you in my office. Give me an hour to greet your mother, and I expect you to be there."

I nod my compliance, glad to have an hour reprieve.

"Gross," I mutter after he walks away and I take a moment to consider why he needs an hour to say hello to my mom.

Lawson chuckles at my discomfort.

My eyes stay glued to the door leading to the hallway, hoping, praying, and wondering if Jameson will come back through it before I have to go face the firing squad.

"Want to tell us what's going on?" My sister didn't allow even two minutes before the questioning began.

"Seems Dad doesn't approve of my choice in men," I tell them without pulling my eyes away.

"He's never approved of your choice in men. Well, not since Jordy. He liked that boy."

Looking away from the hall, I turn my attention to Delilah. "Jordy was the last guy Dad should've ever liked."

Good 'ol Jordy. He was my boyfriend my sophomore year. We dated for eight months, a lifetime in high school years. We messed around after his junior prom. A dreadful attempt at a blowjob somehow transformed into rumors of me sleeping with half the baseball team. My reputation in Farmington never recovered, and neither did my attitude.

"We all have regrets," Ivy says reaching for my hand.

I jerk it away before she can touch me.

"What's done is done," I tell her before standing up and walking away.

At first, I think of running out the front and hitchhiking into town, taking off and leaving New Mexico before Dad can yell at me, but the pull in Jameson's direction is stronger.

Ignoring the whispers at my back, I take the hallway that leads to the guys' rooms. We aren't allowed back here, so I'm not surprised Ivy and Delilah are having a mild freak out in the living area. I realize my mistake when I get to the middle of the long narrow hallway. I have no idea which room is his. Short of banging on every door, I have no other way to determine where he is. I have a million questions. Why is he even here? How did Dad go from hating him to hiring him in a matter of days?

"Jameson," I hiss. No answer, so I say it even louder, but it still doesn't pull him from his room. "Hound!"

"What are you doing?" Shadow's voice snaps my eyes to him just as a door down at the end of the hall opens.

I weaken at the sight of Jameson's gorgeous face, but my world is crushed when I realize he's looking past me at Shadow.

"You're not allowed back here," Shadow reminds me in a gruff tone.

"I want to talk to you," I tell Jameson just as his door closes.

"You need to leave him alone."

"We're both adults," I remind Shadow.

"It's a conflict of interest and not allowed, Gigi. It's been that way since day one, and nothing has changed." Shadow sweeps his hand toward the doorway. "After you."

Without a glance into the living room, I head out the back door of the clubhouse. Going inside my parents' house right now isn't an option.

I'll wait until I hear my mother tinkering around in the kitchen, in order to prevent hearing my dad tinkering inside of her by going inside too soon.

Sitting on the front porch, I notice the always empty field past Jaxon and Rob's house is breaking ground, preparing for another home to be built. It has to be Lawson and Delilah's. There's no one else that would be allowed to build out here.

Homeownership and marriage, which are their plans, seem like an anchor, and would only serve to drown me in obligation I never want to be burdened with.

I have no idea how long I sit on the front porch, but my back has rivulets of sweat running down it when my mother opens the door and lets me know my dad is waiting.

I notice the flush in her cheeks and grin for the first time thinking about my parents getting down and dirty. Maybe their romping will help Dad's demeanor toward me.

"Take a seat," he snaps the second I walk through the door of his office.

"Should I shut the door?"

He shakes his head. "No, your mother will be joining us."

"Why?" I question. "This is a club matter, not a family matter."

I don't want to face my actions in front of my mother even though I know my dad will hold nothing back when he speaks to her about it. They have no secrets. They kept tons of stuff from Ivy and me growing up, but they don't keep things from each other.

"It's both," he corrects just as my mother walks into the room and takes a seat in one of the chairs in front of Dad's desk.

I take the other seat, just wanting to get this over and done with.

"You will stay away from Hound," he commands.

"Why is he even here? How do you know him?"

"It's club business, Georgia, which means it's not yours."

I draw air into my lungs, preparing to let him have it, but my mother speaks up first.

"Maybe explaining Hound will make a difference," she appeases.

Dad makes eye contact with her before steepling his fingers under his chin. He squints when he looks back at me, considering his options.

Decision made, he sighs and leans in, elbows and forearms on the top of his massive desk.

"Hound was heading to work for me when Blade sent him on the fool's errand to collect you from your," he clears his throat, "latest place of employment."

"The strip club," I state, trying to rile him up for no other reason than knowing I'm going to agree to his demands, and this is the only power I have.

"He's off-limits," Dad says reiterating his point.

"He knew who I was then?" His eyes shoot to my Mom's before looking back at me.

"Not the night he met you. I don't think he recognized you with the contacts and wig."

He never would've touched me if he'd known the girl who met him in the alley was Kincaid Anderson's daughter.

It makes my heart deflate, but then I realize that Hound wanted me for me, not the appeal of fucking the boss' kid.

I smile at Dad. "You don't have to worry about Hound and me. It was just one of those things. A couple of wild days. It's over."

"Good," Dad says as Mom releases a long whoosh of air.

"I'm going to Jake's this evening with Ivy and the others."

He nods. I don't need permission to go, but his 'my house-my rules' still sticks even now at twenty. He wants to know where we are. It's the least I can do with the plans I have for later tonight.

Chapter 11

Hound

"Hey, man. I'm Hound." My proffered hand hangs in the air as the younger Cerberus member looks at it in disgust. "Okay."

I draw out the last word as I turn to grab a cold beer from the fridge.

"Nothing personal," he mutters. "But you won't be around long enough for us to spend time getting to know you."

"That so?" I lean my ass against the counter and tilt my beer to my lips.

"Yeah." He grabs his own beer out of the fridge. "Plus, there's no one here that's going to risk pissing Kincaid off by hanging out with you."

I know he's joining all the other guys outside in the garage. They all seem to gravitate in that area.

Word of my fuck up with Gigi has clearly spread from Dallas to New Mexico, and the cold shoulder I've gotten from all of the three members who aren't out on a job is just the way it's going to be for a while. What they don't understand is I have staying power and no plans to go anywhere anytime soon. I hope they change their tune when they realize that Kincaid has enough faith in my skills that even after what I've done, he's allowing me to work for him.

Emptying my first beer in one long swallow, I grab another from the fridge and head to my room. The Cerberus clubhouse isn't super fancy, but it's efficient. My room has a bed, dresser, and a full bathroom. I couldn't ask for much more.

I'm in the middle of stripping out of my jeans and t-shirt when my phone chimes. I smile without even thinking about it. Isabella is the one thing that can always bring me out of any funk.

Izzy: What are you doing?

I fold back the covers and climb between the sheets before responding.

Me: Getting ready for bed.

Izzy: You're such an old man!!

Me: But you love me anyway.

Izzy: With my whole heart.

Me: What are you doing?

I wait and wait for her to respond. A picture precedes her next text. I immediately save the shot of her smiling to my phone. Big green eyes and silky, black hair. She's the most beautiful girl I've ever laid my eyes on.

Izzy: Heading out with some friends.

I clench my fists knowing the kind of trouble she can get into.

Me: Be safe and have fun.

Izzy: ALWAYS!

I almost tell her how much I miss her. I almost tell her I wish we could be together sooner than I know we can be, but doing that will only drag her current good mood down. I'm a big enough person to shoulder the weight of our separation all on my own.

Instead, I go through my phone, looking at each and every picture she's texted me and the handful I've stolen from her social media profiles. The joy of seeing her pretty smiling face in all the pictures is almost enough to forget about the pain caused by the distance and time that separates us.

***

The safety is off on my Glock before the intruder can even get the bedroom door closed. I presumed this would happen. After being ignored so rudely by the MC members that are here, I've waited for their retribution. It wouldn't come in the form of murder, but I figured a late-night roughing up was in my near future.

What I don't expect is the hiccup and feminine giggle.

I stash the handgun back under my pillow and watch as Gigi tries to be quiet as she walks across the room. I should tell her to leave, not let her get any closer, but that's something I don't have the strength to do. I can't let anything progress, but that doesn't mean that I can't let her get close enough to smell her perfume.

She giggles again when her knees hit the end of the bed. Two soft thumps, presumably her shoes falling off, echo around the sparse room.

The scent of liquor on her breath makes it to my nose long before the soft floral scent of her perfume. That doesn't hit until a few seconds later, and rather than it being off-putting, the combination is intoxicating. My cock thickens, even further from the realization that she's brave enough to sneak into my room.

Even though there's limited light in the room, I can see her bright smile and the dark smudges of her makeup under her eyes. I want nothing more than to fuck her so hard she cries, making it run in streaks down her cheeks.

I wait until she's halfway up my body before speaking.

"What the fuck do you think you're doing?"

Startled, her eyes widen as far as the alcohol will allow, and she gazes around the room as if the voice could've come from anywhere else but under her.

She pats around, her eyes clearly not adjusted to the darkness. Her hand slides over my cock, and I growl.

"I'm going to see how far I can take that huge dick of yours down my throat."

Jesus, that sounds like the best thing in the world right now.

A glutton for punishment, I let her stroke me over the thin sheet. Up and down, with soft grips near the base and the tip, I let her continue until I'm half a second away from making another bad choice.

"Stop," I hiss and still her hand on my cock. "You know damn well I'd snap that pretty jaw of yours before you even made it halfway down."

"What a way to go," she coos. "If you're worried about hurting me, you can always just hold it straight up so I can bounce up and down on it."

"You need to go."

Please don't go.

"I'm so wet for you," she says ignoring my orders. "I've been thinking about the way you fucked me in that alley."

What a coincidence, I've been thinking of the exact same thing since I turned off the light this evening.

"It'll still be a tight fit, but I bet I just slide right down."

I keep my grip on her hand, right over my cock, even when she wiggles her fingers to try to get free. I know she has no intention of leaving, so letting her go is only a ploy so she can touch me somewhere else. God, do I want to let her do just that.

"You need to go," I repeat.

"I need *you*."

"Not gonna happen, Gigi. Now get the fuck out."

I hate the sound of her swift intake of air, but I release her hand instead of pulling her against my chest, exactly the opposite of what every single instinct in my body is telling me to do.

"You're an asshole," she whispers, but she doesn't say it in a hateful tone. She purrs it like the sultry sex kitten that she is.

Instead of moving further away, she inches closer. Rum, her choice of liquor tonight washes over me. I love the smell, knowing it probably makes her pliable, even more open to anything I'd like to do to her. I hate the smell for the exact same reasons.

"Seriously, Gigi." I roll out from under her and climb off the bed. "The last fucking thing I need is Kincaid finding out you've been in here."

I flip the light on. Big fucking mistake. Sprawled out on my bed in a tight green dress, Gigi fucking Anderson has her knees bent with her legs open. No. Fucking. Panties. I'm staring at the direct proof of that tight, slick seam she mentioned earlier.

I grip my dick.

She licks her lips.

It's sloppy, not as sexy as I'm sure she thinks, but her wet mouth has more appeal than this damn job does.

"So," she slurs. "You think he'll be mad if he finds out I'm here?"

I narrow my eyes at her, already knowing where she's going to take this. I remain silent, waiting for the drunken blackmail.

"You can fuck me, and he can never find out, or you can deny me, and I'll tell everyone I run into what a great fucking lay you were tonight."

"Not a chance."

I grip her by her upper arm and pull her off of my bed. On the way to the door, I scoop up her shoes and press them to her chest until her free hand reaches up to hold them.

"Blackmail doesn't work for me, beautiful." I swing open the door, praying someone is there, someone to serve as a witness to me throwing her out. The hall remains empty. "You'll only be wasting your time if you try to pull this shit again."

I shove her out of my room and close the door, locking it this time for good measure.

"I hate you," she seethes from the hallway.

"I hate me, too," I mutter.

Stripping out of my boxers, I hit the shower. To prove how much I despise what I've just done, I clamp my balls in my fist to the point of pain as I say her name and shoot my load down the drain.

Chapter 12

Gigi

Rejected. Again.

Always. Rejected.

I sniffle and straighten my back as I walk out the back door of the clubhouse and into the front door of my parents' home. I waited until everyone was asleep before sneaking down the sidewalk to Jameson's room. I couldn't care less if I wake the three people sleeping in this house now. Indirectly, my father is once again controlling my life. I can't even choose Jameson if I wanted to. Dad made sure of that.

My tears have dried, and a sense of calm resolve has settled in that gaping hole in my heart that never seems to be filled with anything else but the need to get away. So that's exactly what I plan to do.

I didn't unpack my bags when Jaxon brought them up the first day I got back, so too much of the room inside is filled with trinkets and shit I have no use for on the road. It takes a mere fifteen minutes to get them emptied and refilled with necessities.

"You're leaving already?"

I'm not surprised to find Ivy standing in the hall when I leave my room. Even the tears on her cheeks and the heartbreak in her voice isn't new.

"I wish I could be more like you," I confess. I blame the rum still in my system for that slip-up of honesty.

She shakes her head. "You're fine just the way you are."

I try to swallow the lump forming in my throat. Saying goodbye to her is always the hardest. You can't really share a womb with someone and not have a connection so deep it's unexplainable.

"I wish Mom and Dad felt the same way."

I put my bags down and wrap her in a hug, holding on just a little longer than the last time I walked away from New Mexico. Something in my gut tells me this time is going to be much different. This time feels like forever.

"You're not running from Dad this time." The truth burns my ear, but I ignore it just the same.

"I'll miss you the most," I tell her as I pull away and reach for the straps of my two bags.

"You can call and text," she offers.

"I will," I lie and walk away.

The cab I called for earlier is idling out front when I make my way around the clubhouse.

The lone Cerberus member standing on the front porch having one last smoke before calling it a night doesn't even faze me. I know he won't try to stop me. There's only one living Cerberus member who ever physically touched me without my father's permission, and he made sure to make me burn.

"Prez won't stop looking for you," he says on a thick puff of smoke.

I ignore him and climb inside of the cab. Just like always, I keep my eyes closed until the bump in the road three miles away. I never look back. I never second guess my decision to leave this place. Well, I never did until tonight.

***

"Hey, sweetie?"

I startle awake, looking right into the soft, tired eyes of the elderly woman that sat beside me on the bus out of Farmington.

"You said you were heading to Phoenix, right?"

I nod, draw in a lung full of air, and stretch my back out.

"We're only a few miles away," she informs me and points an arthritic finger toward the window.

"Thank you."

"Anytime, dear." She begins humming again with her eyes closed. It's what lulled me to sleep to begin with a couple of hours ago when she got on at the Tucson stop.

Even though I don't use my cell phone very often, traveling from Farmington after having tossed it in the trash hasn't been the most pleasurable. At least with a burner and a pair of headphones, I can ignore the world around me. Traveling and circling back, going out of the way has always been how I traveled.

It's how I found myself in an all-but-deserted bus station at three in the morning. Unable to buy a phone then, I knew in daylight hours I'd be able to grab one in Phoenix.

When the hiss of the bus's brakes make their final gasp, I wait for the elderly woman to stand. She manages on her third attempt, and I find myself uncharacteristically worried about her. I help her traverse the steep stairs at the front of the bus and wait for her while the attendants pull her suitcases off.

When she tells me that her son will be there to pick her up in an hour, I forgo my seat on my original bus to catch the one later in the evening.

"Thank you," she says in the sweetest voice I imagine a grandmother would have, as I pull out her chair and hand her a small ice cream cup.

I've always wondered what it would be like to have an elderly family. My dad's mom met an awful fate at the hands of my grandfather when he was only a teen. My mom doesn't have any family to speak of. Ivy and I have had some interaction with grandparent-type figures. Shadow's parents came around often enough, and her obsession with Griffin always ensured we'd be where he was. Doc and Rose have been very active in our lives as well.

"You didn't have to miss your bus for me."

"I have a little shopping to do," I tell her before filling my mouth with a huge bite of chocolate frozen yogurt.

"Where are you heading again?"

I know she's just curious, but cautious no matter who we are around is something that Dad drilled into our heads.

If you're not with family, you're not entirely safe.

"San Diego," I lie, a little weirded out and cautious since I never mentioned where I was heading before, just that I needed to grab some things in Phoenix.

"That's right," she says with a sugary sweet smile before diving back into her ice cream.

My nerves relax a little when she starts re-telling me the story about her travels and the three grandchildren she's visiting. It's the same story she told me when she got on the bus. She speaks of how busy her son is. My heart hurts for this woman. She's closer to eighty than seventy and shouldn't be traveling alone, and yet her family couldn't be bothered to drive two hours to get her.

"The world is heavy," she says in her soft, weak voice.

"I'm sorry?" I put my ice cream down and look over at her. "I was lost in my own head."

"You have the weight of the world all around you," she repeats. "It's too heavy of a burden to carry yourself."

I placate her with a smile but keep my mouth shut. In thirty minutes, I won't have to worry about her rambling. I'll make sure she's safe with her family, and I'll head North-West to Vegas just like I'd planned.

"You'll carry it on your back until you stop running and give someone the chance to love you."

"I'll keep that in mind," I cajole and stir my spoon through my melting ice cream.

"Mother?"

We both look up to see a middle-aged man walking toward us.

"Oh, Dave," she says in a near giddy tone. "Meet my new friend Annie. She's traveling to San Diego."

"Nice to meet you," he placates his mother without as much as a nod in my direction.

Asshole.

He helps her stand, taking no care to allow her to straighten and be firm in her stance before he releases her and reaches down for the handles on her suitcases. I stand, hand near her back, just in case she's not as sure-footed as he presumes she is.

"The next time he finds you," she whispers in my ear. "Stick around long enough that he can prove how much you deserve to be loved."

I watch, stunned and a little confused at her words, as her son shuffles her away almost faster than she can walk.

It's minutes after they've disappeared through the crowd of people buying tickets that I find myself wanting to yell, to chase her down and inform her that *he*, if she's referring to Hound, rejected me just like every guy I got close to did. I wasn't enough for him to go against my father's wishes. I can't imagine him changing his mind.

He's thirty-four years old, and I'm sure has had more woman than he can count. There's no way he'd ever be interested in me for more than what he already got.

Chapter 13

Hound

"Where the fuck is she?" Kincaid says after opening my door with what I presume is the master key to the building.

"What?" I sit up in bed, trying to scrub the sleep from my eyes. I did nothing but toss and turn all night after I escorted Gigi out of here. How I can feel both regret over it and proud I did the right thing is beyond me.

"Where is Georgia?" he asks again.

"She's not here."

"She *was* here." He holds up the shoes I handed Gigi before throwing her out of my room. "I found these outside of your door in the hallway."

"I gave my word to you, Prez. She showed up. She'd been drinking." I swallow and refuse to tell him that she offered herself to me. I squeeze my eyes closed, a futile attempt to block out the memory of the tightest, pinkest slit I've ever had the pleasure of sinking inside of. "I made her leave."

"What time?" he asks, defeat clear in his tone.

"Two-thirty? Maybe three." I stand and pull on a pair of jeans. "Think she took off again?"

"She packed her bags," Shadow says as he steps into my room behind Kincaid. "Misty checked her room."

"Did she tell you where she was going?" Kincaid's eyes are back on mine. He's pleading, grasping at straws, trying to control a daughter who has no interest in such a thing. I want to tell him to lay off of her and maybe she'll stick around, but he's only being a protective father.

I shake my head. "It wasn't...last night wasn't pretty."

"The fuck does that mean?" Kincaid growls, dropping the shoes and taking a menacing step in my direction.

"She made...advances. I didn't reciprocate." He growls, and I know he's torn between her being rejected and his command that I stay away from her. "I kept my promise."

"Are you saying you forced a drunken girl out of your room last night?" Seems the rejection is winning out right now.

I can't win for fucking trying at this point.

"I kept my promise," I repeat. "But, yes. I had to physically remove her. I didn't hurt her, but she wasn't happy when I closed my door on her."

"She ran," Kincaid says with disappointment. "Again. Shadow."

"On it," Shadow says and leaves us in the room.

"Did she ever mention going somewhere? A city? A certain job? Friends?"

I shake my head. "We never really talked about life goals and futures."

I'm disgusted, standing in front of this man and practically telling him I treated his daughter like a whore. Even after knowing who she was, I took her to bed, and if I'm honest, I can admit that the thrill of fucking her, the pleasure I gained from sleeping with the boss' daughter was part of the appeal.

"Pack your shit," he hisses.

I should've seen this coming. Fuck her or don't fuck her. The end result was always going to be the same.

"You, Scooter, and Rocker are heading to Tijuana. Simple extraction. Three days max."

He leaves without another word. My head is spinning from everything that just happened. Gigi is gone, more than likely left because I pissed her off, and I still have a job? Either Kincaid has something planned for me of devious proportions, or he actually is a decent man, and isn't holding a grudge even where his daughter is concerned.

"Fuck," I mutter scraping my hands over the top of my head. "I don't even know if I'm coming or going in this fucking place."

* * *

"This," Scooter says handing over a flash drive, "has all of the forms you have to complete before we can leave Mexico. Send them to Blade so he can finish the mission remotely."

I look at the sleek black device in my hand and then to Scooter's and Rocker's back as they turn to leave the hotel suite.

"And where are you guys going?"

Rocker grins over his shoulder. "Tijuana nightlife is the best thing ever. Sexy-ass girls all half-naked and ready to fuck."

"We're heading to the club," Scooter adds.

"And I'm staying here to do the paperwork?"

They both grin. "Being the boss sucks sometimes."

I look at Rocker, and he just shrugs.

"You can come with us," Scooter offers. "We can show you how Cerberus celebrates a successful recovery, but you'll still have to have that shit submitted before we leave."

My eyes cut to Rocker, who sobers a little, his smile falling to a flat line. He knows as well as I do that this mission wasn't as simple as we all thought.

One of the guys guarding the young girl that was abducted got the jump on him. He also got a bullet to the head, but Rocker was mere seconds from having his throat slit in the basement of a makeshift whorehouse that caters to men who have singular tastes, their sexual proclivities leaning toward pre-pubescent girls and toddlers. He was distracted by the depravity, and it almost cost him his life.

"It's no big deal," I offer. "I'll knock this out and grab some sleep. I haven't slept well in a couple of weeks. I'm sure I'll crash like the dead tonight."

"Your loss," Scooter says and turns back to the door. He turns back when he realizes that Rocker isn't with him. "You coming?"

"Naw," Rocker answers before grabbing a laptop out of his bag and sitting down on the bed. "I'm gonna help Hound fill out this paperwork."

"I appreciate it, man," I tell him. "But you don't have to do that. I can handle it."

"Shut the fuck up. The sooner we knock this shit out, the sooner we can slip inside of some sweet Mexican pussy." I can hear the playfulness in Rocker's voice, and for the very first time since joining Cerberus, I feel like part of the team.

"Dammit," Scooter mutters, but he grabs another laptop from his bag and opens it.

Rocker and I work in silence, but Scooter feels the need to hum stupid ass songs as he works. What would've taken me several hours to complete alone is finished in just under one with all three of us working.

"This is what Kincaid and Shadow spend all of their time on after missions?" I ask as I close my laptop.

I verified all of their forms and made sure they were sent to Blade.

"I guess," Rocker answers. "I only went out with them a few times when I first started. Grinch usually heads up the missions, but since he's in South Africa with the rest of the guys, Prez picked you."

"And if I wasn't an option?"

"More than likely we wouldn't be here," Scooter says as he puts his laptop away. "They only allow the guys with ten or more years in the Corps to head up the missions."

"So the girl we extracted tonight would've just been left?"

"Not necessarily," Rocker begins. "There are other companies. The family would've just gone down the list until they found someone available."

"Cerberus needs a bigger team," I mutter.

"Kincaid is expanding as fast as he can. I know you saw them breaking ground across the street. They have to have somewhere to house the new members. The new clubhouse will look more like a two-story hotel. We'll be able to have three times the amount of men, but until then we have to wait. You took the last available room." Rocker slaps me on the back and heads to the door. "You coming?"

I waffle between building a relationship with these men or just staying the hell inside. Getting laid, for the first time in my life, doesn't appeal to me.

"We can always bunk up together," I offer as a solution to the lack of space back at the clubhouse.

"Never," Scooter objects. "That's Kincaid's view. When we're in New Mexico, we're home, and having to share space with others is something he wouldn't force on us. We live that way when we're working. He doesn't want it to be that way all the time."

I nod my head in understanding but knowing more men means more chances for us to help those in need.

"Besides," Rocker says with a quick laugh. "You'd change your mind the first time you saw Scooter rutting around in some chick too stupid to turn him down."

I laugh. Scooter shoots Rocker a double middle finger.

"You coming?" Rocker asks again. He stares at me when I don't respond. "She always runs."

As if he's reading my mind, Rocker responds to thoughts I'd never verbalize to these men.

"Every once in a while, she'll show up like a lost dog, but she never stays long," Scooter adds.

"Who?" I ask playing dumb.

They both laugh and shake their heads.

"Come on," Scooter urges. "Tijuana is the best place to fuck her off of your mind."

I stand and join them. Not doing so would raise more questions, more suspicion than I'm willing to answer for.

Chapter 14

Gigi

"Order up," Benny says for at least the hundredth time tonight. He slaps the bell in the window beside the steaming plate of chicken fried steak as if I'm not standing right in front of him.

"Thanks," I mumble and drop off another ticket.

I carry the plate of food to the trucker who ordered it. I drop it the last couple of inches unintentionally.

"Sorry. Be careful, that plate is damn hot."

The trucker, unfazed by the hot splash of gravy on the back of his hand smiles up at me. Lifting his hand, he licks the food from it.

"That's alright, darlin." The quick flip of his tongue, I know, is supposed to be seductive, but half of it gets stuck in his ratty beard, and my stomach turns. "You can make it up to me later."

I just nod, used to the sexual solicitations from the clientele this crappy diner pulls in. Three more weeks until I turn twenty-one and I won't have to work for less than waitressing wages under the table. Benny hires all of the women who work here that way, so he doesn't have to pay payroll taxes. If an accountant took a long hard look at this place, they'd question how it operates without staff.

"I still need ketchup," a woman barks when I walk by.

"Coming right up," I tell her with a smile.

"They know your smile is fake," Farrah sneers when I reach behind the counter for ketchup.

"And?" I hiss. "What does it matter if I fake smile?"

"You get better tips if you're genuine."

"The fake smile is the best I can do," I murmur before dropping the sauce off to the female trucker who's looking at me the same way the gravy guy did.

"Thanks, baby," she purrs in a rough smoker's voice. "When do you get off?"

"I work all night," I lie. My shift ends in a couple of hours, and all I can think about is falling into my bed and passing out. Sleep and work. It's all I can manage these days.

"Too bad. I pull out at midnight. Have to make it to Salt Lake City by ten." She winks at me, and I offer my fake smile. "I could possibly be a little late."

I take a step back when she reaches for my hip. "Have a safe trip. Maybe next time you're coming through."

"You bet your tiny, sweet ass, baby," she says as I walk away.

I know I shouldn't give them any hope. I know it's a dangerous line I'm walking, but tips generally suck, or they go to the girls like Farrah, who will either jump from sleeper to sleeper or bring these men and women up to our tiny two-room apartment over the diner.

I have to scrape for every dollar I earn because whoring myself out for twenty bucks isn't something I'm willing to do.

"She would've paid at least fifty," Farrah says looking back over at the lady trucker. "I bet she'd be more interested in getting you off than the other way around."

"No thanks," I say standing near the window and waiting for my next order to come out.

Farrah has been trying to get me to see the brighter side of prostitution since she arrived over a month ago. I started working here less than a week before that, but she isn't the first girl to pick the diner for the extra earning ability. The girl that I shared the apartment with for four days before she took off with a trucker that promised her the world also earned extra cash in the parking lots.

"Not my thing," I mutter when Farrah just stands there staring at me.

"Women?" she questions. "I'd choose the women over the men any day, and one like that one where I'll probably just have to lay back and get licked? Those are the best."

"She's all yours," I offer.

"Sweet," she says turning her back to the patrons eating and waiting for food. She doesn't turn back until she's lifted her already exposed tits up an inch higher.

Shaking my head, I do my best not to judge her. I know some women are forced into this kind of life. They do things they never thought they would because they have no other choice. I also know the probability that Farrah will either end up on drugs or with a pimp that controls her every move is high. I also know the likelihood that she may end up in the sex trafficking trade is even higher. The difference in her and the women Dad has spent his life rescuing is that there's no one out there for Farrah. There's no one looking for her, worried about her, or willing to pay a ridiculous amount of money to keep her safe. She's one of the truly lost ones.

Just like me.

Shaking my head again, I try to dislodge those thoughts. I know all of the risks Farrah is taking with her life, other than the prostitution, are the same ones I take with mine.

The difference is, she's looking for someone to love her whether she admits it or not. I'm running from parents who, in their own weird way, only want what's best for me. I'm running from people who love me and want me around. Tears sting my eyes when I look over and watch Farrah shove her tits in the female trucker's face.

I've managed to keep the money I whored myself out to Hound for, but I know that if something doesn't change soon, there's a real chance I'll be doing exactly what my roommate is doing to earn a couple extra bucks. Farrah truly seems to enjoy the extra attention she gets from the truckers. She's not crying into her pillow when they leave. She's not using drugs to get through the act of selling herself.

I'm the one teary-eyed and questioning every choice I've ever made. I'm the one standing here and ignoring the ding of Benny's bell. I'm the one who's considering that maybe community college and the comfort of my parents' home isn't such a bad thing.

***

The sounds of familiar grunts and a shitty bed frame squeaking wake me up. It's the third time it's happened since I got off work early this morning.

I cover my head with my pillow and wait for it to stop. It never takes Farrah long to escort her Johns from the apartment, so I wait, bladder ready to explode until she's done. I never look up, never wonder what's going on. I've never had any desire to see first-hand what it takes to earn a little extra cash, but today the yelling makes my head pop up.

"Let go," Farrah says clawing at the man's hands around her throat.

"I'm not leaving until I come," he hisses but loosens his grip.

She takes as deep a breath as she can manage, and despite this man, twice her size and menacing as the devil himself, who is in front of her with the ability to kill her in a flash, Farrah never looks scared.

"I'm done," she hisses. "If you'd stay off of the dope, I'd have more to work with than a half-hard dick."

My eyes shoot straight to his crotch. If that's half-hard, I can't imagine what he looks like fully erect.

His grip tightens again, but even with breaths being pulled in on harsh wheezes, she never loses the fire in her eyes or drops the sneer from her lips.

The click, that tell-tale sound of a hammer being pulled back, draws both of their attention.

"Let her go," I command.

Farrah frowns, but the guy immediately releases her and pulls up his pants.

"I didn't sign up for this shit, Farrah," he mutters before shrugging on his jacket.

Farrah glares at me before turning back to him. "We can finish in your truck."

The fuck is going on?

"Next time." He angles his head in my direction. "Make sure that crazy bitch doesn't pull this again."

I watch as the man digs out a few bills from his wallet before handing them to my psycho roommate and kissing her lips. He doesn't kiss her like a man who just had his massive hand cutting off her air supply, but someone he genuinely cares for.

"Unless you want to take this next trip with me?" Hope fills his voice, but Farrah takes a step back and shakes her head.

"Maybe next time." She pecks him one last time before he leaves the room.

I release the hammer on the small gun I got a week ago and shove it back under the edge of my shitty mattress.

"What the hell is that all about, Homeless Barbie?"

"He was hurting you," I hiss. "Well, I thought he was hurting you."

"It's his kink," she offers folding the money and shoving it into a tin cookie can.

"I know that now."

"Did it turn you on?"

I huff a humorless laugh. "Turn me on? Not a fucking chance. I was seconds away from shooting him."

"You'd kill for me?" Confusion draws her brows together.

"No," I lie. "I'd probably shoot him in the leg. I won't sit around and watch any man hurting a woman like that."

Another lie. Yes, I'd kill him. Dad trained us to shoot center mass, and that's exactly where my weapon was pointed.

"You need to go home," Farrah says as she tugs on a t-shirt. "You don't belong out here with girls like me."

"Girls like you?" She better not start in on trying to convince me to be a prostitute again. I've heard all I can take.

"Girls like me would've looked at the reversal of this situation. If I saw you dangling from the fist of some deadly trucker, I would've wondered if I could work my shift at the diner before reporting your dead body up here. Girls like me would've covered my head with my pillow while you died, not out of fear, but because if you die, then I get to keep the money you have stashed under that broken tile in the bathroom."

My stomach turns.

"You'll never be a girl like me, and that makes you more dangerous than the men that choke me when they're not role-playing. I'll take those creeps over some girl running from problems any of us would trade our shitty lives for any day."

I fall back on my mattress, wondering if she's stealing my money when she walks away and closes herself into the bathroom.

Chapter 15

Hound

"Jesus," I hiss when Scooter slams the door to the SUV at least ten times harder than required.

"The day after always sucks," Rocker says with a quick slap to my back.

I cringe harder, the movement jostling my brain that's been swimming in Russian vodka for the last three days.

"It was a three-day bender," I correct him.

"You can't tell me you didn't do this shit in the Corps," Grinch says no worse for the wear even though he put back more alcohol this last week than all of us combined.

"I worked. All the time. I didn't risk getting drunk in foreign countries."

"We worked, too," Catfish says with a little irritation in his voice.

I shake my head. "You spent four years in the Corps. I was there seventeen. You really want to compare our work ethic?"

He flips me off. When I first got here two months ago, I wouldn't have bothered to joke around with them or call them out on their shit. After several missions and a couple of close calls, these guys have finally accepted me into their inner circles.

I can't say the same for Kincaid. He talks at me, barks orders, listens with professionalism when there's a problem, but for the most part, he sends Shadow with information or Blade with intel. I stopped taking it personal weeks ago when I realized he's not really treating me any differently than he does the other guys.

His inner circle: Shadow, Dom, Kid, Jaxon, and Rob are different, but he's been with those guys going on twenty years. I understand that type of brotherhood. I can also accept that I'll never be a part of it.

"You wanna grab a beer?" I glare at Rocker as I walk past him into the clubhouse. "Don't be a pussy."

I growl, no menace in the act. A long hard look at him and I can tell he's fucking with me. He looks tired as fuck, and I bet we all lay down and sleep for the next two days.

The mission to Russia was beyond fucked. The three girls we were sent to recover were dead before the wheels of our plane left New Mexico soil two weeks ago. We didn't find that out, though, until four days ago. All the guys took it hard, but I took it harder.

The trio of seventeen-year-olds were all abducted after softball practice. Same graduating class, same small town. Two were cousins, so that family took a double hit. They just never showed up for dinner that night. Hell, I found out the small-town Baptist church they all attended offered to pay for the recovery. Grinch, the other Cerberus member who leads missions when we split up informed me that Kincaid wouldn't take a dime from them. He said we have funds and accounts to help people like this. Kincaid isn't the type of man to bankrupt a small community just because they wanted their children back.

So the three-day Cerberus bender was about healing, regret, and the stolen lives of three young women who didn't deserve the fate they ended up with. We were waiting for Kincaid to work some things out, giving us the ability to carry home the decomposing bodies so their families will have some closure.

"It never gets easier."

I look up and see Kincaid standing in the kitchen of the clubhouse. He offers me a beer, and even though the thought of turning it up to my lips makes me want to vomit, I take it from him.

"Thanks." I tilt it his direction in salute before turning it up to my lips.

We stand in silence for a long moment, me just letting the weight of the mission hang heavy in the air. He, being the true leader he is, gives me this moment of reprieve.

"It's not my first loss. It's not even my first civilian loss, but it just fucked me up more than I thought possible."

My phone buzzes in my jeans pocket, but I ignore it.

"I was affected when I was younger." His calm voice is like a balm to the wounds our trip opened. "But when I became a father to two precious, helpless little girls it was always more difficult."

"It's why you'll never stop looking for Gigi even when she's adamant that she doesn't want to be found."

It's not a question. I know I'd do exactly the same thing he is. I'd do everything in my power to keep my child safe, even if she fought me every step of the way.

"You'll understand when you're a dad." With a quick nod of his head, he leaves me standing alone in the kitchen.

"Right," I mutter and pour the rest of my beer down the drain.

My phone buzzes again, the second notification from the text I got a moment ago, but I don't pull my phone out of my pocket until my bags are thrown in the corner, and I'm stripped down to my boxers.

My stomach turns, and I nearly vomit for a whole other reason when I finally look down at the message.

Blade: Georgia has an appointment at the abortion clinic in two days. Sending info.

It buzzes again in my hand with the address of a women's clinic on Sahara in Las Vegas.

A cold sweat chills my skin.

My first instinct is to grab the keys to one of the SUVs and make the sub-nine hour trip across the desert.

My second instinct is to allow her to make her own decisions.

Her body, her choice.

I made the same argument once before, and that didn't work out the way I'd expected it to either.

Without a second thought, I unlock my darkened phone and make a call.

"Hey, you."

My eyes close at the sweet sound of her voice.

"Hey, you," I mimic.

"I have a ton stuff to take care of tonight."

I can hear the TV going in the background and other voices close by.

"I just wanted to call and hear your voice, baby."

"My day is pretty busy tomorrow, too."

I nod. "Maybe the day after?"

"Who are you talking to?" The male voice I despise echoes through her phone, and I clutch mine even tighter.

"Nicky from work," she lies.

"Tell her I said 'hi.'"

"Jim says hi," she says into the phone.

"Tell Jim to jump off of a cliff."

I clamp the bridge of my nose with my fingers.

"Saturday will be best," she assures me, ignoring my jab. The noise level lowers, and I can tell that she's walking away from whatever group she was with. "He'll be gone Friday night and won't be back until late on Sunday. I can talk more then, but I'll text you later."

"I love you, Izzy," I tell her.

"Love you, too," she whispers before ending the call.

I haven't told Izzy about my fuck up with the Prez's daughter. I haven't even mentioned her once. She's asked more than once about my job here. I give her the basics, protecting her from my mistakes, but she'll know eventually. If Gigi is pregnant, if I do exactly what my instinct is telling me to do, then I risk losing Izzy altogether. For the first time in my life, I'm honestly torn between two decisions. For the first time in my life, I second guess whether choosing Izzy over all others is what's best. I'm torn between breaking the heart of a girl I swore to love and protect seventeen years ago or a twenty-year-old wild child who spends her life running away from her family just because they want her to grow the fuck up.

My hands clench until they hurt as I lie in bed trying to make a decision, a decision I knew wasn't a fucking decision the second that fucking text came through.

"Fuck," I roar as I climb out of bed and get dressed.

Hoping to find Grinch in the living room where chatter is coming from, I stop dead when I see Kincaid and Shadow having a couple of beers with some of the guys that just returned from Russia.

"Beer?" Scooter asks, pointing to the cooler near his feet.

"No thanks." I turn to Kincaid. "Can I borrow one of the SUVs, and take a couple of days off?"

He watches me for a long moment, analyzing the look on my face and trying to figure out exactly what's going on.

"Can I ask what's up?"

I clear my throat.

"You can."

This isn't going to be pretty.

"And you'll tell me the truth."

"Yes, Sir."

His face softens. "But you don't want to tell me."

"I'd rather not."

"Do you need backup?"

I shake my head. "No, sir. This is mostly personal."

His eyes widen, but only a little. He nods, and I can see a pleading on his face. I've seen that look once before, so I know he knows the nature of my business.

"Be safe." I turn to leave. "Keep your promise."

I walk out without responding. I did make him a promise, but I won't repeat it, especially when I know I may not be able to keep it.

Chapter 16

Gigi

"Seriously?"

I roll my eyes at my new roommate.

"Calm the fuck down," she hisses. "I worked a double yesterday."

I swipe at the angry tears running down my cheeks as I toss another small pile of clothes out of my way.

"You worked a double *two* days ago. Then you got fucked up on pills." I kick the small table between our beds just to make noise. "I worked your double yesterday. On my one and only day off I had scheduled for the next two weeks."

"I'll work your shift tonight," she offers.

My eyes narrow at her kindness.

"I'll work my own shifts, thank you very much."

I'm normally nice to my roommates, but this one has a different guy in her bed sometimes twice a day, and the fucked-up part is she isn't a prostitute. At least with Farrah, I knew she was working to build up a nest egg. Kori just sleeps with guys to sleep with guys, and she's not even courteous about it.

"But today's your *thing*, right?"

Nosy bitch.

"Right?" She sits up in bed. "You won't be able to work after."

"I'll be fine," I hiss, hating that she overheard me on the phone when I made the appointment last week. I even gave them my real name, knowing Blade would probably track me down in whatever IT magical way he finds me.

"I'm not saying you're a weak person, Annie. I'm saying, from experience, working a ten-hour shift on your feet after an abortion isn't going to be possible."

I collapse on my bed.

"I need the money," I mumble.

She laughs. "For what? It's not like you're saving up to take care of a baby."

I stare at her back when she goes to the restroom, but turn my eyes when she doesn't even bother to close the door before she sits on the commode.

"How are you getting there?" The toilet flushes and the water in the shower starts. "I can get Simon to take you."

"I'm taking the bus. I don't want to be anywhere near Simon."

I shudder at the thought of her boyfriend taking me to do something so personal. Technically, he's not her boyfriend, just a guy she keeps around and uses for things like money and transportation. He's head over heels in love with her, has been since they ran away from home together a couple of years ago, but Kori is too wild to see what's in front of her eyes.

"He's not a bad guy," she yells over the sound of the shower.

I know he's not, but today is going to be emotionally exhausting. Simon always wants to talk about Kori and what I think he should do to make her love him. The last time he asked and I was in a shitty mood, I told him to walk away from her. Let her live her life like she wants. Even if she's fucking up, it's her choice.

He wasn't very happy about that. So unhappy in fact, he told her what I said. She was livid with me, which I normally wouldn't have an opinion one way or the other about, but I have to trust this girl enough to at least not slit my throat while I'm sleeping. Praying she wouldn't rob me blind was even asking too much of her.

"Like I said." Kori comes in buck ass naked and drying her unhealthy hair with a sheet-thin towel. "The first one is always the hardest. I'll cover your shift tonight."

"It's the last one," I mutter to myself.

"Huh?" She turns her head in my direction.

"I said thanks. I won't ask you to cover another. I appreciate it."

"Don't worry," she says with a wide grin. "You'll owe me."

I only nod, not willing to argue the point of covering her double shift yesterday while she slept off the effects of the handful of pills she took that should've killed her.

After I find the jeans I was looking for earlier, I scoop up my clothes and toiletries and head to the bathroom, making sure to lock the door. I miss Farrah more than I ever thought I would when she came home three weeks ago and said she was getting married to the choking trucker. She promised to stop by when they drive through, but I haven't seen her yet. Probably never will again.

I shower and dress before opening the door. Steam follows me out of the room, and my clothes stick to my body. There is not one window in this small apartment. If it weren't for both of us having keys to the deadbolt, It'd almost be like a prison cell with only one way in and one way out. It goes against everything my father instilled in us as kids.

"You sure you don't want Simon to take you?" She looks back down at her hands and types away on her phone.

"I'm good, thanks though."

"It's free if Simon takes you." She looks up again.

Why is she hounding me about this?

"It's free for me, not him. I'm not going to owe Simon a damn thing."

"You won't owe him anything. I will."

And she'll never repay him. She uses people. She always has an ulterior motive. Always thinking of deception two steps ahead. I won't owe her by proxy either.

"The bus is fine."

I flip my hair over and gather it in a loose ponytail before twisting it into a bun. I'm in desperate need of a haircut, but I've been so tired. I add keeping my long hair to my mental pro/con list I've been building since the second line showed up on the dollar store piss test. I get too hot with it down against my neck, but I have a raging headache within an hour of pinning it up.

"Suit yourself," Kori says as she tosses her phone on her mattress and tugs a Benny's Diner t-shirt over her head. She doesn't bother with a bra. Hell, I don't know if the woman even owns one. She probably left it back home with her modesty.

"Where did you get the money?"

"Huh?" I look up at her after putting my real ID in my purse.

"For the abortion. You said you're going to the clinic down on Sahara? That's not some back-alley procedure. That's like a legit fucking place. Expensive. Where did you get the money?"

Holy hell. What has this girl been through?

For a second I wonder if she's going to shake me down for the cash, and that's the reason she was pressing so hard for me to ride with her friend.

"The father is paying for it."

"He just handed over six hundred dollars in cash?"

Her head pulls back a few inches as if she's shocked, but then she licks her lips, literally salivating at the thought of having access to that much cash. No doubt she's imagining all of the drugs she could buy with it.

"Fuck no." I release a heartless laugh. "He's meeting me there. Said he didn't trust a whore with that kind of money."

My stomach turns, part with the morning sickness I haven't been able to kick but also at the thought of how Jameson would actually act if he found out that he knocked me up during our little tryst.

Her face falls, filled with disappointment, and I immediately begin to think of moving on soon. She doesn't seem to be going anywhere soon, and there's no way I can stay feeling so unsafe. As soon as I heal from this procedure, I'm on to bigger and better things.

I wait until Kori heads downstairs to work my shift before going back into the bathroom and pulling away the broken tile behind the toilet. Thankfully, the wad of cash I've managed to hang onto for months is still there. I take all of it, even though it's more than today will cost. I have to find a different place to keep it, and I'm thinking outside of this apartment is going to be best.

The trip on public transportation isn't as bad as it could be. At least it's daytime, and no one tries to sit on my lap like the last time I made a trek across town.

I do like always, keep my head down, headphones in with no music. It's a deterrent for people who want to bother me, but still gives me the ability to be cognizant of what's going on around me. I'm closed off, angry look on my face, as unapproachable as possible.

Forty-five minutes and one bus switch later I'm standing near the parking lot of the clinic. I take a deep breath, having already made my decision before today. Keeping a baby while running from town to town isn't possible, so there's only one solution.

I pat my pocket, making sure I didn't get rolled by the teenager who bumped into me on my way off of the bus. Relieved, but for some reason also saddened by it still being there, I walk toward the front door.

For the third time in my life, I'm hauled off of my feet and tossed over a shoulder. Even as embarrassing as this is, when the scent of his cologne fills my nose, I smile against his back, and I don't even argue when he roughly shoves me into the front seat of an SUV I recognize as my dad's. I remain silent as he clips my belt and walks around to the driver's seat.

Chapter 17

Hound

"You look like shit," I spit when I settle in behind the steering wheel.

Fun fact, she actually looks gorgeous. Her long brown hair is more radiant than I remember, and her blue eyes, although not as bright as before, shine.

"Nice talk," she says and reaches for the door handle.

I growl before I even realize I want to. My hand clamps on her thigh, squeezing until she yelps from the unintentional pain.

"Why are you here?"

I angle my head toward the women's clinic.

"You know exactly why I'm here."

She huffs a humorless laugh. "This is a Cerberus SUV."

Small talk isn't her style, and since neither is keeping her thoughts bottled up, I wait for her to get to the point she wants to make.

"I have to say," she begins looking away from me and out the window. "I'm surprised you're still working for him. Figured you would've tried to fuck my mom by now."

"I'm sure my employment will end today," I say not taking her bait and getting riled up at the mother comment.

"Why are you here?" she asks again. "To stop me?"

I look out the window, the battle in my heart and head telling me to beg her to walk away from this place raging like a literal fire.

"I'm here to hold your hand or—"

"You're here to make sure I follow through with what you said in the alley."

"I don't rem—"

She lowers her voice, trying, and failing, to sound more masculine.

"That money is for the abortion if my stupid ass put that shit into motion..."

Chills race over my skin, leaving behind the sting of regret.

She pats her pocket. "I still have the money, so thanks for that."

I bite my bottom lip until I taste tangy copper on my tongue.

"You don't have to go in with me." Her lack of bravery is betrayed by the crack of her voice. She's trying so hard to make me think she's strong, all I want to do is wrap my arms around her and promise her the world. "I'll make sure it's taken care of."

I reach out and clamp her thigh again when she tries to open the door.

"Georgia."

Her tear-streaked face turns, telling me she's listening, but she's looking past me, not directly in my eye.

"You didn't let me finish. I'm here to hold your hand in that clinic if that's what you want."

She nods.

"Or to hold that baby when it's born and help you raise him." Her eyes finally meet mine. "I'm not here to convince you one way or the other, but I'm here for you—whichever direction you go."

"You're not here to stop me?"

I shake my head, but her eyes trail to my throat where I work on the dry lump that has formed there.

"You're lying," she whispers. "You do have an opinion about what I should do."

I follow her eyes when they look down at the hand gripping her thigh, the hand that's keeping her from getting out of the SUV.

"It's your body. It's your choice." I shake my head, fingers flexing against her jeans as I resist the urge to cup her cheek.

She looks out the window, staring at the entrance to the clinic, and I sit in silence with my heart pounding in my chest.

"You want to marry me and raise this baby together?"

I can't stop the laughter that bubbles up my throat. "Fat fucking chance."

I can see mirth in her eyes when she looks back at me. The reaction on my part was natural, but the smile on her face tells me it's exactly what she wanted to hear.

"No happily ever after for us?" She gives me a weak smile. "No handful of kids and white picket fence in our future?"

"That's not what you want either," I add.

"You said you're unemployed after today. Why would you think that?"

Shaking my head with a quick chuckle, I look back over at her. "Fucking you is one thing. I don't imagine your dad is going to be happy that I knocked you up."

It's her turn to laugh. "I'm a grown woman, Jameson."

God, I love the sound of my given name on her lips, the breathy way it falls off of her tongue.

"You are," I agree.

"We can just not tell him," she suggests.

"A baby is kind of hard to hide," I reason with her, but the fact that she's considering keeping the child makes my heart soar.

When she looks up at me, a small smile playing on her lips, the brightness she lacked in her eyes is there once again. She's breathtakingly beautiful.

"We don't have to go back." She shifts in her seat, anxious for the future she's imagining. "We can stay here in Vegas. Get a three-bedroom house or apartment."

My brow furrows.

"One for me, one for you, and a nursery."

I told her there's no happily ever after for us, and I meant it, but for some reason, the thought of us living together sounds perfect until she specifies that it'll be in separate rooms. As if I would have the ability to stay out of her bed. Out of *her*.

I can't live in Vegas. It's too far from Izzy. I've spent years too far from her. When I discharged from the Corps, I told myself, I promised her, I'd never be more than a few hours away.

"I'm not living in Vegas," I mutter. "And I'm sure as fuck not getting a three-bedroom apartment and hiding a grandchild from your dad."

Her mood changes the second the words are out of my mouth.

"Why do you keep running? What's so bad about New Mexico?"

She clears her throat past the emotion that's playing in her tear-filled eyes.

"I hate it there."

"Not good enough." I cup her cheek like I wanted to earlier.

"They want me to be Ivy."

The twin. The one that looks so much like the woman sitting in this SUV, but amazingly different at the same time.

"You're nothing like your sister."

"Much to my parents' disappointment," she mutters.

"You're not a disappointment."

She gives me an incredulous look before turning her eyes back to the clinic.

"My appointment is in five minutes."

"Okay."

What else could I possibly say to her?

Silence fills the inside of the SUV, thick and full of unsaid things.

Five minutes tick by, then another ten.

"Are you going in?"

Her head shakes, and relief fills my heart.

"Not today," she whispers.

I put the SUV in drive and pull away before she can change her mind.

"We have to tell your dad."

"And he's the deciding factor?" I can't ignore the bitterness in her voice.

"It's your choice. I won't force you to make a decision one way or the other, and I sure as fuck won't let anyone else either."

"You'd go against my dad?"

"For you?" I ask. "For that baby? For your right to choose what happens to your body? How you want to live your life? Any day. Every day for the rest of my life."

"Careful, Jameson. You're making me want things I know I can never have."

She refuses something to eat, so we head back to the hotel I checked into late last night. It's better than the one back in Dallas, and I know I got the upgrade hoping she'd come back here with me at some point. I wanted her in comfort if she followed through with the procedure, all the time praying she'd be here under different circumstances.

"You seem way more okay with knocking me up than I ever expected," she says as I open the door for her and let her walk in first.

"I feel guilty," I confess as I toss the keys on the table in the corner. "I should've taken the time to wrap up that night."

She winces and turns so I can't see her face.

"You regret hooking up with me."

I don't even try to stop the laugh that bubbles from my throat.

"Regret? Not a fucking chance." Her shoulders tense, but she doesn't turn around. "I don't know that I'd change a damn thing, even considering exactly where we are right now."

That's the fucked-up truth to this entire situation. Even risking losing my job, even the different scenarios of how Dallas could've ended, I wouldn't change a damn thing.

"I'm tired," she says in a soft voice. "Can I take a nap?"

"Of course. Bed is yours."

I watch, my mouth going dry when she pulls off her t-shirt and jeans. Crawling between sheets I tossed and turned in last night, she sighs heavily before settling into the comfort I know she isn't afforded in whatever shithole she's been staying in.

I don't ignore the text I get from Shadow. I don't pretend like we're living on borrowed time in some bubble like I did before. I don't know how much Cerberus knows, but it won't be long before the cavalry shows up and tries to sweep her away. I imagine they've done it so many times; it's just become part of their routine.

I send Shadow the name of the hotel and room number, then I spend hours trying to figure out a way to make this entire fucked-up situation work for all involved.

Chapter 18
Gigi

I stiffen in the bed, even though it's the best night of sleep I've gotten in months. The last, of course, is the night I slept in the bed with Jameson in Dallas. It's surprising, considering he spent the night on the small sofa in the room. He woke me after the sun had set and convinced me to eat something which I did, but fell asleep again shortly after.

"She's sleeping," Jameson says from the hallway.

"It's noon, Hound. Is she sick?"

Shadow.

I should've known that they would arrive shortly after my knight in biker boots scooped me off of the sidewalk yesterday.

"Kinda," Jameson responds.

I have no clue why they haven't busted down the door and insisted I go pack my shitty apartment. Dad wouldn't let Jameson block the door, so I know he must've bowed out of my latest 'rescue.'

"The fuck does kinda mean, Hound?" Shadow's voice is filled with irritation and only tinted with anger.

You'd think they'd get tired of chasing me all over the damn place.

"You need to get her up so she can go home."

Kid.

Those two always travel together.

"She has a choice to make." I stiffen as worry settles into my bones.

Is Jameson just going to put my business out there with these two?

"Kincaid expects her to come back to New Mexico."

"I'll let her know."

I smile, the concern I was feeling that Jameson was here to drag me back fading away.

I flip the covers back, stretching my back, arms high over my head. The ding of a cell phone notification draws my attention. I don't have a phone right now. Paying for the minutes after I left a couple of months ago seemed like a waste of time, so I didn't buy new minutes when the original ones ran out.

The voices go quiet in the hallway, and I wonder if Shadow and Kid have dragged Jameson away to beat his ass behind the hotel. I can't concentrate on that for very long because I know when my stomach grumbles that the nausea is only a few moments behind. I consider the crackers and room temp ginger ale Jameson went out and grabbed last night.

Even though I know it's a waste because I'll just get sick again, I sit, legs tucked under me on the bed and nibble the crackers, washing it down with the smallest sips of ginger ale I can handle.

When twenty minutes go by without Jameson returning to the room, I turn on the TV and flip through not finding anything I'm interested in. I never watch TV, especially since getting pregnant. There's one in the backroom of the diner, but when I'm not working, I've been sleeping.

I stare at an episode explaining how baseballs are made, but I'm not really watching it. I nap on the couch and eventually crawl back into the bed. Benny is going to be pissed. Kori took over my shift yesterday, but I was supposed to be at work over an hour ago. I'm certain my stuff will be in the dumpster, and another girl will already be living in my space by the end of the day. Too tired, I can't manage to even care. These shitty waitressing jobs are a dime a dozen, and honestly, Kori is so fucked-up, moving on soon was in my plans anyway.

The ringing of Jameson's phone wakes me just after two. I have no intention of getting in his business, but when it silences and rings again, I pick it up.

IZZY CALLING flashes on the screen.

"Hello?" I say after the call connects.

"Who is this?" the caller asks.

"I could be asking you the same damn thing," I mutter.

I didn't have grandiose plans about a charmed life lived in bliss with Jameson, but I also didn't consider another woman being in his life.

The call disconnects without the woman saying another word.

I move to put the phone back on the bedside table, telling myself, pregnant or not, I have no say in anything he does. He didn't insist we be together. Hell, he was adamant that there was no happily ever after where I'm concerned.

Anger builds, and irritation grows exponentially as I stare at his phone.

"Not your business," I say out loud trying to convince myself.

Curiosity and the need for full disclosure win out just like I knew it would.

I swipe the front of the screen, surprised that a man like Jameson doesn't have a lock code on his phone. Then I'm hit with the insidious thought that he left me here alone with the phone so I can discover things he doesn't have the balls to just come out and say.

First, I see the text to Shadow giving him the address to this hotel and the room number. It may not say 'come get her' or anything like that, but the text is bad enough. I realize he's on my dad's side, loyal to the end even though he knows when we disclose the pregnancy that he may be fired, if not strangled.

The next text thread is with the woman who just called. Without remorse, I tap and pull up the thread. Picture after picture of a young girl, duck lips and all assault me.

I stare, disgusted at what I see. I'm young, but there is no way this girl is even out of high school. With majestic green eyes, surrounded by lush lashes, and so much dark hair it's almost a curtain over one in many of the pictures, I can't deny that she's gorgeous. Even in tank tops with puckered lips, there's an innocence about her that I can't see Jameson being attracted to, but the proof is in the evidence. He's saved every one of the pictures she's sent in a folder title MY HEART.

That stings.

The texts are cryptic, not really saying anything specific about meeting or hooking up, but the I LOVE YOU staring at me right in my face is hard to stomach. It's not only said once but comes at the conclusion of every texted conversation that they've had.

Jealousy, other than directed at my perfect twin, isn't an emotion I'm very familiar with, but it rumbles in my stomach until nausea hits me in the chest. Unable to ignore it, I'm off the bed and over the toilet a second later. The small meal of crackers and ginger ale rebel in my body and I get sick.

Trying to convince myself that it's the morning sickness I've had for the last couple of weeks, I rinse my mouth out and stare at my face in the mirror. Rosy cheeks and that dull look in my eyes I hate so much stare back at me.

For the first time since Jameson practically abducted me in front of the clinic yesterday, I doubt my decision to let him drive me away from that place. Walking away from him right now would be so much easier if the deal was done, and I only had myself to worry about.

Sure that I'm not going to get sick again, I crawl back in bed and ignore his cell phone on the floor.

I don't know how long it's been since I laid down, but it feels like hours I've been trying to fight the tears that want to fall.

"Still sleeping?" he says with a chuckle as he closes us in the room.

The walls feel like they're closing in all around me. I sit up, needing to run, but knowing I have to face him.

His brow crinkles when he reaches down and picks up his phone.

"Izzy called," I say with a nonchalance I don't feel.

"I'll call her back later," he replies and places the phone back on the nightstand.

"She didn't seem very happy that another woman was answering the phone."

I stare into his green eyes, challenging him and waiting for a reaction of some sort.

The cocked eyebrow isn't exactly what I expect.

"You answered my phone?"

I shrug. "It was ringing. Ringing phones get answered."

"I see."

I have no idea why he's so aloof and cryptic but he sure as fuck isn't giving anything away. The red-hot anger I felt earlier bubbles from just under my skin. It was as far as I could push it down while waiting for him to return so he could give me the answers I need before I leave him and this fucking city far behind.

"She seems a little young." I shoot for an easy, conversational tone, but my bitterness is hard to hide. "What is she fifteen? Sixteen?"

"Seventeen," he corrects with his stance just a hair wider and arms crossed over his chest.

"She let you fuck her hard?" He sneers. "Up against the wall? Does she enjoy your cock? Your piercings?"

"Georgia," he warns.

"You think I would keep this fucking baby around you worrying what you'd do to her since you like them so fucking young? You've lost your mind."

I expect his anger, but what I don't expect is his hand around my throat.

Chapter 19

Hound

"That's my daughter you're talking about you filthy-mouthed bitch!"

Her eyes widen, but she doesn't try to pull away.

The anger and jealousy fade away, and when she whimpers, I can see the arousal in her eyes. She gets off on the brute force, the power I have over her. My cock thickens, going from half-mast at her jealousy to full-on steel in my jeans.

"Jesus, you make me insane," I hiss, letting her go to fall back on the mattress.

"Daughter?" she asks as her hand comes up to the base of her throat. She doesn't touch it in inspection from injury but caresses it almost like she's missing the clamp of my fingers. "You're only thirty-four."

"Yeah," I say and sit down on the couch. "I didn't like condoms at sixteen any more than I like those fuckers now."

I don't miss the way her hands flow over her lower belly.

Her eyes fire with need, and I shake my head at her.

"No, Gigi." It's what my mouth says, but my eyes stay pinned to her when she shoves down the satin covering her pussy. A second later her tank top hits the plush carpet at her feet.

"No?"

She prowls, graceful like a panther across the room with the same elegance and sure moves I've watched her use on stage. This woman knows exactly what she's doing, exactly how she needs to move to entice a man. It's early, and the pregnancy isn't showing at all, but there's a fullness in her perky tits that wasn't there months ago.

I swallow, eyes sweeping from her toes all the way up to her messy hair.

Her shift in mood, going from disgusting insults about Izzy, saying things I'd kill any man who even considers doing to my daughter, to the sex kitten now standing directly in front of me, is concerning.

"No," I repeat, this time with my hands on her slender hips.

When she tries to move closer, I tighten my hands, but the grip of my fingers into the plush flesh of her ass stirs a need in me I never feel unless she's around. It's then that I start to question my own mental health. I should tell her to get dressed, tell her we're going back to face her father, but I've already sent Shadow and Kid away, assuring them I'd do my best to get her back to New Mexico. Even speaking with them, I know it's a long shot. I won't force this woman to do anything she doesn't want to do.

I'm struck with the thought of shoving her head so far down on my cock that she chokes, but from the gleam in her eyes, I don't think it would be unwelcome. Punishing her for making me want her so fucking bad only entices her to seek more punishment.

Her teeth scrape over her bottom lip, and her hands find the top of my head.

"Fuck," I grumble when her nails dig into my scalp with just the right amount of pain and pleasure. I roll my head on my shoulders until her nails are scraping over my beard and onto the sensitive skin of my neck.

Her arousal is thick in the air, filling my lungs, drowning me in a heady need I can barely keep control over.

I know I'm going to cave long moments before I actually do it. The anticipation is nearly unbearable, but I know the prize is going to be a bliss I can only find with her.

My skin is itchy, tingling with need and desire, but I wait. I just watch, looking at her lithe body until her breathing grows heavy and her eyelids droop with a sexiness I know I'll dream about for nights to come.

She's trembling by the time I spread my legs and allow her to stand in between them. She's gasping for much-needed air by the time I press my lips to the flatness of her lower belly. And she's barely able to stand by the time I snake my tongue out and lick her from her slit all the way to the top of her throbbing clit.

"Ja-Jameson," she stutters, and the sound of my name on her lips ignites a fire in my gut that can only be extinguished with her taste, her scent filling my body until I've wrung her dry and she's trembling beneath me.

"Fight it," I command with another harsh lick to her most sensitive flesh.

"I can't," she objects. "It feels too good."

She's shaking, near convulsing in my grip, so I hold her tighter, so tight that my fingers will be imprinted on her skin for days to come. My cock thickens painfully, leaking at the tip with the knowledge.

"I'll spank your ass if you come before I give you permission."

Her moan filters through the room as her body begins to quiver in earnest. She's fighting the one thing her brain is telling her to take, and it pleases me like nothing else ever has.

I toy, tease, and tangle my tongue around the epicenter of her desire. I'm relentless, challenging her to obey my command, but hoping she's unable. The idea of pinking her ass warms my palm against the fleshy part of her thigh with anticipation.

"Please, please, please," she begs.

The beseeching inflection of her voice is enough to make me cave. This is Gigi I'm drinking down my throat. It won't be long before she presents another situation where I can take my frustrations out on her beautiful ass.

"Now," I hiss, my breath hitting her marvelous cunt and forcing goosebumps to race down her legs. "Come for me."

"Only for you," she whispers and splinters apart.

I honor her submission by extending her pleasure with quick, pulsing swipes of my tongue.

Unable to wait, unable to care about what happens tomorrow, my hand is releasing its punishing grip on her thigh and working open the zipper of my jeans. The next second, the denim is pushed down past my balls, and I'm stroking, with a brutal fist, the length of my metal-studded cock.

"Oh God." The awe in her voice draws the pre-cum from my shaft until it's glistening at the tip. The lick of her tongue over her lips is enough to make me forget every woman before her, a victory no one else can claim.

"It's yours," I offer with my grip at the base.

"No," I tell her when she makes to straddle my thighs on the couch. "Take my boots and jeans fully off."

I know how hard I want to fuck her, how hard I need to fuck her. She's athletic, but she's not going to have the stamina I'll demand from her taut, little body. I plan to punish her, to assault her, to push inside of her so deep and so hard that she'll feel me tomorrow and the day after. When I watch her squirm, I'll know it's the echo of my cock that's pushing the blush up her chest and on to her cheeks.

Eager hands unlace my combat boots and tug my jeans down. The only help I give her is the slight lift of my hips so she can get my jeans down my thighs and eventually off my legs.

She stands, impatiently waiting for my next command, and fuck if that doesn't stir something deep inside my chest. My cock jerks in my hand, reminding me that it's not the time or place for introspection. The sight of her swollen clit peaking past the delicate lips of her slit is glorious.

I'm an undeserving asshole, but I'm going to take what never should've been given to me in the first place.

"Come here," I shift my gaze down, indicating the throbbing cock I'm holding straight up. "Have a seat."

A coy smile plays on her lips but her feet move quickly, and her knees hit the couch cushions at my thighs with a speed that rivals Olympic sprinters.

"Condom?" She blinks up at me.

A harsh breath leaves my lips. Not at the thought of wrapping up, but with the memory of why we won't.

"I'm already so deep inside of you." The thumb of my free hand rubs the soft skin below her navel. I lift her hips, kissing her sensitive flesh with the tip of my cock. "I'm already a part of you."

I ease her down, the gravity of the situation and unanswered questions, decisions that have yet to be made and verbalized is the weight that forces her to sink to the base.

The need to fuck her wild, fuck her until she's nothing but liquid in my hands fades away. She whimpers at the fullness, shifting her hips, rocking with small sweeps side to side to help her body accommodate the thickness of mine.

I rock up, enjoying every centimeter of her gripping cunt as it flexes, tightens, and pleads for more. The ache in my balls is bearable. The tension gnawing at the base of my spine just as willing as I am to take my time.

Her eyes flutter, but she's able to keep them open. The shine, the glisten of wetness near the corners of her eyes draw me in. I revel in the keen ability to pull such emotion from her, but when one lone tear crests and rolls down her face, the demon in me wants a hundred more. I want to see them gushing down her face, while she begs me to stop, while she's chocking on my cock, while she loves every aspect of every deranged thing I want to do to her.

But, it isn't until her forehead rests against mine, and she looks down at the carnal union of our bodies that my restraint begins to crack. The tension at my spine, the ache in my balls is no longer bearable.

The slow and steady, the feathery ripple of her pussy along my erection has become a tease. The soft huffs of her breath abrade my skin rather than flush it with satisfaction. The delicate noises she makes are contradictory and insufferable to what my body is demanding I take.

Then, it's the puncture of her teeth in the hard flesh of my pectoral that makes my head snap up.

"You feisty bitch," I hiss and stand from the couch.

I bite my tongue as her fingernails seer a hole into my back. She knows I have her, knows I'd never drop her so the aggression, although welcome, will be punished.

"Yes," she moans when I walk her to the bed and lay her on her back.

I chuckle at her greediness when her hips flex, and she's fucking herself on my dick the instant her back hits the mattress.

"No." I pull out, the whimper she emits landing in my gut.

After flipping her over, I'm almost tempted by the arch of her back, so much so that I don't resist the temptation to run my hand down the ridges of her spine and trace the heart shape of her ass. Fucking her from behind becomes my only mission, but the disappointment in not seeing her face isn't something I'm going to tolerate. She squeals, a gleeful, silly sound in this moment when I lift her, back to my chest and stand. Her giggle turns to a brutal moan when I impale her down my shaft and position our bodies, so we're standing in front of the full-length dressing mirror.

"Jesus," she hisses as I hold her aloft, the bends of her knees cradled in the bend of my elbows.

She's spread open, the pink of her pussy a sharp contrast to the angry, purple hue of my brutally hard cock. The glint of the light in the room radiating off of the barbells along my cock adds to the depravity we're both so wrapped up in that nothing else in the world matters.

Her head rocks back on my shoulder, eyes mere slits as she continues to watch me fuck up into her like a man possessed.

"You need to fucking come," I demand as her hands find the furled tips of her nipples. Her face scrunches, and I love that she's causing the bite of pain to get her off. "Now."

Like a genie rubbing a golden lamp, my words, my insistence to put an end to both of our misery is obeyed the second the words push past my lips.

I hold her closer as her small body curls in on itself. I groan my own release at the sight of her stomach ridging and flexing with the force of her climax.

"God damn," I cry when I explode inside of her, the force of her pulsing leaving no room for my own release.

Warm, thick liquid, a combination of both her and I, slicks her thighs and the length of my shaft and balls. I need to get us into the shower before we ruin the carpet any more than we already have, but it's not even an option.

As carefully as I can manage, I walk us the few feet to the bed, setting her down before climbing in behind her.

"I just need a few minutes," I explain when she looks back over her shoulder at me.

She laughs at the weakness in my voice, the words nearly slurred like I'd been drinking whiskey all night rather than feeding at the offerings of her body.

The stroking of her fingers up and down the arm wrapped around her stomach calms my pounding heart, if only for a second because true to form, she opens her mouth, and the world spins again.

"Tell me about your daughter."

Chapter 20

Gigi

I expect him to release me, to climb off of the bed and refuse to talk, and as the silence drags on, I imagine him telling me to mind my fucking business and never ask him about her again. Then, to my surprise he sighs, his body settling in closer to mine, heavier into the mattress, his fingers twisting until our hands are joined, and he begins.

"Isabella Roze, with a Z, not an S," he explains, "Montoya is everything I never knew I wanted."

Did he rub our combined hands over my lower belly on purpose? It's not the first time tonight he's touched me there in a way so loving it's almost out of character for the man I hardly know.

I shiver at the soft press of his lips on my bare shoulder.

"Gabriela Montoya showed up in the middle of my sophomore year. There was only one high school in Kaufman, Texas at the time. All of the rich kids, all of the poor kids, and every kid in between were thrown together. Her dad was some executive for a nearby refinery, so if there was an opportunity for her to go somewhere else, I'm certain her upper-class parents would've made sure she did."

I let my eyes close, loving the soothing tone of his voice, but I hang onto every word, hurting as he begins to speak of another woman, but too curious to tell him to stop.

"She showed up in clothes that cost more than my rusty old pickup truck with a gleam in her eye that drew in every boy, made every teenage cock rock solid at first glance. I wasn't immune. I fantasized about her for days before I built up the courage to approach her."

"What did she look like?" I need to compare her to me, to see if he's attracted to traits we may share.

"Long, rich brown hair." He kisses the back of my head, and I stiffen. He either doesn't notice my unease, or he ignores it. "The thickest, most luscious ass I'd ever lain eyes on. Eyes so dark, you couldn't tell the iris from the pupil."

"She sounds lovely," I mutter.

He releases my hand and grips my thigh.

"Be careful, Georgia, your jealousy turns me on."

I huff as he continues.

"She was new and exotic. Colombian. She came from San Antonio, the big city compared to our quiet little town. I wanted her the second I saw her. Needed her the second I smelled the sun on her skin."

"Did you love her?" Sounds a lot like fucking love to me.

"At sixteen? I sure as hell thought I did but looking back I realize there were things I loved *about* her. I loved her body, the way she moved with sensual grace whether she was dancing to David Allan Coe or Shakira. I loved the way my hands would tangle into her thick hair as if once I touched her, she refused to let me go. I loved the way she welcomed a terrified virgin boy into her body and taught me things no seventeen-year-old girl should've ever known in the first place."

I whimper, his words and the sensual way he described his young lust turning me on.

"You got her pregnant."

"Almost immediately," he says with a quick chuckle, his hand grazing low on my stomach again. "I didn't ask if she was on the pill."

"Seems to be a problem for you."

He pinches the lips of my pussy until I moan with need. "Can I finish my story?"

I nod, unable to speak while he has my clit clamped between his thumb and forefinger.

"All the girls at school talked about birth control. The first time I slid inside of her, a latex barrier was the last thing on my mind. Every time after, I couldn't imagine anything dulling the sensation, so I didn't bother. Figured she'd tell me if there was a problem. That problem," he sighs and releases my clit. I hiss when the blood flow returns in the form of a throbbing pulse. "Came a couple months after we started dating. I was ready to quit school, go to work, do anything and everything for her and our child."

"What did you do?"

"I made plans. We made plans. When she started to show and her parents got suspicious enough to ask, we sat down and told them. She'd hidden it too long for an abortion. We'd talked about it in passing, but it wasn't something either of us wanted. We were a family. We were going to raise our child in a happy home and give it everything that it could ever want."

He swallows, I'm certain remembering the time when life was easier. When he faced things with pride and determination without being bogged down with the reality that only maturity and age can bring, or in my case growing up too fast.

"Her dad was livid. Her mother cried the whole time, upset that her Catholic soul may never recover. I offered everything I had, which amounted to less than a complete sophomore education and a shitty truck that didn't crank more days than it actually did. I should've been a junior, but I have a late birthday, and my parents made me repeat kindergarten. I couldn't offer her that extra year of education.

"Her dad pointed all of that out of course. Convinced Gabby that a life with me would be lived in poverty because he sure as hell wasn't being financially responsible for some poor ass white boy. He gave her an ultimatum, and I've never seen a girl who claims to be in love make a decision so fast."

I don't miss the tremble in his now unsteady hand or the deep breaths he pulls in to calm his anger.

"She chose the money, the life I now know I never would've been able to give her. She chose the support of her family even to the detriment of our relationship. I knew she'd love that baby, that her parents wouldn't fault a child for the sins her teenage parents committed. I was told to take a step back, to leave her alone."

His laugh is bitter, filled with years of something akin to remorse or regret.

"I couldn't though. I convinced my parents to let me drop out of high school. I was a year behind on paper, but I was smart enough to pass my GED. They let me join the Marine Corps at seventeen. I was in Miramar, California when my parents called to tell me that the letters I'd been sending to Gabby had all been returned to their house, unopened. They'd promised me a relationship with my child. I never would've walked away, joined the Corps if I knew they were going to pull some shit like they did. When they drove by, the place was deserted by the Montoya's and another family was already moving in."

"That's so fucking shitty," I whisper even though he knows it and doesn't need it spoken out loud.

"Yeah," he agrees.

"How did you locate her?"

He tugs the sheet over us when I shiver, half burning up from his heat at my back, but frigid where the air conditioner is drifting over my shoulders and chest.

"Her dad was easy enough to track. They didn't live a secret life, just a nomadic one because of his line of work. I saw Izzy for the first time when she was four. She was doing her best to kick around a soccer ball on a field. Her long brown hair flowed behind her, and when her eyes turned in my direction, they were *my* eyes, and I never knew love like I found on a children's soccer field that day. She's everything wonderful about Gabby and me. None of the bad, none of the struggle. She's pure and beautiful, and now she's nearly a woman, and that scares the fuck out of me."

I clasp his hand again in mine.

"So Gabby let you have a relationship with her?"

"Hardly," he spits. "She'd gotten married to some pompous asshole. She made threats. I made threats. Hers were backed up by a team of attorneys. There's not much you can do with a military salary, and her family, her new husband, knew that. The only faith I had in life that day was the saddened look on the nanny's face when she carried my daughter away."

"You just let her walk away with Izzy?" I can't help the disdain in my voice. What parent just lets someone steal their child?

"That day? Yes. I let Gabby think she won. I let her new husband keep the smug smile on his face as he walked out, hand gripping the curve of Gabby's ass tight, the same ass I used to obsess over every night before her parents ripped my life apart. The crazy thing is, all I felt was anger. I wasn't bitter he got the girl. I was upset she'd so easily tossed me away. My only concern was the brown-haired, green-eyed girl who was just strapped into a car seat in the back of a nanny's minivan.

"I sought out that nanny, having a buddy run the license plate. I explained that I needed a relationship with my child, and she agreed. It started with pictures at first. The letters, written in the heavy hand of a child, came next. On her fourteenth birthday, Gabby got her a cell phone for her birthday. She'd written and given me her number. We texted at first. Her stepdad isn't as bad as I made him out to be. She's happy, but I'm one thing he would never budge on. She learned early on that my name, the subject of her actual paternity isn't on the table in any shape or form."

"You've only seen her in person once?"

"We video chat, and we've met a few times. She's on a protective leash and isn't allowed much leeway, but we find time to see each other."

"That sucks," I say honestly.

"She wants to move in with me when she graduates, and God, do I want that. The ability to actually get to know my daughter has been all I can think about since she mentioned it about a year ago. It's why I served seventeen years rather than staying in for twenty. It's why I was so fucking excited about the job offer in Farmington. She's currently living in Flagstaff but wants to attend college in Albuquerque. It seemed like the best fit."

"Sounds like you have it all figured out." I don't even know how I should feel right now. His separation from his daughter is shitty, but at the same time, I wonder if all of his energy is going to be used to the point he wouldn't have any for the baby I'm carrying. It's selfish and greedy, but I can't lie and pretend it's not part of the deciding factor in the direction my own life is going.

"I did. It's all fucked now."

I tense, anger so close to boiling over my vision starts to blur.

"Shadow and Kid instructed me that I'm to head back to Farmington and pack my shit. Cerberus can't trust a man who can't be honest with their President."

"My dad is an asshole."

"He's really not, Gigi. He's trustworthy, protective, and he's doing what he thinks is best to protect his daughter. I promised him I'd never touch you again, and here I lay with my cock between my stomach and your back, my fingers drifting over this perfect little cunt." He drives his words home by slicking his thumb over my clit. "He can't trust me because I can't trust myself when it comes to you."

"What will you d-do?" I stammer, moaning my displeasure when he stops.

"Pack my shit. I have other job offers. They aren't Cerberus, more private security, boring shit. Mainly in the LA and San Fran area. It's almost twice as far away from Izzy and even further when she goes to college. But," he says as he turns me in his arms until my sore breasts are pushing against the t-shirt he never bothered to take off. "My next step depends on yours."

Chapter 21

Hound

I shake my head when she buries her pretty face into my t-shirt.

"That came out like pressure, and I promise you I'm not pressuring you. I won't lie to you either." I tilt her chin until her tear-stained eyes are looking directly into mine. "I can't make a move until you make yours."

I release her chin, my hand falling naturally to the place her body holds my precious child, the tiny bundle of cells I may never get to meet.

My heart constricts at the thought.

"You'd want to raise this baby?" I hate the uncertainty in her voice.

"I told you it's your choice." I've said it more than once, and it gets harder each and every damn time.

"And I'm asking about your stance."

"You know where I stand. I told you yesterday in the truck."

"Dammit," she says as she pushes away from my chest until she's sitting crossed-legged on the bed. "You told me I have options, but I need to know that if I keep this baby, you'll want to be involved. I don't want to force you into anything."

"Force me?" I can't help but laugh at the ridiculousness. "Are you sitting there and telling me that I'm the deciding factor."

My lip curls in rage at her stoic posture and the way she refuses to answer my question.

"It's your fucking choice!" I yell and climb off of the bed.

"I can't do this alone," she screams, just as angry as I am.

I tilt my head and swallow the words I want to say, the ones that won't be received well and speak slowly. "You. Don't. Have. To."

"You'll help raise this baby?" She's asked that now several times, each one like a jackhammer to my heart.

"I want to raise this baby." Tears streak her face. "More than anything, I want the chance to be a dad. From start to finish. From day one until the day I die, I want it."

She nods but doesn't say a word. She doesn't calm my fears or attempt to appease me with even a small smile.

"I'm tired."

Two simple words.

Seven letters that do nothing to hint at where her mind is at.

I want to rush to the bed, shake her, and force her to make the right decision. I want to beg her to keep our baby. I want to redden her ass for even contemplating an alternative to bringing that precious child into the world. I want to tease her, suck her clit, and keep her orgasm just out of reach until she agrees that there is but one choice in the matter.

I do none of those things.

I watch the sway of her naked ass and the swish of her gorgeous brown hair as she lies down on the bed, back pointed in my direction. I run my hands harshly over my head as she tugs up the sheets and covers the silkiness of her back, hiding herself from me.

Her breathing is still ragged as I tug on my jeans, boots, and t-shirt.

"I'm going to grab something to eat." She doesn't move. Doesn't look over her shoulder. Doesn't offer one word. "Can I get you anything?"

A simple shake of her head. "I can't keep anything down."

I turn and leave the room because the alternative of climbing in behind her, wrapping her in my arms, and soothing her until she falls asleep isn't an option.

The small store in the hotel has nothing to offer other than shitty Vegas memorabilia and antacids. A quick internet search on my phone is so uninformative, I'm wondering how women have managed to have healthy babies at all. The information provided is always contradicted by another post. Do this. Do that. NEVER do this. It's overwhelming. The only thing that seems to have the least objections is that ginger ale and crackers seem to be a lifesaver. She had that last night, so I set out to grab myself a burger and supplies to settle her stomach.

While at the burger joint, I go ahead and grab one for her as well, hoping she'll be up for something more than carbs and soda.

Just like when you're buying a new car and narrow it down to one or two, and you start to notice that car everywhere, for the first time in as long as I can remember, I notice every child. I focus on their laughter, their crying, the innocent questions they ask their parents while standing in line at the pharmacy.

Back at the hotel, trying to wake Gigi is pointless. She's out like a light and isn't interested in ginger ale and crackers, so I sit on the couch and eat, never taking my eyes off of the soft rise and fall of her back. I can't help but wonder if my child in her stomach is the reason I'm so drawn to her.

I shake my head, clearing it of the ridiculous thought. She was a sleek piece of metal and I a magnet, feverishly attracted to her long before I knew about the baby, long before I put that child in front of her. The memories of seeing her on that stage for the first time flood my brain and all of my other senses. The slide of her athletic thighs on the pole. The roll of her abdominals. The perfect sway of her hips.

I run a rough hand over the erection tenting my jeans. It's pure physical attraction, unadulterated need from knowing just what it feels like to slide inside of her. It's carnal, instinctual biology to be attracted to, to crave the person who's continuing your bloodline.

After eating, I lie back on the sofa, arms behind my head, feet propped on the end because it's way too fucking small for my body. How I fall asleep with the distance between us, I have no clue, but my slumber is short lived.

I snap awake, unsure of what pulled me from a dreamless sleep until I hear a small whimper fill the silence in the room.

The once soft up and down of Gigi's back as she slept has been replaced with jagged jerks with her sobs.

I don't consider the ramifications. I don't worry if she wants me to touch her or not. I climb off the couch, hitting the lights and enveloping the room in darkness before climbing on the bed behind her.

"Shhh," I purr in her ear. "I'm here."

My comfort only makes her cry harder, so I don't say another word. I don't ask her what's wrong. I don't offer advice. I don't tell her what she should do or remind her of her options. I hold her, as close to my chest as I can manage without suffocating her. I lean my head in and breathe in her scent, nose pressed deep into her hair. At first, she's a stiff board in my arms, but as the sobbing ebbs away her body relaxes and she settles into my hold. She allows herself the comfort of my embrace until her breathing begins to match mine.

Not a word is spoken. Not a promise is made, but I reassure her with the light sweep of my fingers on her arm. I touch her hip, pushing her legs until she's curled in a ball, I mirror her position and nestle her even closer.

Just when I think she's asleep, she speaks with a hint of devastation and sadness in her voice.

"I'd be a horrible mother."

I squeeze her. I can't object to her assessment. I don't know hardly anything about her, and lying isn't really my thing.

"My mom is the greatest," she continues. "There's no way I could ever even come close to being like her. Bake sales, PTO, and fucking classroom chaperoning?"

She gives a humorless chuckle and shakes her head a little.

"That's not me. I can't even picture myself doing those things."

I open my mouth to tell her I'd do all of those things in her place. The idea of taking a handful of rowdy kids to the zoo and experience everyday sights through the brand-new eyes of a child sounds like a great time to me. I close my mouth again, only opening my lips slightly to brush them over the soft skin of her naked shoulder.

She begins crying again, torn with her decision.

"I don't want to abort this baby." I smile against her skin, my heart filling with eagerness. "But I can't see myself as a mother either. I thought it was instinctual. I thought once my suspicions were confirmed with the positive test I would transition from who I am into someone different."

All she gets is silence from me, and since she hasn't called me out on it, I imagine it's just what she needs.

"But I'm not different." She shakes her head slightly to punctuate her point. "Other than the sickness I don't even feel different. I still want to run. I want to take off and put it behind me, but no matter where I go this baby will be right there. I can't run from this."

She clasps my hand and lowers it to the flatness of her stomach. She doesn't say another word. She merely takes one last shuddering breath and falls asleep.

My eyes stay on her until the pink hue of the dawn stabs across the room. It's only then that I take my eyes off of her, that I stop counting her breaths and allow myself to get a little rest. Later today, no matter which way she decides, she's going to make a life-altering decision. One that's going to change the course of my previously decided future.

Chapter 22

Gigi

Oppressive heat surrounds me, blanketing me to the point my stomach rolls, urging me to get out of bed. In the split second I have before my body revolts against the emptiness in my belly, I look back over my shoulder at Jameson. He reaches for me, hand skimming over the warmth my body left behind on the bed. My smile turns into a grimace as I run, as quietly as I can to the bathroom.

Dry heaving is the devil's work I'm certain by the time I lift my head and rinse my mouth. Rinsing the smell of his skin from mine is the last thing I want to do. His scent, the combined smell of our wild sex last night coats me like a living being. I revel in it, running my nose over the soft skin of my shoulder before giving in and turning the dials of the shower.

The warm blast on my now cool skin sends pinpricks over every inch of my skin. It's not altogether different from the way my body responded watching Jameson fuck me in front of the mirror. I sigh a breath of remembrance and wash him off of me.

My cries. The pleas. The whispered confessions in the dark last night.

I laid my heart bare to him, and unlike all the others so quick to give me advice, he held me. He didn't try to bring me to his side. He didn't give his opinion. He embraced me and let me draw my own conclusions. As much as it pained him, he gave me exactly what I needed.

After the suds from the hotel soap disappear down the drain, I turn the water off and steel my spine. I know exactly what I have to do. I've known it all along. It's just that being an adult, actually making those decisions on my own, the ones others have been so quick to make for me all my life, is much harder than I had ever anticipated they would be.

I dress, right back into the clothes I wore to the clinic what seems like a lifetime ago, and take one last look at Jameson asleep in the bed. His hand is still stretched out, searching for me even in his sleep. The crinkle of his brow is calming as I imagine he's missing me even in his sleep.

Instead of brushing my lips against his to wake him up like I want to, I jerk the floor to ceiling curtains open, bathing the room in the blinding sunlight.

He jerks in the bed, almost violently, as he's ripped from his dreams.

"The fuck," he grumbles, sitting up on the bed and swiping harsh hands over his tired green eyes.

Why I didn't see it last night, why I didn't recognize his eyes in Izzy's pictures on his phone is beyond me. It's clear as day right now as those amazing green orbs are turned on me in almost angry agitation.

"Get your boots on," I instruct, hating that he's fully clothed.

I resist the urge to once again strip naked in front of him and taunt him with my body. There will be plenty of time for that later.

He sighs, leaning his back against the wooden headboard. "What's the damn rush?"

I smile at him. "What's the delay?"

He growls. "I got you more crackers and ginger ale last night."

His large hand motions toward the mini fridge against the wall.

"That's very sweet of you."

"I got crackers with peanut butter. That way you're eating more than just shitty carbs and soda."

I cock an eyebrow at him. "A little controlling, don't you think?"

My question is playful, not annoyed like it would normally be.

A passive look fills his eyes as he glances my way. How he can look so apathetic and dominating at the same time I have no idea. The single look makes my skin itch. The same way it did last night when he challenged me not to come on his tongue until he gave me permission to do so.

"You're growing my baby," he says, voice flat.

"Our baby," I correct.

"Until you make your decision, you need to take care of it. The protein in the peanut butter is good for him."

"Him?" I question. "So sure we're having a son."

I don't miss the hopeful swallow of his throat as mine clogs with some of the same emotions I was unable to shove down last night.

"You still haven't made a decision." I hate the break in his voice, the opinion he was terrified to give power to last night.

"But I have," I correct. "It's why you need to get dressed."

I turn my gaze down to the boots on the floor.

His hands tremble as he shoves back the sheets that cocooned us last night.

"Back to the clinic?" Pain washes over his face even as I can tell he's doing his best to fight it.

"Nope," I say, both hating and loving that I'm keeping him on edge with such an important choice.

"To your apartment?"

Just the thought of that shitty place and my deviant roommate makes me shiver.

"There's nothing there for me. There's nothing from this life that I want to remember."

"Where are we heading?"

I turn to the mirror, the one that finds me swiping my fingers through my sleep-messy hair and not splayed open for both of our pleasure like I was last night.

"I'm going home," I whisper.

"Home?" His voice cracks with hopefulness, a smile spreading his cheeks in the reflection of the glass.

I woke up this morning a new woman if that's even possible. I woke up with renewed faith in not only life but also my ability to be the best mother I can be. It may not look exactly like my mother's did, but it'll be me and Jameson and our child. We'll make the best of it. I won't have to do it alone, and that was my one and only true fear because I knew motherhood in the form of single parenting isn't something I could ever manage.

"Someone has to tell my dad that you knocked me up."

I turn back to him expecting to see the smile still in place and hope in his eyes. Instead, I find him nearly green, resembling my face every morning before I get sick. I can't help but laugh as he turns white at the mention of telling my dad, even though he's the one who pressed the point yesterday.

***

The normally eight-hour trip back to Farmington takes closer to eleven with the multiple stops we're forced to take because my stomach doesn't agree with the miniscule rocking of the SUV over the interstate. When I wasn't dozing, I was getting sick.

"I'm going to go pack my room," he says as we pull into the gravel lot in front of the Cerberus clubhouse.

"I think that's a little premature," I object.

"I have my orders," he says with a sigh as he places the vehicle in park.

"I'm going to go talk to my dad," I inform him.

He clasps my thigh in a soft but dominating grip. "If you get the feeling that he plans to kill me, give me a heads up. I'm more than willing to face what's coming my way, but I at least want to be prepared."

I laugh but stop when I see the seriousness in his eyes. I caress his face, loving the feel of his rough beard under my palm. My body is on fire for this man.

"That look in your eyes right now is exactly what got you fucked against an alley wall," he warns.

"Mmm," I purr.

"Stop." I snap out of my horny daze. "Packing my shit while you lay all of this at your father's feet is one thing. Doing it with a swollen cock is another."

"You have nothing to worry about," I offer, but he doesn't seem to think the outcome will be pleasant.

"Twenty-years-old or not, I'd kill any man that fucked my daughter and got her pregnant," he advises. "He's already been more forgiving by letting me work after he found out about the sex than I ever would've been."

"My back was as sore as my pussy after that night." My eyes flutter closed. "The brick was as unforgiving as your cock."

"Jesus," he hisses, mouth meeting mine in a brutal kiss before I can even open my eyes.

We're panting by the time he pulls away.

"I'm going to sneak in your room tonight." He swallows and nods. "Will you turn me away again?"

Doubt, uncertainty, and the memory of his rejection last time fill my voice.

"I doubt I'll still be here, baby, but you're welcome in my bed no matter where I lay my head down to sleep."

I peck his lips one last time, youthful glee filling me to the brim even when the news that I have to share with my father burdens me.

"See you in a little while," I promise as I climb out of the vehicle.

Less than five minutes later, I'm standing, heart racing at my father's office door. When I entered the house, my mother pointed in this direction and simply said, "He's waiting for you."

I raise my hand to knock, praying he's asleep, which is ridiculous, or on the phone. Hoping that he's busy and I'll have to wait just a few minutes longer.

"It's open," comes the gruff voice I've learned to despise over my many years of fucking up.

I turn the knob, ignoring the near sting of the metal against my palm, and push the door open.

"Close it." His gruff command is obeyed. "Have a seat."

I sit in the chair across from his desk. How do these same types of things being barked at me from Jameson make me wet, yet with my father only make me want to cower in fear?

I guess having the same response to my father would be inappropriate.

"How long are you home for this time, Georgia?"

He looks as exhausted as I feel. The sun set long ago, the second half of our trip spent in darkness and silence.

"It depends on how this conversation goes," I answer honestly.

"A threat?" He tilts his head, the same motion that a few years ago would have me quivering in my chair.

"No. I'm not a teenager any longer. I've lived in hell the last couple of years. I—"

"You chose that life. I never wanted that for you."

"I know that." He raises an eyebrow at me. "I know that *now*. I'm grateful to you and Mom. You don't have to put up with my shit. You don't have to continuously chase after me, trying to rescue me from myself."

"Parents do everything they can for their children. We love you. Taking off and leaving will never change that."

"I love you guys, too." I love the smile that tugs at the corner of his mouth and brightens his eyes. I don't say it often enough, not even close to as often as I feel it.

"You didn't fight Hound in coming back." I'm not surprised he's well aware of my agreement to return to New Mexico. "Is there a reason you're so agreeable to being here?"

Moment of truth.

"I'm pregnant."

He stops breathing.

"The baby is Jameson's."

I've never seen that color of red on my father's face in all my life.

It seems like a millennia before he releases a long, jagged breath.

"Hound's?" he finally says like Jameson and Hound could possibly be two different men.

He types something on his phone, and I crane my neck to try to see if it's the execution order Jameson is so sure is coming.

He waits, only looking up from his phone when the door opens. My mother's softly scented perfume hits my nose, wiping away all hope that Jameson has been called in here to face this with the Cerberus MC President right along beside me.

I can't look at her, not when she sits in the chair beside me, not when she clasps my hand in her lap, and especially not when the tears that have been threatening since my truth spilled from my lips, begin to fall.

"Your daughter is pregnant," Dad spits as if I may not stay that way for long.

My free hand protects the innocent life cradled there, and my head snaps up.

My mother gasps, her hand clenching mine even tighter.

"The baby is Hound's."

The grasp loosens, but I squeeze tighter, unable to lose her touch in the face of what comes next.

"A baby?" she whispers.

I nod, eyes evaluating my father's face, still unable to look at her.

"I'm not ashamed." I raise my head higher, my spine stiffening with the same steel I found in the Vegas bathroom earlier in the day.

"So you're keeping the baby?" Is that hope in my rigid father's voice?

"Yes," I answer.

My mother releases a breath in a long whoosh, relief evident in the gesture.

"And Hound?"

"He's on board with my decision."

"I'm not okay with you sleeping with my men."

Here it comes.

"I've only slept with Jameson." A knot forms low in my stomach, and I beg it not to start turning. Getting violently ill right now is the worst thing that can happen.

"I fired Grimlock a mere two months after he started working here your senior year," he reminds me.

"Okay?" I don't hide the confusion in my voice.

"I fired him because rumors of you two together spread through my club like wildfire."

I can't help the chuckle that slips out.

"That's why he was here one day and then gone the next?"

My father nods. "I don't like you sleeping with my men. It's dangerous. I can't take the risk that they think they can disobey orders because of their connection to you."

"Man," I correct.

He shakes his head. "What?"

"I slept with one man. I've only slept with Jameson. No others, not from this club. He's the only one." I take a long breath and release it slowly. "Ever."

"Really?"

I hate the disbelief in his voice. Hate that I'm going to have to explain the rumors that started in high school and ruined my reputation. How I fed those fires because people already had those opinions so why argue with them. It seems my parents aren't even immune to the talk of the town.

"I will stay as long as you'll have me." My mother begins to cry silently beside me. "So long as Jameson is still employed with Cerberus."

"No," my father hisses. "I can't have it. I didn't even want to keep him after Dallas, but Dominic talked me into it. This just cements that I should've followed my gut instinct in the first place."

"Yes, Sir," I say as I stand. My father has made my decision for me.

"Diego," my mother sobs as she catches my wrist on my way out. I look down at her. "Go take a nap, honey. I'll be up in just a few minutes."

I leave the room closing the door on the hushed voices of my parents arguing.

Chapter 23

Hound

I think waiting for the confrontation is worse than the actual confrontation itself. It's the anticipation. The worry about what will happen. The hundreds of scenarios you work through in your head are never what actually happens.

I'm not startled by the knock on my door. I'm not even surprised that it's both Kid and Shadow on the other side when I tug the door open. A show of force. It's exactly how I'd handle the situation.

"Kincaid wants to speak with you," Shadow says, his gruff voice not giving anything away.

I grab the straps of my two rucksacks and follow them from the room. It may seem overdramatic, but I could be walking toward my death, yet, even knowing that I trudge along with my head held high the short distance to the conference room. I don't miss that Kincaid is waiting for me in a room that leaves no chance of my seeing Gigi before I face him.

Smart.

It's also what I would've done.

Kid pushes open the right side of the double doors, but he doesn't follow me inside. He and Shadow turn, hands clenched down by their sides. The fact that they're both standing at attention isn't lost on me. It's another show of force, one of unity with their president.

I swallow thickly, but enter the room and close the door behind me. At the end of the table, Kincaid sits silently with his hands steepled, index fingers resting against his bottom lip. I step forward, and resisting the urge to salute him, I reach into my pocket and pull the lone key to my room down the hall from my pocket. Once within arm's length, I pass it to him.

"Room's clear, Mr. Anderson."

He accepts the key, turning it over and over in his palm. I take a few steps back, hands gripping my rucksacks so hard they begin to ache. Time stretches for what seems like hours before he speaks.

"Mr. Anderson?" He clears his throat. "Now you treat me with respect?"

When his eyes meet mine, the fury in them is enough to make my blood run cold. My eyes dart, looking for an escape. There's one way in, and one way out. The passage to safety is guarded by two of Kincaid's Marines, two of his closest friends, men so close Gigi considers them uncles.

"My intention was never to disrespect you, Sir." Dressed in civvies or not, this man deserves my respect, not only as the leader of the club I'm fixing to be booted out of, but also because he's my child's grandfather.

"Georgia is keeping the baby."

"Yes, Sir." This isn't news to me.

"And you plan to stick around?"

I nod. "I may not be a part of Cerberus any longer, but I'm not walking away from my child."

"Just your child?" I shake my head, but he continues before I can argue with his wording. "Do you plan to marry her?"

I shake my head and wait for him to come off of his chair and pummel my face with both fists. When he doesn't, I try to do my best to explain.

"This isn't the fifties, Sir. The last thing any of us need, including our unborn child, is to be brought into a loveless marriage."

At this he growls, so deep and so long in his throat, my life nearly flashes before my eyes.

"That's my daughter you're talking about," he hisses, and I reflect back on the way I responded nearly the same way last night when Gigi was saying horrific things about Izzy. I commend his restraint, the control over his instincts I wasn't man enough to have myself.

"Can you tell me that you loved every single woman you touched before you met Mrs. Anderson?" He narrows his eyes at me. That's just as scary as the growl. "I'm not saying I hate her, but I hardly know her. Standing here and confessing something to you that I never even considered telling her would be a lie. I'm not, by normal practice, a liar, Sir."

"My wife thinks you sticking around is a good idea." My burden lifts, if only a fraction of an inch. "I wholeheartedly disagree with her."

The burden increases tenfold.

"Georgia will leave if you leave." I nod, knowing it's true. I promised her that raising the child together is what I wanted. She's the one who suggested the awful idea of a three-bedroom apartment. "I let that factor into my decision about you."

Silence grows heavy between us once again. I can tell he wants me to ask, to plead, but it would only show weakness. He's both hoping for it, so he can prove himself right, and wishing against it because his daughter and I are having a baby whether he likes it or not, and needs me to be a man he can trust her and his grandchild with.

The moments stretch on, lasting an eternity in the already late hours of the night.

He clears his throat. "You still being a part of Cerberus changes nothing. You impregnating and dating my daughter doesn't give you any allowances the other men don't have."

My eyes snap from the front of his shirt where I've been staring at for what seems like hours to his eyes.

"Dating," my voice cracks, "Sir?"

"Dating," he affirms.

There are worse things than waking up to Georgia Anderson's body against mine.

I shake my head to clear the thought.

"You don't want to?" he asks questioning my physical response to thinking of his daughter naked and splayed out across my chest.

"I will," I agree so hastily I forget the last part. I swallow again. "Sir."

"Do you want to?" he asks again.

"Yes, Sir. I'd like nothing more than to date your daughter."

"She may run again." This is something I know about her.

"I'll chase her and our baby to the ends of the Earth."

He nods, the only physical approval he's shown other than his words.

"Maybe Dominic was right to vouch for you."

"Thank you, Sir." I step forward to thank him and shake his hand, but he just passes me the key to my abandoned room back.

"Rack up. You have shit to do tomorrow."

"A new mission?" Why I ask I have no idea. Being allowed to stay in Cerberus, the privilege of being this close to Gigi is more than I could've ever expected.

"Georgia has a doctor's appointment. Shadow is taking her."

"I'm taking her," I insist.

His eyes narrow at the challenge, but there's something else there, something akin to pride or expectation.

"So be it," he agrees.

Backing away, I open the door and step out into the hallway in one swift move. Shadow is as stoic as ever standing sentry over the room, but I don't miss the slight twitch of Kid's mouth as I walk past. I ignore the groups of guys, the ones I've spent numerous months with in foreign countries as they hover near the hallway door to the conference rooms.

Those nosy fuckers are just as bad as teenage girls. I should know. Izzy prattles on relentlessly about the girls in her school.

I don't bother unpacking once I get inside my room. It's a simple task and can be completed in mere minutes. I hit the shower, scrubbing every inch of my body, preparing myself for Gigi's visit later. Her sneaking into my room will do nothing but anger Kincaid, even though I'm now *dating* his daughter, but he didn't lay out any ground rules, so I'm going to play ignorant to the fact that fucking her in his clubhouse will piss him off. Gigi is irresistible, and I promised her I'd never turn her away again. My promise to her is more important than any emotion her father could face with the news.

The damage has already been done, right?

I wait.

And wait.

And wait some more.

I wait until sleep drags me under and the erection that sprang up just thinking about my dark-haired girl deflates in desperate sadness.

Chapter 24

Gigi

"It's late," Mom says with a yawn when she finds me sitting on a stool at the breakfast counter.

"Couldn't sleep," I say and stare down at the uneaten peanut butter and jelly sandwich on the counter in front of me.

"Want some milk," she asks as she tugs the fridge door open.

"No thanks. Where's Dad?"

"At the clubhouse," she answers.

"Doing what exactly?"

She turns in my direction and frowns. "You know exactly what he's doing."

"Firing Jameson? Getting his guys to hide his body?"

She chuckles, but it's guarded as if she knows what Dad is capable of when he's protecting his family.

"I doubt he's going to kill that man."

"He wants to," I mutter.

"I'm pretty sure that's not the way your father was leaning when he headed over there." She places a cold cup of milk in front of me. I eye it with disinterest.

"Why are you staring at me?" I ask when I look up and find her leaning against the counter, arms crossed over her chest, and her eyes drilling holes into me.

"We only want what's best for you, Georgia. We want you to be happy."

"Is this when you tell me that marrying Jameson is what is best? It's what will make me happy?"

I don't know how to be a wife or a mother, but I can't deny the pain I get in my chest at the thought of having both.

She shakes her head, a soft smile playing at the corners of her mouth. "Marrying a man you don't love just because you're pregnant is the last thing you need. It's not a decision to be made lightly."

I spin the glass of milk around on the counter, concentrating on the ring of condensation it leaves behind as if it's the most interesting thing in the world. I usually run from serious conversations, opting to ignore anything that may resemble an adult choice.

"Marrying a man for anything less than being madly in love is a huge mistake." I look up to find her eyes distant, pain pulling at her previously smiling eyes. "You don't marry out of fear or some obligation to another person. Love. Love is the only reason you stand before your friends and God and say vows, commit to one person for the rest of your life."

I've heard Dad, Shadow, and Kid talking about Mom's first husband, the same man that came after her after abusing her during their entire relationship. He died for his efforts less than a hundred yards from where we are right now.

"I can see myself loving him," I confess.

I don't know if my appeal is merely sexual or if it goes deeper than that, but there has been a pull, low in my gut that confuses me whenever he's around.

"That's a start." The smile that was disappearing with her memories is renewed the moment the front door opens, and Dad appears in the kitchen.

He's not happy, but the black cloud of anger that rained down on all of us in his office earlier seems to have dissipated some.

"You need to eat," he huffs on his way to wrap his arms around Mom. "You're too skinny, and the baby needs the nourishment."

"How quickly you accept my delicate decision." I pick up my previously ignored sandwich and take a hearty bite.

"I'm a realist, Georgia. No matter how much I wish things were different, I can't ignore the truth of the situation."

"Different?" Irritation marks my tone enough that he leans in, head on my mother's shoulder, arms wrapped tight around her, and his eyebrow cocks up. "And exactly how do you wish my life was different?"

"I'd prefer you educated, married, and mentally, financially, and emotionally prepared. Parenting is hard even for those that plan on the children they conceive."

My mom's smile grows wider as she turns her head and kisses Dad on the jaw.

"Your dad struggled a little in the beginning. Two babies are a handful with everything else going on."

I've heard those stories as well. Only these were told around Thanksgiving tables and near the fireplace at Christmas. The stories of him coming to terms with being the father of not one, but two, little girls were told to family and friends in rooms filled with friendly taunting and laughs.

"I remember." I smile at both of them, so in love even after two decades, is something I've longed for for a while, although I'd never admitted it out loud.

"Blade made you a doctor's appointment for tomorrow. Thankfully, Dr. Davison had an opening, but it's first thing in the morning," Dad says nuzzling into Mom's neck.

Her cheeks flush, and I want to groan at the arousal he's building in her, but that's what kids do, and I'm no longer a child.

"Dr. Davison is old as the hills, and besides, he's a general practitioner. I think an OB/GYN is better suited for this situation. Don't you?"

"Dr. Camryn Davison, his daughter, is in her residency. I hear she's better than the OB she's working under."

The pride he has in his eyes for his friend's daughter hurts more than it should. I haven't seen it pointed in my direction since stealing home once at a softball game in middle school.

"Sounds good," I agree and laugh when shock runs across his face at my quick agreement.

I never give in that easy. Normal Gigi would argue, throw a fit about him running her life and making decisions for her, but I know, even though he may not be happy about my out-of-wedlock pregnancy, he'd never send me to a doctor he didn't have full faith in.

"I trust you, grandpa." I slide off of the stool, still unable to stomach the half-eaten sandwich and laugh again when he begins to look sick.

"Too soon, honey," my mother chides as I kiss them both on the cheek and head up to my room.

Maybe making Dad freak out means whatever sexual tension that was building between them will have faded away and they'll just go to bed. Although I'm exhausted, I know I'll sleep better in Jameson's arms. My skin tingles at the mere thought of his hands not just wrapped around me, but his hand wandering lower.

I shake my head.

"Soon," I mutter, kicking off my shoes and climbing under the warm sheets.

When I hear my mom giggle on their way upstairs, I groan and settle in, knowing they won't be going to sleep anytime soon.

I spend an hour staring up at the ceiling in my childhood bedroom, mind racing with worry and doubt. There's nothing I could be doing right this second to make things easier, but I'm still restless at the idea of being back in Farmington. I have no prospects. The only plan on my horizon is hanging out at my parents' house and growing a baby. The truth of the boredom I'm facing agitates me. I'm not an idle person. I'm not lazy. I can't stand being stagnant, just sitting around and not doing a damn thing.

Turning my head, I glance over at my dresser. Usually, when I'm dragged back home, I've got a suitcase and a stray bag or two. This time, I was honest with Jameson. There was nothing back at the apartment that I wanted to keep. The vacancy on the carpet across the room is unsettling as my itch to get up and do something claws at my skin.

It's how it has always been. I'm finicky and make decisions pretty quickly. It's why I just up and leave sometimes. I don't even have to be annoyed or pissed at my parents. Some days, I just feel like leaving.

I bite my lip at the thought of Jameson chasing me, hunting me down after I've left Farmington in my dust. Smiling, I turn to my left side, closing my eyes, and I let the fantasy of him finding me, punishing me for my insolence invades my mind. That thought, that idea carries me into sleep and keeps me warm all night long.

Chapter 25

Hound

She never came to me last night. I have no idea what happened in her house last night after her dad returned.

"You really know how to fuck shit up don't you?"

I turn to look at Scooter who is smoking just outside of the front door of the clubhouse.

"Clearly," I mutter, glancing to his cigarette and remembering a time when smoke in my lungs first thing in the morning was what I lived for.

I lick my lips unconsciously, and Scooter offers his pack in my direction.

"No thanks," I tell him and look over at the construction crew that's already milling around across the street.

"They work fast as hell," Scooter says, his eyes focusing across the street as well.

"Kincaid going to build you a house out back now that you're family and shit?"

"Not likely. I'm pretty certain I'll end up a casualty on our next mission. It'd be easier to explain than a corpse in the clubhouse."

He chuckles, but he's shaking his head. "If Prez didn't kill you in the moment, he won't do it later. Well…"

"What?" I turn back to look at him.

"He may if you fuck her twin and knock her up too."

I punch him in the arm hard enough to nearly knock him off the side of the small concrete porch.

"That shit's not funny. I have no intention of fucking her twin."

"Who's fucking whom?"

We both turn to see Gigi walking down the sidewalk toward us.

Scooter clears his throat, tosses his cigarette butt into the ashtray, and apologizes for his language before he turns and walks toward the garage.

"Hey." It's the best I can manage at the sight of her in a dress that hits the middle of her thighs and clings to the perfect globes of her breasts.

"I see you've made friends while I was gone." She smiles, but I can see the exhaustion playing near her eyes and the same pink on her cheeks she gets when she either gets sick or orgasms.

Betting that the glow is from morning sickness and not coming, I step closer to her.

"I missed you last night," I confess and wrap my arms around her. I press a soft kiss to her forehead before pulling my head back to look into her eyes.

"I fell asleep waiting for Mom and Dad to go to sleep," she says, her eyes beaming up at mine.

"What's that look for?"

A sheepish smile spreads across her beautiful face, the pink in her cheeks doubling.

"I dreamed about you last night," she confesses.

"Did you?" My cock thickens at the salaciousness in her eyes. "Dare I ask what this dream entailed?"

"Well," she says turning, breaking my hold on her, and walking toward the SUV we drove back from Vegas in yesterday. "There were ropes."

"I'm good with ropes."

"There was a ball gag."

"Not my style," I whisper in her ear as I tug open the passenger side door so she can climb inside. "I want to hear you whimper, moan, and come loud enough to make the neighbors bang on the wall."

Her breathing grows shallower, eyelids lowering.

"There were also nipple clamps and a butt plug."

My cock, ready for all of it, pushes against the zipper of my jeans. Since I go commando, I know I'll have indentions from the teeth in a line right down the length of it.

"We're going to the doctor's office," I remind her.

Her pretty white teeth clamp on her bottom lip as she fights a smile. "We can always stop off at the park. We have time."

I lean in close, her breath mixing with mine. "It's your first visit."

"It is," she agrees.

"I looked on the internet, and your first visit includes an exam," I inform her.

"Okay," she says watching my mouth and only half listening.

"We can stop at the park."

She nods, pink tongue sweeping across her lip. I can feel the echo of the action in the throb of my cock.

"Please," she begs. "I dreamed of you fucking me all night. I needed it so much, I fingered myself the second I woke up."

"Did you?"

I groan at the frantic nodding of her head. "And again in the shower."

So the flush on her cheeks wasn't from morning sickness.

"You have an exam in an hour."

"We have time," she urges.

"Then you'll be the one explaining to the doctor why my come is dripping out of you during your exam."

Fuck do I hate she has that damn exam.

Her eyes widen at realizing what a stop at the park will mean, and I can't help but laugh.

She shoves at my shoulder. "You asshole. You got me all hot and bothered, and now we can't do a damn thing."

"You're wet."

"So wet," she pants.

"We can take care of that."

I close her door and walk around to the driver's side, thankful there isn't a soul in sight to see the pole trying to escape my jeans.

***

"That smirk," she says with a quick shake of her head.

"You're beautiful after you come." I shift, not finding any comfort in the motion. My cock was ignored in the park when I lifted her off her seat of the SUV and forced her pussy to my mouth. She came twice, and I licked her clean, my dick going untouched the entire time. It seemed like a good idea at the time. I regretted it the instant we got inside the exam room, and she stripped naked only to cover her amazing body back up with a thin, paper gown.

"I could've sucked you off."

I groan and shift again.

"You'll get your chance," I promise just as a soft but authoritative knock hits the door.

"Come in," Gigi says, an expectant look on her face.

A female doctor, too damn young to have already gone through medical school walks in with a bright smile on her face.

"Hello, Georgia." She offers her hand, and my girl shakes it.

"Gigi, please," she corrects, her eyes narrowing at the doctor.

"Your dad called this morning. Gave me a little history. I noticed in your chart that it's been a few years since your last pelvic exam."

"Listen, Cam," Gigi begins, and I can tell she's suddenly irritated just by her tone.

"It's Dr. Davison, now," the professional says with such sharpness I recoil then dart my eyes to Gigi, fully expecting her to come off the table and claw the doctor's eyes out.

Instead, Gigi laughs. "You've been Cam all my life."

"Don't remind me," Cam says with a familiarity I'm just now catching onto. "Babysitting you is something I'd rather not remember."

"You were mean," Gigi says.

"You stuck bubble gum in my hair." Her arms cross over her chest, nose tilting up in defiance.

"You had your boyfriend over and ignored us. Ivy hurt herself in the bath because you were too busy sucking face with that Benelli boy!"

Cam closes her eyes and takes a deep breath. "That was ten years ago. Your parents forgave me, and you should too. I babysat you for several more years after that."

"Hi," I say standing and trying to diffuse the situation. I offer her my hand. "I'm Jameson Rawley."

"The father, I presume." She shakes my hand, full professional mask back in place.

"Let's get started." She turns back to Gigi like they weren't enemies years ago. "Yearly exams are vital for your health, Gigi."

"I know. I won't miss another one."

When Dr. Davison asks her to lie back for a breast exam, I nearly get up and walk out. The pictures marking the walls don't help either. Breasts, albeit rendered with an artist's hand, are everywhere. I look down at my hands instead.

"Please don't talk to my dad about me," Gigi says in a pleading voice. "I'm grown."

"Of course," Dr. Davison says.

The breast exam is complete, and I finally look up when Gigi covers her chest.

"Let me get the nurse for the next part. I'll be right back."

"You know her?" Why I ask I don't know. Clearly, they have a history.

She just nods, but I pay attention when her teeth strike her bottom lip. "I'm going to be imagining it's you when she slides her fingers inside of me."

"God damn," I hiss. "You need to stop."

There's a soft knock, and now two people dressed in scrubs make their way inside the already cramped room.

My throat is dry, and I only stare when the nurse tries to make casual conversation.

I'm hard as steel by the time Dr. Davison asks Gigi to lie back.

I'm leaking from my tip when the request is made for her feet to be placed in the stirrups.

I nearly come as Gigi moans when Dr. Davison inserts her fingers into my girl.

"Are you experiencing discomfort," the doctor asks, concerned.

"No," Gigi pants. "It's just a little weird with you being the one to do this."

Dr. Davison laughs. "I assure you. We're very professional here."

I'm not a ménage kind of guy. I can admit I've had my fair share of fucking several girls at once, but it wasn't something I ever sought out, rather something that just ended up happening. I sure as fuck don't want to share a second of Gigi's time, but her words and the knowledge that she's inappropriately turned on right now would bring me to my knees if I were standing.

"Is sex safe?"

I choke out a disbelieving cough.

The doctor laughs again. "That's the most asked question we get when a couple finds out they're expecting."

I fucking blush when she looks over at me, at least two fingers deep inside my girl.

"Sex is safe. I suggest lots of showers beforehand and no douching. Pregnant women's hormones are all over the place which makes you more prone to yeast and urinary tract infections."

"What about piercings?"

I can feel the heat creep up my chest to my face. She's fucking with me. I just know it. These are questions we can Google, yet she's asking them in a room with two women I don't know. I'm not a shy man, but their professionalism makes me uncomfortable.

Dr. Davison tries to cover a laugh with a quick cough. The older nurse just looks bored.

"You've got what?" Gigi looks over at me, and grins, knowing I'm going to paddle her ass later for this. "Four or five piercings."

"Seven, total," I correct.

Dr. Davison looks impressed, but it's the nurse's "Oh my," that earns Gigi another couple of slaps to her naked ass.

"Piercings are fine." Dr. Davison's voice is a little higher than it has been so far today. She gives me a serious look. "So long as they're taken care of, not infected, and clean."

"Of course," I respond.

Dr. Davison pulls off her latex gloves and tosses them to the used instrument tray before turning back to Gigi.

"Do you have any more questions?"

I watch Gigi's throat work on a swallow, and I try to prepare myself for what's coming. My palm is already warming, and I know I'm going to redden her ass before we even leave the parking lot.

Yet, all thoughts of distributing punishment fade away when her mouth opens.

Chapter 26

Gigi

"Will cocaine hurt the baby?"

I avoid Jameson's eyes even though I can feel the fire from them burning into the side of my face.

"Any drugs including cigarettes, excessive amounts of caffeine and some over the counter medications can be harmful to the fetus," Dr. Davison explains. "How often are you using? There are programs—"

"I haven't." I shake my head, the only thing I can think to do to keep the tears burning my eyes from falling. "The night..."

I look over at Jameson, but he's looking down at hands knotted together in anger, not in disappointment. His anger I can handle. Knowing he'll meet my eyes and I'll see the same disappointment that's been so familiar on my parents' faces will be unbearable.

"The night I conceived. I used cocaine that night. I haven't used since then."

I'm speaking to Cam, but my eyes stay on Jameson, begging him to look at me, praying he'll still want me. I wasn't going to say anything, but I vowed to be the best mother I can be, and I knew I'd worry relentlessly if I didn't know.

"Look at me." I feel Cam's hand on my shoulder. When I turn to face her, she pushes a tissue into my hand, and it's only then that I realize the tears have begun to fall. "Your baby will be fine. There's minimal risk so long as you don't use again."

I nod, and she continues.

"Is it something you're struggling with? There are programs I can refer you to."

I shake my head. "I'm okay. I haven't even thought about drugs in months. It was something I did to make my life easier. It made doing my job easier."

I look back at Jameson. His face is a passive mask, and I realize his indifference is much, much worse than disappointment.

"Okay," Cam says with one final rub to my back. "Are you taking prenatal vitamins?"

I shake my head. "They made me sick, and I couldn't keep them down."

"They're important. Try eating a few crackers and drinking some juice or ginger ale before even getting out of bed in the morning. According to your paperwork, you're nine weeks along. Morning sickness tends to ease up in the second trimester, so you only have a few more weeks to go."

"Thank you." I give her a weak smile.

She hands me a card from the front pocket of her white coat. "My cell number is on there. You call me if you have any questions. Tell your mom I said hi."

Thickness fills the air when Cam and the nurse exit.

"Jameson," I begin.

He stands, and I pray he'll walk up to me, comfort me, and tell me everything will be fine, but he turns toward the door. "I'll wait outside while you get dressed."

It takes twice as long to get my clothes back on as it did to take them off, even when I did it slowly to tease and taunt Jameson. I get sick, emptying my stomach into the trash, so overcome with worry that I can't even feel sorry for whoever has to deal with it. I swish my mouth with mouthwash I've been carrying in my purse since I get sick all the time.

When I finally make my way out of the room, Jameson is leaning right outside of the door. I can't speak. I don't even know what I would say to him, so I just walk past him and Dr. Davison who's standing up at a computer kiosk and typing in information. My dad will find out about the cocaine use if he wants. Blade can gain access to just about any database in the world. Farmington Women's Clinic would be child's play for him.

I feel his heat close, but not close enough as I step up to the business counter to make my next appointment.

"Your co-pay for the exam is thirty dollars," the nice receptionist says as she hands me a card for an appointment in a month's time.

"Co-pay?" I ask, but shake my head. Of course, my dad still has me on his insurance. That information would've been helpful when I sprained my knee on a new pole routine six months ago. Blade would've tracked me down, but I would've saved a couple thousand dollars. I would've left Dallas before Hound even showed up had I not had to use my savings to pay medical bills.

"I got it," Jameson says and hands cash over my shoulder.

"No," I tell him and reach into my purse for my own money.

"Now is not the time to test me," he growls in my ear.

I step out of the way, thanking the woman when she hands me a printed receipt.

"See you next month," she says with a bright smile before turning to help the next person behind me.

"Not likely," I mutter.

He doesn't touch me, doesn't say a word as we exit the doctor's office and make our way down the long hall of doors that lead to other practices.

I yelp in surprise when he pushes open the door to the family restroom and drags me inside. He doesn't even bother to flip on the light, but I can still see how angry he is in the glow of the red exit sign above the door.

"You planning on running?" I shake my head. A lie. It's my first instinct at his reaction to my confession in the exam room. "I'm pretty fucking sure that's exactly what 'not likely' meant."

I snap my head up, not realizing I said it loud enough for him to hear.

"I'll find you," he warns as his hands go first to the buckle of his belt, then the top button and zipper of his jeans. "I'll chase you clear across the world if I have to."

"I'm not running."

"Damn right you're not," he hisses as one hand strokes his now exposed cock and the other one presses down on my shoulder. "Get on your knees, Gigi."

I obey without second thought.

The second he presses the glistening tip of his cock against my lips, I moan, knowing this is the very first time I've had a dick in my mouth since Jordy convinced me to try to suck his in high school.

"Go slow," he groans. "Don't want you to chip one of those pretty teeth."

I open my jaw wider, but his invasion is still too much. My eyes water as he presses deeper without withdrawing. Breathing through my nose is nearly as unrelenting as his fist in my hair. It may be the hottest thing I've ever experienced.

"Fuck," he whispers on a pant when I gag. He pulls back an inch or so but then presses in again. "Close your mouth and suck or I'm going to fuck your throat."

I whimper, hating the choice because fuck if I don't want to experience both.

I tighten my lips around the shaft, sucking until my cheeks collapse. The unique feel of the metal against my tongue and my lips when he pulls out and pushes back in makes me wet. The saliva dripping from my chin goes ignored as his grip gets even more brutal in my hair.

"I'm not going to last," he grunts but doesn't slow the now driving force of his hips.

I press my palms against his tense thighs and relish the feel of the muscles jumping and flexing with his exertion.

"Swallow it all," he hisses just as his cock jerks in my mouth.

The first thick, salty burst makes me squeeze my watering eyes closed, and I try to focus only on his pleasure. Letting myself actually consider what I'm doing would probably make me puke, so I push it to the back of my mind, sucking and swallowing until he slips free of my mouth.

"Don't," he snaps when I raise the back of my hand to my mouth to clear away some of the mess.

He flips the light switch, and we both squint at the sudden illumination of the room. When I can focus again, I see him staring at me, cock still half mast, and hanging from the opening in his jeans. His chest rises and falls in harsh breaths, but he's looking at me differently. Different from the way he watched me while I danced on stage the first day we met. Different from the way he focuses on my face when I come. And thankfully, different from the way he looked at me when Cam left the exam room after my confession.

There's danger in his eyes and damned if my body isn't begging him to do his worst.

"Please," I beg, standing so I can get closer to him.

"You need something?"

His thumb sweeps over the corner of my mouth before dipping inside. I toy with it against my tongue, the tang of his orgasm renewed in my mouth.

I nod and squirm, shifting back and forth in my ballerina flats.

"No." One simple word. An order he expects me to obey without questions.

I watch, mouth hanging open at the rejection, as he tucks himself back into his jeans and washes his hands.

"I'm wet," I purr, running my hands over the muscled expanse of his back.

"I know," he says as he dries his hands. "You'll wait."

"I don't want to," I huff, arms crossed over my chest for emphasis.

"You won't get another chance to come until you've taken your punishment."

"Punishment?" I laugh at the absurdity of his words, all the while my pussy clenching against the soft satin of my panties. "For what?"

"For those orgasms I gave you at the park." He turns facing me with a damn paper towel and runs it under my eyes. "For those comments and the striptease in the exam room, but more importantly for letting me fuck you in an alley while you were high on coke."

"Dr. Davison said the baby will be fine."

"I know he will." I smile at his insistence that he's having a son. "But that doesn't negate the fact that you were a virgin and made the decision to no longer be one while you weren't at a hundred percent capacity to make fucking decisions like that."

"I knew what I was doing," I argue. If anything, the coke made the sex in the alley even better. I would've called it euphoric, but every time he's rammed inside of me since has been just as good.

"Still isn't going to keep me from spanking your ass later."

He grabs my hand, flipping the lock on the door and pulling me back into the hallway. A mother with a toddler in a stroller and another baby strapped to her chest glares at us while tapping her mom sandals on the linoleum.

"That's not what the family restroom is used for," she hisses.

Jameson shrugs. "What can I say? She's insatiable."

We don't hear her response over my laughter as we make our way outside to the SUV.

Chapter 27

Hound

"So we're heading back to your room?" I love the eagerness in her voice. It almost makes me not want to make her cry with quick successive swats to her ass. Almost.

"Nope," I tell her and crank the vehicle. "We're going on a date."

I look over at her to find her beaming at me.

"A date?" The joy on her face, in her eyes is palpable. "Like you fingering me in a dark movie theater?"

My spent cock twitches in my jeans at the prospect.

"Like lunch. That's what people do when they date."

"We're dating now?" She huffs as she clicks her seatbelt in place.

I pull mine across my chest, never taking my eyes off of her.

"I bet my dad is going to flip over that." She turns her head in my direction with a mischievous look in her eyes. "Let's do it."

The only thing that's missing is a creepy laugh and her rubbing her hands together.

"It was your dad's idea." Her face falls.

"Really?" She shakes her head. "Not possible. He may have said it, but he can't possibly be okay with it."

"You don't like the idea?" I tilt my head and wait for her answer.

"That my dad is okay with us dating?" She laughs. "Not at all."

"Because you're only happy when you're fighting him?" That devilish smile is back on her lips. "What about us dating? You okay with that idea?"

She shrugs now, but the pink on her cheeks and gleam in her eyes betrays her apathy. "I'm okay with lunch, even though I'll probably just puke it up."

"Doctor said just a few more weeks," I remind her and put the SUV in drive.

***

"Is this okay?" I ask as I back the SUV into a parking lot.

She laughs. "You're just like my dad. He always backs in also."

I shrug. "Never know when you'll have to get away. Backing in now makes it easy to leave in an emergency later."

"Always the soldier," she mutters.

I climb out and make my way around the front of the vehicle, frowning when she opens her door and jumps out before I can open the door and help her down.

"This is a date. I'm supposed to open the door for you."

She huffs. "You just fucked my face in a bathroom at the doctor's office, and now you want to be a gentleman?"

I pin her to the door, leaning in close, the press of my hips against her stomach tantalizing in the heat of the sun.

"You have earned so many slaps on your ass. I may have to split it up over two days." Bending my knees, I press my thickening cock against the apex of her thighs.

"Yes, please," she says, eyes focused on my mouth.

"You forget," I say backing away. "You don't get to come until they're all done."

"You're a monster," she says exactly like the gingerbread man in Shrek when the king is taunting him with his broken-off legs.

I can't help the laugh that bubbles from my throat. "I love that fucking movie."

I grab her hand and usher her toward the door of the chain restaurant that's exactly like every other damn chain restaurant in town. It makes me wish for that taco bar I ate at with Rocker and Scooter on our way back from Denver last month.

"You like Shrek?" she asks softly as the hostess gathers menus for us. It's early, the lunch rush imminent but not in full swing.

"Don't tell Izzy. I make her think I hate all those kinds of movies, but in reality, most of my favorite movies are animated like that. Shrek, Minions, any Disney movie, except Frozen, that's where I draw the line."

"Will I get to meet her?" We sit across from each other in the booth the hostess guides us to.

"Thank you," I tell her accepting the menus she offers and orders our drinks. "Who?"

Gigi huffs again in agitation. "Izzy. Will I get to meet her?"

I haven't mentioned anything about Gigi or the baby to Izzy even though I've spoken to her twice since I found out about the pregnancy.

"Of course," I say and wait for the dread to settle in my stomach. It never does. "We're meeting up in a few weeks in Albuquerque. She'll be disappointed that I don't bring the bike because she likes to ride, but I think she'll be excited to meet you."

"And when you tell her about the baby? How do you think she'll respond?" We pull our hands back when a waitress walks up and places our Cokes on the table.

We haven't had a chance to look at the menu, but we both tell her cheeseburgers and fries.

When she walks away, and my attention is back on Gigi, I find her still waiting for an answer.

"I honestly don't know. I imagine she'll be shocked."

"Not upset?"

I shake my head. "Why would she be upset?"

She looks down at the table, wasting time not answering by rearranging the silverware roll and positioning her drink just right.

"I'd be upset if my parents told me they were having another baby." She shrugs. "She's not much younger than I am, just figured it would be the normal response."

"You spoiled little brat," I tease with a wide grin.

"You'd be upset if your mom got pregnant."

"Well," she says taking a moment to think it through. "Not now, but when I was younger? Absolutely. They had Ivy to dote on. My sister is a pleaser by nature. They were always so proud. Second place sucks. Third would be even worse. Third could mean they wouldn't have any love left over for me at all."

"It doesn't work that way." I reach for her hand, cupping it between both of mine. "When you told me you were keeping the baby, even before you made your mind up if I'm being honest, I knew I would love that baby just as much as I love Izzy."

"Your heart can only hold so much love," she says with sadness in her voice.

"Also false." I squeeze her hand until she looks up at me. "It just grows bigger or holds some in reserves until it's needed. Your parents don't love Ivy more than they love you. They're good people. Your dad is a good man. You're difficult. A pain in the ass on your best day, but that doesn't cancel love. I promise you."

She takes a moment before responding, and I don't know if she's accepting what I said or trying to think of a way to counter my truth.

"So what? You're Team Kincaid now?" She's grinning, and I feel the heaviness of the conversation drift away with her quip.

"I'm a man with one daughter and a son on the way. I know what it's like to love two kids so fiercely that I can't imagine loving anyone else." The sadness returns. "But then I think about it, and I know I could love twice as many kids just as much. If we had a second kid, if you're pregnant with twins I'd love them both, equally."

"Don't even fucking joke about shit like that," she hisses, and the smile on my face is so wide my cheeks ache.

"Twins are hereditary."

"My mom had IVF." She winks at me, maintaining the upper hand.

"Thank fuck," I say and sit deeper in the booth. "I was seriously freaking out at the possibility."

Her laugh is music to my ears, a calming salve to my injured ego. When I'd heard her mutter 'not likely' to the receptionist my blood ran cold. Getting her on her knees, my cock down her throat to show her who's in charge was my only thought.

"How about we get to know each other?" she asks.

I grin, finally letting myself believe that all of this is real. "What do you want to know?"

She's nervous as she picks at the cuticle of her thumb nail.

"Out with it, gorgeous."

"When will you tell Isabela?"

I smile, knowing how my oldest daughter is going to respond with the news and pull out my phone. I type out a quick text to her and frown when the phone immediately begins to ring.

"You're supposed to be in class," I say when the call connects rather than a normal greeting.

"It's gym class," she explains. "No one does anything but sit in the bleachers on their phones. What's this big news?"

Gigi rolls her lip between her teeth, chewing on it.

"I've met someone."

I hold the phone away from my ear as Izzy squeals like the teenage girl that she is.

The worry that creased Gigi's brow suddenly disappears, her lips turning up in a smile.

Was she worried Izzy wouldn't be happy? I should've explained to her long ago that Izzy has always wanted me to be happy, the point of near harassment to look for something long term.

"There's more," I begin when she finally calms down. "We're having a baby."

The squealing begins anew.

"I'm going to be a big sister!" Izzy screams to those around her.

I reach across the table and squeeze Gigi's hand before bringing it to my lips and kissing the tips.

"I'm so happy for you," Izzy says, voice softer. The emotion is clear, and I couldn't be happier to be the father of such a loving young woman.

"Thank you, Iz. Call me later this evening if you can and we can discuss it more."

"Love you, dad."

"Love you, sweetheart."

I put my phone back in my pocket.

"That went well," Gigi says with a bright smile.

"You were worried?" She shakes her head, but I can tell that's not the entire truth. "She's an amazing person. She'll love you."

I swallow, the words I've not even spoken rolling from my mouth easier than it should at this point.

"When she finds out I'm less than five years older than her, she may not be as happy as she is right now."

Shaking my head, I reject her words. "You'll see," I promise as the waitress begins to unload our plates from the serving tray.

We eat slowly, the burgers better than I anticipated, but maybe it's her company, her smile, and the way she's quick to laugh at stupid jokes that adds seasoning to the meal, making it the most palatable thing I've consumed in a while. Other than her pussy of course.

"Really?" I ask as we walk to the SUV, my hand on her lower back, my cock twitching with the innocuous touch.

"Seriously," she verifies. "My cousin Kaleb has named every one of his dogs after some sort of weapon. "They have Remington now. Their cat is named AK, but I think the kids named it that years ago. Mia was his first dog, his partner at the police department. She's gone now, but they had like fourteen years with her."

I hate the pain in her voice, but my heart sings at the compassion she has for the animal. Somehow this amazing woman thinks she's going to be a terrible mother, but knowing she gets upset over the death of a relative's dog says a lot about the person she is.

"Mia?" I say hoping to draw her out of her sadness. "Doesn't sound like any weapon I've encountered."

I open the door for her, looking down at her perky ass in her dress as she climbs up.

"Well, M-One-A," she corrects. "M1A."

"Oh," I say with clarity. "That makes sense now. Pretty clever name."

I cross in front of the vehicle as quickly as I can so we can continue our conversation.

Before she can ask me another favorite dish, color, or childhood memory, I turn to her the second I get inside with her. "I want to go to every single doctor appointment you have."

"Are you waiting for more confessions? I don't have any."

"No. I want to experience everything. The sound of the first heartbeat, the tiny black and white pictures. I want to be there the second they prove to you that my boy is in there."

"And if it's another girl?"

I sigh playfully and put the SUV in gear. "Then I'll have to buy a fuck ton more guns, won't I?"

Her laughter fills the cabin of the vehicle as I pull out into traffic. "You're going to be a great dad."

I stiffen.

"I mean," she begins.

"I know what you meant. I'm thankful that Izzy's stepdad is super protective of her. As bitter as I want to be about another man raising my daughter, she really lucked out in that department."

"That's good," she says.

I hate the silence that swarms around us. Gone is the teasing and laughing. Gone is the happiness that filled both of us while chatting at the restaurant.

"Give me your phone," I tell her as we pull into the gravel lot of the clubhouse.

She hands it over, and I type my cell number and send a quick text to my phone.

"Now you can reach me." I hand it back to her.

"We seem to be doing everything backward."

"We'll catch up." I kiss her on the cheek and hate the sound of the door when it closes me back inside alone.

Something catches in my chest when I watch her disappear around the corner toward her dad's house. I have a single room in a clubhouse with more than a handful of other guys. No real privacy. No real home.

"Her suggestion of a three-bedroom apartment doesn't sound so crazy," I mutter as I climb out of the SUV and head to the garage.

Chapter 28

Gigi

Me: I can't wait to spank your ass.

I stare down at the text Jameson sent from my phone inside of the SUV debating if going to him is what's best for me.

Do I want the promise he eluded to several times today? Fuck yeah, I do, but the mood changed into something dark and depressing after our incredible meal. That's not something I'm sure I can face again.

I sigh and climb out of my bed. My parents disappeared into their room over an hour ago with no peep, giggle, or other noises I refuse to examine. Yet, I stayed in my bed trying to talk myself into going to him.

Creeping down the stairs, I head out of the house and use the backdoor to the clubhouse. Thankfully unlocked, the door leads just off the kitchen to the hallway of rooms. When Ivy and I were brought home from the hospital, this is where we made our home. Until we were six and Dad finally broke down and had our house built, we roamed these halls with all the other kids.

I let myself into Jameson's room, locking the door securely behind me. I expect to see his sleeping form on his bed, and he's there, but he's sitting on the edge of the bed, in all his naked glory.

"I've been waiting for you." The low gruff of his voice sends shivers over my entire body, and I realize debating even coming here wasn't what I wanted at all. I wanted this, this man looking at me like he both loves and hates the sight of me.

"I wasn't going to come," I confess. "Afraid you wouldn't let me come and wondering if my entire night is only going to be filled with pain, my morning consumed by the aches you're sure to leave on my body."

"Yet here you are." He hasn't shifted, hasn't moved his body one single inch since I stepped inside, and his calmness makes me shiver harder.

"Yes," I pant.

"You have much to atone for," he says crooking his finger and drawing me closer. "All the lies. Running from me after Dallas, keeping the secret about my baby, the way you acted at the doctor earlier, but most importantly the idea in your head that you could ever run from me again."

"I want to run right now," I admit. "Will it hurt badly?"

"If I do it right."

I'm trembling, my knees barely strong enough to hold my weight when I finally make it within arm's reach.

"And if I do it right, you'll beg me not to stop, plead with me to redden your ass every day for the rest of your life."

I moan, not at the idea of him spanking me, but because the idea that he would be around every day turns me on more than anything.

"I want that."

I flinch, the anticipation of his touch incomparable to the actual feel of it on my hip.

"Strip," he directs as his hand falls away.

I scurry out of the same dress I wore to the doctor's office earlier.

"No panties?" The approval in his voice is enough to keep me from ever covering my pussy again.

I stand before him naked as the day I was born, eyes roaming over the taut flesh of his stomach, the rippling muscles of his arms as he runs his hands up and down his muscular thighs.

"I didn't want anything to get in your way." I'm nearly breathless, longing for him to put his hands back on me.

"You walked through a clubhouse full of horny bastards with my pussy bare?" The possession. God, I crave it. To be needed, to be wanted by this man is almost incomprehensible, but his words ring true deep down in a place I don't bother to examine often. "I think that only adds to my count."

"Oh God," I mutter.

"You're going to feel me all over for days," he promises. His hand runs up my bare thigh, over my hip, until his huge hand is testing the weight of my breast. "On your ass for being so petulant."

He twists my nipple until I cry out in either pain or pleasure, at this point I'm not even sure myself.

"Deep inside where I'm going spend the night fucking you. You'll beg me to stop; you'll think you can't take anymore." The tip of his index finger runs delicately down my sternum, a contradiction to his dark vows.

"I won't stop. I'll take what I need because whose pussy is this?"

His finger ghosts over my clit. My hips move seeking more pressure. It earns me a slap to the sensitive bud.

"Whose is it?" he growls nudging my legs further apart.

"Yours," I pledge.

"Remember that."

Next thing I know I'm slung over his lap, face buried in sheets that smell like him, ass on display.

The first smack comes out of nowhere, and like any other time I'm in pain, I try to scramble away from it. The hand pressed low on my back ensures I stay exactly where he's positioned me.

"Do I need to add more?"

I shake my head as his hand rubs over the injured flesh of my right ass cheek.

He smacks and rubs, three strikes and fifteen seconds of stinging massage, repeatedly for what seems like days.

Then, he's spreading my sore cheeks, the cool air in his room licking at the entrance to my body. I'm wet, embarrassingly so, and I didn't even know I was turned on. The cacophony of sensations leaves my head spinning.

I need more.

I never want to be hit again.

"So filthy," he praises, fingers sweeping through the slickness of my desire until they stop, toying with the virgin flesh of my anus. "Whose ass is this?"

"Mine," I argue at the unfamiliar burn as he dips the tip of his finger inside.

Three more strikes; fifteen more seconds of massage.

"Whose?" His finger begins to dip inside again.

"Y-yours," I hiss as he presses deeper.

"Not tonight." I moan when he pulls free. "But soon it will be."

My mouth is dry, the heavy breathing from my punishment and the unsure emotions running through my head have left me delirious, unsure of what's coming next, but knowing that I'll die without it.

"Hurt?" he asks gripping my abused ass cheek in his hand.

I wince, but the warmth of his hands and the sting combine until I'm panting and hoping he hits me again.

"Yes," I admit. "So good."

His dark chuckle turns me on, too.

"Knees and elbows," he commands releasing me and standing me up on wobbly legs. I scramble to mind him, arching my back, feet hanging off the edge of the bed.

He rams inside before I even realize he's positioned himself behind me. The intrusion of his cock and the metal lining the bottom of his shaft is sensation overload. I cry out, uncaring of who in the clubhouse may hear. There's no one that exists in this world but him and me.

"Fuck, your ass is so red." He drives his statement home by gripping my tender flesh and thrusting even deeper.

Howling when he grips a fistful of my hair and forcing my back to arch even deeper, I'm left as nothing more than sensation.

I come. I burst wide open, the darkness disappearing behind the bright flashes in my vision, yellows, and purples, pulsing in time with my release.

Then the sting of his hand on my already tender ass brings me back around.

"I. Didn't. Give. You. Permission." Each word is underlined with another slap to my ass and another brutal shove of his cock.

I come again.

He punishes me.

And I realize I could do this every second of every day for the rest of my life.

"You fucking bitch," he hisses as his cock kicks, and he starts to come.

I smile at both the pleasure he's found with my body and the words he said in awe rather than in a derogatory way.

His weight leans over my back, and I collapse, the cool sheets a needed relief against my sweaty skin.

"You weren't supposed to come," he mutters in my ear. Biting nips of his mouth on my shoulder is enough to stir my overused body until I'm squirming under him once again.

"Your fault," I say on a moan when his tongue sweeps out and licks the shell of my ear.

"You're making me hard."

He's still inside of me, hips moving his cock in and out in lazy strokes.

"You never went soft," I argue.

"I'm always hard around you."

I smile against the mattress.

Suddenly his weight is gone, and I'm being shifted to the center of his bed on my back.

He's back inside of me, chest to chest, mouth hovering near mine, a second later.

I realize as his breath becomes mine that we've never kissed. My tongue has never tasted or felt the roughness of his. And more than anything, more than breath or food or water, it's what I need to survive.

He's watching my mouth, and I pray he needs it as much as I do.

He doesn't lean in; he doesn't press his mouth to mine. He leaves me hanging, gasping, slowly dying in his arms as he hitches my leg up. I press my heel into his back, urging him harder, deeper because it doesn't matter that I'm slowly fading from the deficiency of his mouth, I can't imagine a kinder death than one where he's buried deep inside of me.

When my eyes flutter closed, then and only then does he resuscitate me. Only then does he press his soft but firm lips to my mouth.

The jolt of electricity, the renewed life force is an arrow down my body. It begins to pulse in my clit. My orgasm, another one I didn't get permission for, takes over, clenching and gripping around him while he takes over my mouth.

The lazy sweeps of his tongue don't match the now hurried thrusts of his hips. The soft words he whispers against my lips are a contradiction to the punishing grip of his hand on my ass as he angles my hips just right.

"Perfect," he praises just before he stills, the hot jets of his come coating my womb.

We lie, his weight held up by his strong arms. The kisses we share are calm and satiated.

"You're sleepy," he chuckles against my mouth, and I realize that I'm so dazed and exhausted that I'm sliding in and out of consciousness.

I grumble my dissent when he pulls back and leaves the bed, only waking enough to grumble at him when he begins to massage a soothing cream into the skin of my abused ass.

Chapter 29

Hound

When my eyes open the following morning, the sun is high in the sky, peaking around the side of the curtains and washing the amazing woman beside me in enough of its rays to make her glow. She breathes softly against my chest as one of my hands grip the ass cheek of the leg she has hitched high up on my own thigh. My other hand is resting on my stomach, but the backs of my fingers are nestled against her lower belly.

Emotion clogs my throat knowing that as she sleeps, our child grows, gets stronger, and readies himself to join us. I pull Gigi even closer when she takes a deep breath. She mumbles something incoherent when her stomach growls.

Wincing, she raises her head from my chest when my fingers flex against her ass.

"Ouch," she pouts.

I smile down at her. She's perfection personified, even with messy hair and breath that could use the aid of a toothbrush and mouthwash.

"I loved spanking you last night," I admit to her.

"I loved kissing you."

Jesus, the way she clamped down on me, coming when my mouth met hers. There was no greater feeling than that alone.

"I could tell." My cock is hard, part pure biology, part waking to a naked woman plastered to my side.

"Round three?" she asks with a delicate swivel of her hips.

Her stomach growls again, interrupting my agreement.

"I'll get you some crackers and juice." I try to pull away, but she clings harder to me.

"I'm not hungry." Her stomach cries out again.

"Lying to me will only get your sore ass spanked again." Another swivel of her hips, the heat and slickness of her pussy nearly burning my thigh.

"Mmm," she hums.

"The doctor said you need to eat before you get out of bed," I remind her. "So you don't get sick."

She smiles, sleepy but horny at the same time. "I have no intention of getting out of bed."

Her hand trails down my stomach making the muscles jump and beg for more attention. She gets dangerously close to my cock, and I know the tease of her fingers will be enough to make me ignore her hunger.

I grab her wrist but ease the rejection by brushing my lips against hers.

"Crackers and juice," I tell her against her lips before sliding off of the bed and pulling on a pair of jeans. I don't bother with the top button or shoes.

"Hurry back. As soon as I drink my juice, I'm going to drink your juice."

I ignore the twitch of my still half-erect cock and laugh as I walk out into the hall and close her inside of my room.

"Drink my juice," I mutter. The ridiculous and immature words still making me chuckle as I walk into the kitchen. I choke on them when I see Kincaid, Kid, Shadow, and a couple of the other guys drinking coffee at one of the long kitchen tables.

"What's so funny?" Scooter asks before popping a piece of biscuit in his mouth. "Gigi say something funny?"

Fuck. My. Life.

Kincaid's eyes narrow, and the second Shadow clears his throat, the guys, Scooter included, stand up and clear out.

"Grab a cup of coffee," Kincaid says. "Then have a seat."

I don't argue. I don't tell him that I'm only out of my bed because his naked daughter is hungry. I sure as fuck don't mention the two servings of juice she wants this morning.

"Yes, Sir," is all I mutter as I turn my back and pour coffee into the biggest cup I can find. I don't bother with cream or sugar, knowing bitterness is all I'll be able to taste anyway.

I sit across from him, facing all three members, Kincaid in the middle, Shadow to his right with a look of impassivity on his face. His eyes tell a different story. Kid is on Kincaid's left with a mischievous sparkle in his eye. Classic Kid.

"Morning," I mumble.

"Almost midday," Shadow corrects with a quick glance down at his watch.

"Late night?" Kid asks.

I choke and sputter on the sip of coffee I attempt to take.

Kincaid's eyes close, and his jaw ticks, muscles flexing as he clenches his teeth.

I ignore the taunt, praying it's the right direction. Most people would deny, but even though through omission, I've lied enough to the men of this club. The man sitting in front of me will be a part of my life for the foreseeable future, and I don't want to ruin that so early on.

"How did the doctor's appointment go yesterday?"

I look up at Kincaid. "It went well."

Do not think about the blowjob in the family restroom. Do. Not.

"Well?" He raises an eyebrow at me. "That's all I get?"

"Dr. Davison seems nice, knowledgeable. She confirmed that Gigi is nine weeks. She says her morning sickness should start to fade after she hits the second trimester."

"Her next appointment?"

I look from Shadow to Kid wondering why they're even here for this but then consider Kincaid may need them if I say anything that makes him want to jump across the table and choke the life out of me.

"In a month," I repeat from what I remember the receptionist telling her yesterday. "She's covered by your insurance."

He nods.

"I'd like to take that over."

Kid leans in but doesn't say a word, and I wonder if this is it. If requesting to take care of his daughter, asking her parents to give up that final hold on her is what will make him snap. Kincaid, however, doesn't look upset but contemplative.

"What does Georgia say about it?"

"I didn't ask."

Kincaid huffs a laugh. "That child—"

"Woman," I correct.

He rolls his bottom lip between his teeth before speaking again. "That *woman* has been bucking any type of authority, any person who makes decisions for her long before she ever hit puberty. What makes you think you can just do something like take over her health insurance?"

Because she's mine, and I'll spank her ass if she gives me any shit about it.

"It's a simple thing," I counter.

"For me it's simple. For you it's simple. For Georgia," he tilts his head, and I already know his train of thought.

"It's enough to make her run," I finish for him.

"Exactly," he confirms.

"Even still. I want that responsibility."

"Responsibility?" I hate the snark in Shadow's tone. "Now you want to be responsible?"

"The fuck is that supposed to mean?" If he even mentions the alley back in Dallas, I'll bust his fucking nose.

"Didn't get it right the first time you knocked up a chick in high school? Want a second stab at abandoning your *responsibility*?"

Izzy.

"There's more to the story than the information you think you have."

"I sure as fuck hope so," Shadow spits.

Annoyed, I cross my arms over my chest and sit back in my chair. Kincaid just looks on, not saying a word but I can tell he's curious about the rest of the story as well.

"You seem a little too invested, Shadow." His eyes narrow and I forget he's the club VP. I've got three ranks above his ass where it counts, seventeen years in the Corps compared to his four. "Upset Gigi is with a man that's not you?"

Kincaid is on his feet, rough palms against his best friend's chest as Shadow, furious, tries to push him out of the way to attack.

"She's like my daughter you piece of shit."

"Enough," Kincaid hisses, but Shadow only calms slightly. "Go."

Kid, already on his feet mumbles, "I'm sure as fuck glad I only have one son. Girls are too much fucking trouble."

"You wouldn't understand what it's like to take care of a child, yours or not," Shadow spits before he raises his hands in surrender. Kincaid, still between us, removes his hands. "She sure as fuck deserves better than you."

I nod because it's the truth. Gigi deserves to be worshipped, deserves to have everything laid at her feet. She sure as hell doesn't deserve to have her ass beat in the darkness and her mouth fucked in restrooms.

"I was out of line," I concede because all I see is protective fire and love in his eyes, not jealousy or his own sense of sexual ownership.

Shadow joins Kid who has been hovering at the entrance to the kitchen, and they leave. The front door slams, and it seems to bring Kincaid back to his senses.

"Has making friends always been hard for you?" He takes his seat, and I follow his actions.

"I usually do better on my own," I answer.

"We're a fucking team here, Hound. Pissing off your VP, sleeping with the President's daughter, getting her pregnant isn't winning you any awards in the club right now."

"I know." What else can I say?

"Tell me about Isabella Montoya." It's not a question. I knew the truth would come out. I never planned to hide it deliberately from him, but the fewer people who knew about my daughter, the easier it was to keep her safe.

I spend the next twenty minutes explaining all of the same things I confessed to Gigi just days ago. He nods at some parts, jaw clenching at others, but he never interrupts me.

By the time I'm done, my eyes are glistening with the renewed loss of Izzy, the pain always just under the surface.

"We, as a club, can help you fight for custody," he says when I sit back in my chair emotionally exhausted.

I shake my head. "She'll be eighteen next summer. Then she can make her own decisions."

"That stepdad of hers seems like a complete asshole."

I chuckle. "He fucking hates me that's for sure, but he's good to her. I think he despises me more because Gabby wouldn't let him adopt her. Izzy doesn't have my last name, but at least she doesn't have his."

"A small consolation for missing out on your child's entire life. I couldn't even fucking imagine." He twists the cold cup of coffee on the table in front of him. "I hated being away from the girls, even for short-term missions. It's why we expanded and brought new guys in."

"It was easier when I was overseas fighting. I could push missing her out of my mind. I could focus on the job."

"So much for juice and crackers."

We both snap our heads up at Gigi walking into the kitchen. I clear my throat, a natural response to the sway of her tits under her thin dress. She's rumpled, sexy as fuck, and it's clear she fell back asleep after I left the room.

"Hey, Dad." She gives him a quick wave before walking over to the coffee pot.

"Let me help you," I say standing from my seat. I pull crackers from the cabinet and hand them to her with a quick kiss on the forehead. "Take a seat. I'll grab you some juice."

"Ginger ale," she specifies. "I've already gotten sick."

"How are you feeling, sweetheart," Kincaid asks as she joins him at the table.

"Sore," she says with a chuckle as she sits.

I hold my breath, waiting for her to taunt her dad with our activities from last night.

"Getting sick every morning is like an ab workout for people training for a damn triathlon," she adds.

She winks at me when I hand her the ginger ale. See? Even Gigi can make adult decisions.

Chapter 30

Gigi

I roll my eyes at my mom when she gasps, clutching at the base of her neck like I've ruined her delicate sensibilities.

"What else was I supposed to do?"

Misty busies herself with pouring another glass of wine for my mom.

"You can always come home," Mom answers.

"I'm here, unmarried and pregnant."

"And if Hound didn't sweep you off the sidewalk? You think you would've walked into that clinic and just... ended things?"

"That's what I was there for," I mutter. The thought of aborting my baby less than a week after I had made that final decision makes me sick to my stomach now.

"You would've changed your mind," Misty says as she sits beside me at the dining room table. "I did."

"What?" My eyes snap in her direction.

"I was in the room, sitting on the table talking with a nurse about my options before I realized it wasn't what I really wanted."

"Griffin?"

She nods, swallowing, her throat working under the effort.

"I thought I had no way out, no other choice."

"But you did have a choice."

Just as I had.

"I did," she agrees. "I thought adoption was better. The baby would have a chance to thrive, have someone who loved him, put him first when I wasn't capable."

"Adoption?" I'm confused. This is the first time she's ever said anything about any of this. Griffin is a few years older than us, and he's always just been around. I don't have a single childhood memory without him, Josephine, Samson, and Delilah in it. I know Samson and Delilah were adopted, but I don't recall when they came to live with Jaxon and Rob.

I laugh at the thought. "So Shadow found out and made you change your mind?"

"I wish," she mutters.

"Even though I'd already found a wonderful adoptive couple, the moment I held Griffin for the first time, I knew there was no way I could give him to someone else. I snuck out of the hospital and came here."

I smile, imagining Shadow welcoming her with open arms. He's one of the most loving men I know aside from Dad and Uncle Dom.

"I bet he was excited. A son and you. All of you together."

My mom laughs. Well, it's more of an incredulous snort.

"Hardly," Mom says.

"Shadow welcomed Griff with open arms. He made Misty fight and claw for his attention, for his love." She shakes her head. "It was pretty tense around the clubhouse for months."

I look back to Misty to see her smiling. "He finally came around."

"What made him?"

Her lips form a flat line, and I can tell she doesn't want to tell me exactly what pushed him into action. Misty looks at Mom who just tilts her head as if saying, *"You started the story, might as well finish it."*

"I left. I packed mine and Griff's things while he was away. When he came home, he found out we'd left. Showed up at my new apartment like he owned me and demanded I come back."

I lean in closer and grin when she shrugs.

"What did you do?"

"Within twenty-four hours, she and Griffin were back at the clubhouse. They were madly in love and inseparable," Mom says.

Misty chuckles. "We didn't fall in love overnight. It was growing for months. He was a stubborn ass and just wouldn't consider it."

"It took you leaving for him to come to terms with it." I look past my mom at nothing in particular as I let the information soak in.

"I know that look," Misty says as she touches my arm. I look at her, a small smile playing on my lips. "What worked for us may not work for you."

"What?" I recoil, my head pulling back a few inches. "I'm not going to run to make Jameson fall in love with me."

"But you want him to?" Mom asks.

"I don't want to raise this baby alone," I tell her. "But love doesn't necessarily play into that, I guess."

"Do you love him?" Misty asks.

I shrug. "I don't know. I really like him, but I don't have much dating experience, so I don't really know."

I crave him. My body needs his. But my heart? Who the hell knows?

"It may be too soon just yet. You'll know when you do. You won't be able to think of anything else. It'll consume you until that's all there is." Mom has this faraway look in her eyes, and I know how much she loves my dad. I want that. One day I want to look exactly like her, so in love with another person, that joy is all I feel when I think about them.

"Sounds like prison," I mutter, not ready to let anyone know what my heart desires.

They both laugh.

"Just you wait," Misty says with a pat on the top of my hand. "It's all-consuming. It's not like prison at all. More like a cocoon. There's nothing better than waking up every morning knowing half of your soul is lying right next to you."

I picture waking up this morning in Jameson's arms. All consuming is right. It was unbelievable, but it wasn't my heart that was clenching with love, it was my clit throbbing in need. I may be young, but I know there's a difference between lust and love.

I'm totally in lust with Jameson Rawley.

"Your birthday is in a week and a half," Mom reminds me as she stands to grab the bottle of wine off the counter.

I watch, not saying a word as she tops both her and Misty's glasses off.

"Planning a kegger?" I finally ask.

"Hardly," Misty laughs.

"I'll be twenty-one."

"Then we'll let you buy the alcohol for the party," Mom teases.

"Savage," I mutter, even though it doesn't really upset me. I always preferred coke over booze anyway, even though the hangovers were pretty fucking similar.

"So you're okay with a small party in the clubhouse?" I roll my eyes again.

"Or no party," I murmur.

"We have to do something," she insists. "I just didn't know if you were planning on hanging out with your friends."

"Really? I don't have any friends left in town," I remind her. "Is Ivy coming home?"

"She can't. Has some internship she signed up for."

I frown. I'm always in Ivy's shadow, but the thought of spending our first birthday apart makes me sad. I blame it on fluctuating hormones, and plaster a fake smile on my face.

"Can you make it earlier than usual? The thought of having to be awake past ten entertaining people makes me exhausted just thinking about it."

"I remember those days." Misty stands from the table and carries her empty wine glass to the sink. "I was tired the entire time I was pregnant with both boys."

"Speaking of your son, where is Cannon? I haven't even heard him mentioned since I've been back."

Misty looks down at her watch as if she expects him any minute. "He's still at school."

I may be the only one from Cerberus that never had any intentions of college. Cannon is in San Diego at college.

"Is he doing well?"

Cannon was almost as wild as I was in high school, but the same rules didn't apply to him since he has a dick. The double standard was always a subject of contention for me.

"He's struggling," Misty says. "College is just one party after another for him. He's missing class, failing most subjects. Shadow has spoken with him, and things get better for a while, but I suspect they'll kick him out soon."

Mom rubs a hand over Misty's back, but she only looks down into her wine glass as if it holds the answers for her son's future.

"And Samson?" Changing the subject is all I can think to do. I have no advice to give on Cannon.

"Still in Denver working some sort of internship with Ian Hale," she advises. "He should be home for Thanksgiving."

"I've missed so much." She gives me a weak smile.

"But you're home now." She kisses my forehead before walking toward the door. "That's what counts. See you ladies later. Shadow is going to want dinner shortly."

"See ya," I say as Mom says, "Later."

"I guess Khloe is at school also?"

Mom stands at the sink, handwashing both wine glasses.

"Yeah. Kid is losing his mind because she's been moved up to advanced placement English."

"Why would that bother Kid?"

Mom laughs as if she's remembering some inside joke. "Well, it seems some of the high school boys find her attractive."

I nod my head with a smile. "I can see that. She's beautiful."

"She is," Mom agrees. "Kid is spitting nails, doing his best not to get arrested for beating up children at school."

"Geez," I huff. "Dad, Kid, Shadow...every one of them are like alpha Rambos."

Mom laughs hard. "Don't think for one minute that Hound isn't exactly the same way."

My thighs clench at the memories of just how controlling Jameson is.

Chapter 31
Hound

"He's trying to keep us apart," Gigi mutters from the bed as I grab clothes out of the dresser and shove them into my rucksack.

"It's just work," I counter. "I have to work."

"He knows my birthday is in a week, and he's making sure you're not here."

Her brow crinkles, and damn if she isn't adorable.

"You want to celebrate your birthday with me?"

She gives me a small, sad smile. "I just don't want to spend any time apart from you."

Her confession makes my pulse thrum in my ears.

"Not tired of me yet?" I stuff the last of my clothes in the bag and pull the cord to close it. "You'll miss me?"

Her head tilts, and she looks at me as if I'm an idiot.

"I'll miss your cock," she teases a few seconds later.

"Really?" I prowl toward her, arms on either side of her crossed legs. "You know I can deny you my cock even if I'm here."

Her breathing slows, growing erratic. "But you won't."

I nip at her bottom lip. "You know better than to challenge me."

Her delicate, pink tongue sweeps out to the injured flesh of her lip. "You know I like everything you give me."

The tips of her fingers run down my chest, still naked from our shower not long ago, to the button on my jeans.

"I think you cause trouble just so I'll spank your ass."

She smiles, soft and knowing. "You're a very smart man."

We've spent the better part of the last two weeks barricaded in my room, only leaving every once in a while to 'date.'

Her dad hasn't cornered me, but he still has that look on his face, as if he's tasting something nasty, when he sees us together. Shadow's attitude from the kitchen has disappeared, so I'm certain Kincaid has told him the story about Gabby and her parents and the true reasons I'm not a father to my daughter.

I've heard bits and pieces about his and Misty's story and the fact that she didn't tell him she was pregnant. He missed the doctor's appointments, feeling the baby kick, and his birth. Because of this, I know he has to have some apathy for my situation. Although he may feel bad for me, he hasn't extended any courtesy or offered more than a working relationship. The guys hang out in the garage, and I chill in my room with Gigi.

This next mission, the first since we arrived back from Vegas will be a test. I was able to get along with the Cerberus men on missions before, but I have no clue how things are going to go now.

Scooter and Rocker have at least been courteous, but I can tell they're keeping their distance, no doubt following their Prez's leadership.

"One more time before you leave?" Gigi all but begs.

I chuckle. This woman is insatiable, waking up with sex, not going to bed until I've come inside of her, not to mention the times I wake in the night with her mouth or hands on my cock.

"You're going to kill me," I mutter against her lips.

"I'm just trying to keep you young."

She moans, breathy and ragged when I slip my fingers under my t-shirt she's taken to wearing for bed. Her heated flesh against my fingertips, the feel of her tight cunt fisting my cock is going to be hard to go without.

"I'll let you come one more time," I concede. "But you don't get to come once while I'm gone."

"No promises," she pants against my mouth.

"Fine." I shrug and pull my hand from where it was cresting her entrance.

"No," she whines and reaches for me.

"If you plan to get yourself off while I'm gone, then you can just start today."

"It's not…" she sighs and crosses her arms over her chest, leaning and pressing her back against the headboard. "It's not the same. When I come alone, it's nothing like when I do it with you."

"I know," I agree because fuck if jacking off is anything like orgasming inside her mouth or pussy. I've only come with my hand on my dick once since we returned with news of her pregnancy, and even then I was edging her, teasing her as I refused to let her come.

"Please," she begs.

"Now or later?"

Her eyes narrow and damn I hate leaving her.

"Now," she decides.

I press my fingers back to her slit, toying with the bundle of nerves at the top. She whimpers, rolling her hips, begging me without words to enter her.

"I'll know if you masturbate, Gigi." I press the tips of two fingers inside. "And if you do, I'll make you wait months before you get off on my fingers..."

I press deeper, my middle finger rubbing over that spot that drives her crazy.

"Or my mouth." I lick inside of hers enough to tease her. "Or on my cock."

"You wouldn't," she moans.

"Try me and find out," I warn, before bending my head and biting her nipple through the t-shirt.

She's lost, giving in to her release. By the time her eyes focus, my mouth is on her, and I'm licking her through a second orgasm.

She's weightless, completely pliable, and begging me to stop when I'm done fucking her through a third and coming inside her.

"Remember what I said."

I kiss her again, knowing we're already on borrowed time.

"I'll miss you," I confess against her lips before turning to the bathroom to get cleaned up.

"You'll miss this pussy," she mutters, and I can tell she didn't say it for me to hear.

We've been inseparable for weeks, and yet she's still waiting for me to disappear, to toss her out and replace her. What the beautiful woman sitting on my bed doesn't realize, is for the first time in my life I'm not planning on my next chick to fuck, because she's the only one I can imagine fucking, now and in the foreseeable future.

"You, Georgia Leigh Anderson." I give her a solicitous smile. "I'll miss your pussy too, though."

One last kiss and I pull away, lingering against her mouth. Feeling the heat of her body will only make things worse later.

"The guys," she begins, but she's shaking her head when I look over my shoulder at her.

"What is it?"

"The guys look for women after the missions are done."

"Okay?" She's right. They normally stay one extra day and use it to do the paperwork wrap up and finding pussy is on the top of the list for most of the guys.

"Will you be, you know, looking for a woman?" If she were jealous, I'd be turned on, but the insecurity in her voice nearly guts me.

"Will you go out and look for someone to fuck while I'm gone?"

Her head snaps up. "Of course not!"

"Why not?"

"Because you're all that I want."

"Exactly," I tell her and walk out of the room.

Staying aloof and never really talking about the emotional side of what's going on with us is difficult. Yeah, we can mask what we're feeling with sex and depravity, but the heart side of things is always right there on the cusp. Well, it is for me. Unsure of how she feels about what's going on between us is what keeps my lips closed tight.

"About fucking time," Scooter complains when I walk down the front steps of the clubhouse.

"Listen, guys." I look over to see Kincaid, Shadow, and Snatch standing near an SUV. It's then that I notice that there are three, rather than the usual two, ready to leave. "This should only take us five days, six tops."

"They're going along with us?" I whisper to Scooter.

"Looks that way." He claps his hands, rubbing them together in excitement. "Working with those guys is the highlight of my fucking year."

"It was my understanding that they no longer did this sort of thing."

"Like I said," he repeats. "Highlight of my year."

"Children," Kincaid chides as he looks in our direction. "If I may continue?"

I shift my rucksack from one shoulder to the other and give him my full attention.

"This job is domestic. This isn't a rescue."

Scooter is all but bouncing around like an unmedicated child with ADHD.

"This is—"

"An assassination," I interrupt.

Both Shadow and Snatch look in my direction, but it's the hard look Kincaid gives me that makes me stand up straighter.

"I'm giving you a chance to opt out," Kincaid says, and no one moves. "Your dossiers are in the trucks. Load up."

I move in the same direction as Scooter and Rocker. They've been my men since our first mission.

"Hound," Kincaid says just before I lift my boot to climb inside the SUV. "You're with us."

Scooter snickers. "Like a visit to the principal's office." He laughs again. "Maybe he'll spank you like you spank his daughter."

"Fuck off," I hiss before turning back around and walking toward the Prez's SUV. "We need to get our own place." I mutter.

It's not the first time I thought it, but Gigi hasn't brought it back up, and I know I can't do it without her dad's permission. Hopefully, I'll get a chance to ask him during this trip. When I climb in behind Shadow who's driving and meet the tattooed stare coming from Snatch, I realize I may not get the opportunity.

I busy myself with the folder of information that was left in my seat.

"The President?" I ask. Knots form in my stomach.

"Ever met him?" Snatch doesn't even look at me when he speaks.

"I—" I release the folder and run a rough hand over the top of my head. "We served in Glein together, when all of that Carpathian shit was coming to a head."

"Fuck," Shadow says from the driver's seat.

"Yeah," I mutter. "Melwas Kocur is a piece of shit."

"That's putting it nicely," Snatch mutters on my right.

"I went to the boat with Colchester and Moore to save the kids while the fucking church burned to the ground. My best friend died outside of the church that day." I shake my head trying and failing to stop the flood of memories. "Severe food poisoning and a two-day hospital stay is the only thing that probably kept me alive in Badon. Colchester lost more than two-thirds of his men that night."

"He's our assignment."

My eyes snap to Kincaid. Surely I didn't hear him correctly.

"He's our Commander in Ch—"

"Keep reading," Kincaid orders.

I do, finding that my assumption is all wrong. We're not there to assassinate the President of the United States but prevent an attempt on his life.

I look up nodding. We've all carried out commands in the military, and even now as a former Marine, my service to God and country doesn't end. When I met Maxen Colchester, he wasn't the President but a Captain in the Army.

"Does this mean what I think it means?" There's only one way to get close to the President without causing questions and a media uproar.

Snatch smiles over at me, giving me his full attention this time.

"Yep." Kincaid chuckles. "We're gonna be Secret Service."

"Dream job?" Shadow asks looking at me in the rearview mirror.

"Hardly," I confess. "Don't get me wrong, they have a serious fucking job to do. I'm more of an action man myself, but I can admit that it's always been sort of a bucket list thing for me."

Protecting the President? What soldier wouldn't jump at that opportunity?

"This is the second time we've been called to do this. Once with Fitzgerald after Monica, and now with President Colchester," Kincaid informs.

"Wait," I say looking over at Snatch. I circle my face and point to his. "You just gonna stand in your black suit with all that ink and metal on your face?"

He laughs. "The jewelry has to come out. We can't have anything metal on our persons. We have to go through security before we suit up with Secret Service issued weapons. The tats will be covered up with theatrical makeup."

"That means," I begin.

"The metal is going to have to come out of your cock, too." Kincaid shakes his head at Snatch's information dump and looks out the window.

"Joy," I mutter as we near the airport housing the Cerberus private plane.

* * *

"He even kind of looks like a wizard," I mutter to Scooter as we stand in the background while Kincaid and Shadow speak with Merlin Rhys about the night's objectives. "Maybe because of his dark eyes?"

"I don't know what it is about him, but he doesn't look like someone I want to cross," Scooter replies.

"Definitely not," I mutter just as those dark eyes look from Kincaid in my direction. As if he's somehow looking into my soul, I can't break the hold he has on me.

I'm locked in his stare as he nods at Kincaid and walks past him, right in my direction.

"Lieutenant Rawley," Merlin says as he holds his hand out.

"Sir." I'm confused as to how he knows my name when I've never set eyes on this man before. He's some sort of adviser to the Party, so I'm certain it's his job to know everyone who has the chance of coming into contact with Colchester. I take his proffered hand, and a chill runs over my body at the contact.

"A moment of your time?" He tilts his head in the direction of a quiet corner.

I sidestep Scooter and turn in the direction Mr. Rhys indicates. Once in the abandoned corner of the room, he looks around, exhaustion crinkling the corner of his eyes.

"Mr. Anderson has your team's directions, and he'll go over those with you momentarily, but I need to speak to you about your expectations when the President dies tonight."

***

"Thank you for having me as your President," Colchester says as he concludes his side of the debate. "It's been the greatest honor I can imagine."

My eyes scan the crowd, searching for any sign of discord. I look in people's eyes, watch their hands, trying to find someone, anyone that is disgruntled or pissed about any of the men standing on the stage at my back.

I can't see the President, but his words echo in my ears. He sounds resigned, as if he knows what's going to happen tonight. Having this debate, knowing there is such a serious threat to his life or the life of the former Vice President is a stupid idea, but I'm not a politician, and those decisions are way above my pay grade, which is exactly what Merlin Rhys said when I informed him of my opinion during our conversation.

A man in the corner rolls his eyes at Colchester's words, but before I can inform Rocker, who's closest to him, there's a commotion to my right.

I'm moving the second I see the cameraman nearly knock over his camera, the dolly getting trapped around cords taped to the ground. I'm mere feet from him when he reaches into his pocket, like it's the most natural thing in the fucking world to pull out a utility knife in the presence of dozens of Secret Service and the President of the fucking United States.

Shadow is taking action as well as one other Service member. The camera crashes to the ground, a deafening sound, as people scramble and scream all around us. Once we get our hands on him, he's easier to wrestle to the ground than I presume a would-be assassin should be.

I stand once the cameraman is subdued, but as Shadow is talking into his mic, I hear a different kind of scream at my back. Turning, I see commotion erupt on the stage. The blood-curdling scream came from Greer Colchester, the First Lady.

"It was a diversion," I yell.

Kincaid, Shadow, and I swarm the stage along with several other Service members.

"Strength in the Mountains," the man under the President chants. The familiar Carpathian motto sends a shiver up my spine.

"There's strength here, too," Mr. President claims, and I've never felt prouder of a soldier in my life.

I notice a knife wound bleeding on his bicep, as the First lady and Embry Moore cling to him.

"The ambulance is ready. The paramedics are coming now," Kincaid says as he pushes in closer to the injured President.

It isn't until I slide in closer that I see the ceramic knife sticking out of Colchester's stomach. My blood runs cold even while my body acts. Kincaid grabs Embry Moore who looks like he can't decide between staunching the blood flow and cupping his President's jaw. The First Lady is sobbing uncontrollably and whispering to him.

The gurney arrives, and Colchester is lifted from the ground in less than ninety seconds after the attack. Mrs. Colchester clings to her husband, kissing him frantically before I pull her away. This wasn't part of my plan for tonight. Rhys told me to stay with Colchester no matter what, so after I grab her, I hand her off to another agent and go back to the President's side.

I see a flash of a fist, as Embry Moore tries to fight Kincaid who is wrapped around his front. The punch doesn't land, but it only takes seconds to get him under control and whisked away.

Protocol is protocol. We're trained to act, to ensure the safety of both of them, and even though going one way while President Colchester's bleeding body is pushed in a different direction is the last thing either of them wants, it's exactly what has to happen.

"This way," Mr. Rhys says as he directs paramedics who look more military than medical down a dark hallway.

They don't question the man. They act, just like everyone did on stage, just like we're all clearly trained to do. Seconds later the President's gurney is being pushed into the back of the ambulance.

"Hurry," Merlin urges when I go to step back.

Recognizing his intention, I climb in the back with them. I watch, stunned, as a man in scrubs works on Maxen Colchester. An IV is inserted, and blood from a bag begins to replace what's spilled both from his arm and stomach wounds. The guy in scrubs works, the paramedics providing him with help before he even asks for it. I'm stunned by the silence, confused why we're racing down dark city streets with no sirens, yet not having to slow once for traffic.

"We lost him," I hear Merlin say into a phone I didn't even know he'd pulled out. "Protocol says we head to the funeral home. He'll be cremated immediately. Those were his wishes. Thank you, Belvedere."

He ends the call and grasps the ashen hand of the President.

After no more than five minutes, the ambulance stops and the back doors are pulled open. I step out and take in my surroundings. A field hospital, one so advanced and equipped, it rivals many metropolitan ones I've been in.

The President, now with a solid heartbeat according to the machine connected to the gurney, is pushed further into the room where half a dozen medical staff wait, leaving Merlin and me alone.

He pulls an envelope from his pocket and hands it to me. "This is your debrief on what happened tonight."

I take it, but I'm too stunned to speak.

"Maxen thanks you for your service, both here tonight and in Glein."

I swallow. "I didn't think he remembered me."

"He remembers everyone. You were a Patriot then as you are one again tonight. You're the reason Cerberus was called in." And then he's gone.

Chapter 32

Gigi

"Thank you," I tell Khloe with a small smile on my face.

"That spray hose is the best thing ever. This version is much better than the one we had."

"Sweet."

I place the baby bath beside me as Mom hands me another gift. Why we're doing this in light of what happened a few days ago, I'll never understand.

Everyone has been upset, the news of the President's assassination making it to us before Cerberus even returned from DC. Those of us in New Mexico had no clue that is where the guys went, but we, along with the rest of the nation, watched in horror as a Carpathian rebel stabbed Maxen Colchester in the stomach, the wound becoming fatal on the way to the hospital.

"Happy Birthday," Mom says and kisses my forehead. "This is from Misty."

It's my birthday. Although twenty-one today, there is such a heaviness in the room and no one seems to want to address it. Jameson was with President Colchester when he took his last breath, yet he refuses to talk about it, citing it's club business and shit about national security. I pull apart the wrapping paper and look down at the gift in my lap.

"What in the world?"

Mom chuckles and comes back to stand beside me. "It's a breast pump."

"Okay?"

Misty laughs along with Mom, and it seems out of place even though a week ago things would've been different.

"Sometimes when you're new to nursing, you get sore. The pump will be a lifesaver."

"Actually, I'm not going to have a problem with sore nipples. The fuck," I hiss when Jameson pinches my thigh.

"You don't plan to breastfeed?" Misty asks. "I mean it's your choice, but your mom did, so I just figured you would."

"We," I turn my head to glare at Jameson as my thigh burns from his warning. "I haven't decided yet."

He kisses my cheek, not giving a shit that we're in the middle of the clubhouse. The first ring of people around us are the women, and the outer ring is filled with irritated Cerberus men, new and old, who've been forced, by my mother no doubt, to help me celebrate my birthday.

The real reason I earned a pinch on my thigh was that he knows me well enough, even after just a couple of weeks spending time together that I was going to blurt something about my sex life. He knew there was the possibility of mentioning the nipple clamps, or how I come so hard when he's fucking me as his teeth are nearly cutting into my puckered flesh.

I shift in my seat.

"She's uncomfortable," Dad advises the entire room. "Em, let her open those more private gifts while she's alone."

I'm not embarrassed but every one of his men are here and no doubt imagining my tits after the explanation of the pump. *He's* the uncomfortable one.

"Last one," Mom says and hands me a small box.

"That," Jameson says snatching the box from my hand. "Is for later."

Dad groans again, this time walking right out the front door. The other men follow as Mom, Misty, Khloe, and Aunt Mak start cleaning up.

"When are you going to let me have my gift?"

"Maybe never if you don't get out of this birthday funk you're in," he warns.

"I miss my sister," I confess. "This is our first birthday apart."

He looks confused. "You were on the phone with her for two hours earlier."

"I know." Standing from the chair, I begin to gather the gifts. "She's usually the sentimental one, yet I was the one crying about her not being here."

"You're hormonal," Aunt Mak says with a soft pat on my back as she takes the gifts from my hands. "It'll pass."

"About two months after the baby is born," Misty says.

"If she's lucky," Khloe mutters, and I know she's remembering the post-partum depression she struggled with for a while.

"That's not all that's bothering you," Jameson whispers in my ear as we make our way back to his room.

"I don't have any right to bitch about petty shit," I mumble and flop down on his soft bed.

"Never stopped you before," he teases as he props my feet on his lap, drops my flip flops to the floor and begins rubbing the soles.

"Before, the country wasn't in mourning. Before, I wasn't pregnant. Before the things that seemed petty to others weren't petty for me."

"Still." I moan when his thumb presses hard, working at the knot in my arch. "Tell me why you're upset."

"Every one of the gifts I got today was a baby gift."

"Okay." He keeps rubbing.

"It's my birthday, Jameson. Yet, they turned it into a baby shower."

"Ever think that the reason they got things for the baby now instead of later is because they're worried that you're going to take off again, and they want the baby to have the things it needs?"

"Well shit. I'm not going anywhere."

"I know that, but you've taken off too many times for them to believe that." Releasing my foot, he leans in and presses his lips against mine. "My gift isn't for the baby."

When he pulls away, my tongue licks against the tingle his beard left behind.

"No?"

He shakes his head, the playful twitch at the corner of his mouth making me narrow my eyes, suspicion growing low in my gut. I shake the box, smiling when it gives off an interesting rattle.

"Car keys?" I beam up at him.

"Fat chance. Open it and see."

I tug the ribbon and let it fall into my lap. I can't help but laugh when I take the top off.

"My dad would've killed you if I opened that out in the living room," I say with a chuckle.

"I have plans, devious plans for you tonight," he warns.

"And they include this?"

I look down again at the *gift*. The shiny butt plug looks innocuous nestled in tissue paper, but I know it's not. He's threatened to take me there, vowed that it will happen sooner or later, but he's not gone any further than the tip of one finger.

"I want you to wear it." He gives me a heated stare, and who am I to object?

I nod, the corners of my mouth lifting into a smile to match his.

"We're going to Denver. You'll wear it on the drive."

I shift my weight on the bed.

"Denver?" He nods. "That's over seven hours away."

Without a word, he takes the plug from the box and disappears into the bathroom. When he comes back out, he's holding a small bottle of lube I've never seen before. It's not something we've ever needed before. I'm always wet and ready for him. It doesn't matter if we're teasing each other for hours or he just gives me a certain look. I always slicken for him, my body ready for him all the time.

"Turn over and pull your dress up."

I obey, gasping when he hitches my hips up forcing me to my knees. Wasting no time, he tugs my thong to the side. Fingers, already slick with the cold gel, sweep over my backside.

"Fuck," he mutters. "Seven hours is a long ass time."

"Forever," I agree and push back into the fingers he's pressing into me.

"I don't know that I can wait."

I hiss and try to scoot away when the cool metal of my gift brushes my anus.

"Settle down." His tone doesn't leave room for objection. That husky growl is just like when I'm riding him, and he's so close to coming but doesn't want to give into the explosion of pleasure just yet.

I yelp when his heavy hand slaps the crease where my ass meets thigh.

"I didn't move," I complain.

He ignores me. "Push back into it. Ah fuck, yeah Gigi just like that."

There's a burn that somehow is also pleasurable. I feel the toy slip into place, and the fullness is only a tease. I wiggle, adjusting to the intrusion, and groan when he taps on it.

"How does it feel?"

I begin to answer him, but then his fingers are in my soaked pussy, and I'm left speechless.

"Dammit," he grumbles. "There's no way I can wait."

I smile at the sound of his zipper.

"What about delayed gratification?" I tease.

"Never been good at it," he confesses before slamming inside of me.

"Oh, God," I cry.

I'm so full as the ring through his head taunts that spot deep inside, and the fullness of his cock presses against the thin layer of skin separating him from the plug.

I'm a writhing mess. He's everywhere, inside of me, fingers bruising my hips in his grasp, mouth biting at the delicate skin of my shoulder blades.

"You can come," he offers.

And I chuckle at the absurdity of his permission. As if I could prevent the orgasm that rushes through my body and explodes in a blinding light behind my eyes.

"Fuck, fuck, fuck," he chants before stiffening, buried to the base of his cock. I'm so full of him and the toy, I can easily feel each pulse of his dick during his release.

I whimper when he withdraws and purr like a happy little kitten when he cleans me with a warm washcloth.

"Not a chance," he whispers against my lips.

My eyes flutter open to find him leaning in close. "Just for a minute."

"You can sleep in the car," he offers. "We have an appointment."

Biting my lips when he helps me off of the bed, I can see both satisfaction and longing in his eyes.

"I think this is doing just as much for you as it is me."

I rock from one foot to the other, not having a damn clue how I'm going to leave this room and out of the front of the clubhouse without everyone knowing exactly what's going on.

"You have no idea."

Walking to the door, I stop just before my hand grabs the knob.

"What's wrong?" he asks as his hand sweeps down my back and over my ass coming dangerously close to my gift.

"I think I'll come before I make it outside."

"Your mom and dad are out there," he reminds me. "You really want to explain that?"

I walk, slowly and deliberately, and much to my embarrassment the guys that left the party earlier for cleanup are back inside. The entire Cerberus MC is here to watch my plugged walk of shame.

"You guys heading out?" Dad asks as we enter the living area.

"Yeah," Jameson answers, but I just ignore him, face scrunched in concentration as I walk to the door.

"She not feeling well?" Dad asks behind me.

"She's tired," Jameson says making my excuses. "I'll make sure she gets plenty of rest."

"Drive safe," Dad says as Jameson joins me, hand at the small of my back.

"No," I say as we come down the front steps and I see the Jeep waiting. "I'm not getting into that."

"Your dad thinks we're heading to Denver to have the seats reupholstered. We have to take it."

He opens the passenger side door.

"Jameson, this thing bounces all over the road."

He just stares into my eyes.

"I can hardly walk and keep it together."

Mirth takes over his smile, and I realize this vehicle is as much a part of his game as the plug is.

"Imagine how many times you'll come between now and Denver." He nips at my bottom lip. "Play along, and I may even make a half-way pit stop to fuck you again."

Chapter 33
Hound

"What is this place?" Gigi asks with her neck craned so she can see out of the side window.

I don't answer, rather just watch her, loving the pink blush on her cheeks from the drive over. I promised we'd stop once so I could take care of her needy pussy. We ended up stopping twice. The plug in her ass, the tiny whimpering noises she made relentlessly as we drove was enough to drive me mad.

"The Hale-ish Retreat and Spa?" She turns her head, looking at me over her shoulder. "I could use a massage."

"Maybe next time," I offer. "Tonight is going to go a little different than you're thinking."

I adjust my cock behind its denim confines and climb out of the crappy Jeep. She has the passenger-side door open by the time I walk around the front.

"It's a spa," she whines. "I'm sure they specialize in massages."

"The spa is closed."

Confusion draws in her brow as I help her jump down from the seat.

"You've never heard any of the guys talking about this place?"

She chuckles. "Cerberus men aren't the type to get facials and hot stone rubdowns."

I smile, loving the innocence I'm going to command tonight.

"They don't go through the front door," I say as I reach down for her hand and walk around the corner of the building.

She sighs, pulling another smile to my lips. "This night is weird. Why are you making this weird?"

"It's only going to get weirder." I turn to face her, arms on her shoulders, so she knows to pay attention. "If you want to leave at any time, all you have to do is say the word."

"Yep, weirder." She tries to look over my shoulder at the nondescript door at my back, but I shift her again so she can look into my eyes.

"I need you to wear this." I pull a thin mask from my back pocket and begin to tie it around her head. It's soft and looks like a gorgeous monarch butterfly. "If it got back to Garrett or Alexa that I brought you here, your dad would probably gut me."

She gasps, eyes searching mine. "As in Garrett Hale?" I nod. "Oh, God."

My cheeks hurt with the size of my grin. "You know where you're at now."

She nods quickly, her throat working on a rough swallow. "I've always been curious about this place."

"So you have heard the guys talking about it?"

"Yes," she whispers.

I turn, grabbing her hand again and taking another step closer to the door.

She doesn't budge.

"What's wrong?"

She shakes her head. "I don't..." Another thick swallow. "I can't have sex in front of people. Stripping is one thing, but this—"

My lips are on hers before she can say another word. I lick into her mouth, bite at her lips, all the while my hands are tight on her ass and grinding her on my rock-hard cock.

"I'd never share the sight of your pussy with another person," I pant against her mouth when I'm finally in control enough to pull away. "Trust me?"

She nods, and this time when I take her hand and pull her toward the door, she follows.

Having made an appointment last week, the sign in process is quick, and before long we're led into a wide-open room. I hold her against my chest as we stand just inside letting our eyes adjust to the dimly lit room.

The soft thump of music surrounds us, as does the heat and humidity of more than a dozen people in all stages of sexual activity.

"Wow," Gigi mutters.

"What do you think?" I ask with my head bent close to her ear. The shudder that runs down her spine is familiar. It's the same way her body reacts to mine when I look at her with need and desperation. For good measure, I dip my legs and press my erection against her, knowing it's rubbing against the plug in her ass. I started her out small but increased its size both times we stopped to quench my thirst for her pussy.

"I'm wet."

Two words, with enough power to make me nearly come in my jeans.

"Happy birthday." I kiss her temple and try to get my libido under control.

"No one's ever given me an orgy for my birthday before."

My grip on her middle tightens. "I sure as fuck hope not."

"Let's go to the room," I offer.

"Room?" She tilts her head to the side to look at me. "I want to watch."

"Believe me, gorgeous. You'll get to watch."

I direct her down a darkened hallway, thankful for the instructions I got in an email when I made the appointment. Nothing is less sexy than having to stop and ask directions when all you want to do is get naked.

I type in the passcode I was given, and the door opens with a soft beep.

"No," she says and stops no less than two feet inside of the room.

"They can't see us," I promise as we both look across the room and see another couple on the other side of a large window. "They want to be watched, but they don't want to see us. We want to watch but not be seen."

"Th-they can't see in here?" She hasn't moved, legs locked and refusing to get any closer.

Stepping around her, I wave my hands near the glass and try to get their attention.

"Look," I say motioning to a small TV in the corner. "All they can see is their reflection. They know there's a chance someone will be in this room, but they can't be one hundred percent sure."

She closes the distance between us until her palms are flat against the glass. The swipe of her tongue on her perfectly pink lip makes my cock jump.

"She looks like she's having a good time." Her words are breathy, arousal clear in the tone.

I crowd her, leaning over her back, every inch of my body I can manage touching some part of hers.

"We can turn the sound on, listen to her as he tongues her to orgasm."

She nods, almost erratically.

Leaning to the side, I grab the remote on the small table and hit the sound button. The woman's gasps fill the room. The man devouring her releasing guttural grunts as he feasts on his woman.

Gigi is entranced, squirming and needful as she watches the illicit show. Unable to wait another second longer, I tug down the zipper of her dress and pull it over her head. I hate that her breasts have been too sore to wear a bra the last week, but fuck if I don't love the sight of her gorgeous tits. The nipples, a shade or two darker than her stage days, are puckered and beading, reaching toward the glass and the other couple.

With a slight push of my hand against her back, I press until the tips of her breasts touch the cold glass. She hisses, but it turns into a moan matching that of the other woman as she orgasms.

"That's so fucking hot," she mutters.

I don't respond, too busy working her thong down her thighs. Instinctually, she arches her back and angles her ass out, presenting herself to me, exactly the way I like, only this time is different. This time the bright red jewel on the plug in her ass reflects the soft light in the room. It's my turn to swallow and breathe.

"Fuck," I grumble when two fingers sweep at her seam, finding it soaked and swollen for me.

"She's..." She doesn't finish her sentence, but I look around her, and I know immediately what she's seeing as the man pulls his mouth from the cunt he's been eating and spreads her legs even further.

"The plug in your ass is bigger," I say with a punctuated press of my erection against her ass.

"Your cock is much bigger. It scares me." Those are her words, but her ass is still pushing against me, rotating ever so often in a tiny circle.

"It will be uncomfortable at first, but by the time it's over, you'll be begging me for more."

My fingers roam down the front of her stomach, pausing briefly over my growing little boy before sliding through the slickness of her desire.

"I need you on the bed."

She nods but doesn't make to move there until I turn her shoulders in that direction. She goes, eyes never pulling from the action on the other side of the room. When she lies on her back, and her thighs fall open, I can feel my cock weeping in my jeans.

"We're going to mimic them," I inform her as I pull a small bottle of lube and a condom from my pocket before shedding my clothes.

"You missed the first step," she says petulantly referring to the oral.

"I've made you come several times today with my mouth," I remind her.

Fuck, the way she looked sitting on the steering wheel with her pussy right in my face. I'll never forget it.

"True," she agrees. "Better hurry."

I follow her eyes and see that the other woman is wrapping her mouth around his cock. I shake my head. "If you put your mouth on my cock right now, I'll come." I crawl up her body, licking at her knees, thighs, and tits on my way up. "And I'm coming in your ass tonight."

She whimpers with another delicious rotation of her hips.

"Stop." The unfamiliar voice throws me for a second before I turn my head and watch the man grip a pile of the woman's hair and pull her off his cock.

"Seems he's having the same problem," she says with a chuckle.

We watch, entranced as the woman is thrown to her back and the guy slams inside of her. Flexing my hips, I'm only a few seconds behind him, groaning when Gigi's cunt only opens enough to fit the head of my cock inside of her.

"Oh God," she pants. "So full."

With the larger plug in her ass, there's no way to sink all the way in without hurting her.

"Feel good?" She nods, but the glint in her eye tells me she's not exactly sure.

I press my thumb to her clit as the moaning of the couple fills the room around us.

"Can they hear us?" she whispers.

I shake my head, my hips moving, my cock looking for just one more inch of her glorious heat. I inch forward again when her mouth finds mine. I'm breathless when we break apart, shattered in her arms, and thinking about a future I haven't allowed myself to imagine in a very long time.

Her head tilts, and I utilize the opportunity to suck at the soft skin on her neck.

"Mmm. He's taking the plug out."

I turn my head to see the guy back on his haunches, thumb toying with the woman's clit as he works the plug from her body, so I do the same.

I press harder with my thumb when she whimpers as the largest part of the toy stretches the tight ring. With my hand still against her body, I tear the rubber open with my teeth and roll it down my cock.

She looks at me confused.

"The condom is for easier cleanup," I explain, working the bottle of lube open with my mouth and coating the tips of my fingers. I'm obsessed with the frown on her pretty face, knowing how much she loves my come dripping out of her. "Don't worry. Next time I fuck your ass, I'll fill you up."

Her bottom lip rolls between her teeth when I press my slickened fingers against her ass. It doesn't stop the moan when I dip two and then three fingers in her prepared opening.

"You ready?" I ask as I pull my hand from her pussy and add a thick layer of lube to my throbbing cock.

She nods, glancing quickly at the other couple. Either the guy is incredibly eager or anal sex isn't new for them because he's pounding away in her like his ass is on fire.

Her eyes widen when I press the tip of my cock against her. "Please," she begs. "Go slow."

"Of course," I say to calm her nerves. Now, I pray my body complies.

I lean over her, my mouth breathing in her shallow pants as I press deeper. When she tenses, I lick at her lips, grip her hips in assurance, and still my hips.

"Give it a second." I bite at her lip when she squeezes her eyes closed. "Look at me."

I watch her, search her eyes for the level of discomfort that will make me back away.

"More," she moans after an endless moment.

I give her what she asks for, sliding my aching cock forward another inch. When she doesn't tense up like the first time, I keep going, pressing into her, teeth grinding from the softness, from the heat, and from the grip she has encased my cock.

"All the way?" she asks with a quiver in her voice.

"Yeah, gorgeous. I'm all the way in." She nods, the sheen of tears forming on her lower lashes. "Is it too much?"

She nods at first, but then her head shakes back and forth.

"I have to move," I warn.

"Please," she begs again.

The first couple of slow thrusts are met with tense, tight muscles, but they evolve until she's pressing against me, meeting my movements with her own.

"You're mine." I push as deep as I can go. "Your beautiful mouth. This tight pussy."

Turning my hand face up, I push two fingers inside of her and stroke the front wall of her clenching cunt.

"This ass." I pull out and slam back in. "My baby inside of you. Every part of you belongs to me."

I lean forward, pressing my lips against her left breast as my hips surge and my fingers plunder.

"This amazing heart." I kiss the flesh, my lips trembling against her skin. "I own all of it."

"I'm going to cum," she hisses, but I knew this already. Her pussy clenches, her ass tightens, and her eyes roll back into her head.

"Mine," I grunt one final time before spilling inside of the condom.

I stay inside of her, fingers working in tandem with the flutters of her pussy as she comes down from her orgasm. It isn't until she whimpers, finally coming back to reality that I give in and drag myself out of her.

"Happy birthday," I whisper against the crown of her head as I pull her into my arms.

"Best. Birthday. Ever."

Chapter 34

Gigi

"Hey," I look up when something taps against my foot. "It's the holidays. You aren't supposed to be sad."

I look over at my twin and smile.

"I'm not sad." The response is immediate, but I know deep down it's a lie.

Jameson has been gone for last three weeks, and I haven't spoken to him in two days. The aura around my dad and Shadow is thick. I know something is wrong, but they won't speak to me about it.

All I get is "It's confidential club business."

"Well, you seem mopey. We should go to Jake's."

I roll my eyes at her. "Right. Sorry."

I watch as she tips her wine glass to her lips. Not drinking isn't a problem for me, but the torture of knowing I can't even if I wanted to is like sandpaper to my skin.

"How's my nephew doing?" I smile and look at her only to find her eyes focused across the room.

Griffin.

Of course, her attention is with him even though she's sitting and making small talk with me.

"They found out he has two heads. So it's more like Siamese twins than just one baby."

She smiles. "I bet he's going to be adorable."

"He has hooves like a zebra. Hurts really badly when he kicks."

"Sounds good," she says standing without warning and crossing the room.

I hear a chuckle on my other side, and I turn to find Lawson and Delilah cuddled up together. I'm hot with jealousy that they get to spend all of their time together.

"You know she doesn't hear or see anything else when he's within a fifty-mile radius," Lawson says with a huge grin.

"At least it's two heads," Delilah teases. "That's much better than two butts."

I grin, grateful for her attempt to lighten the mood.

"So," Delilah says leaning in closer to me. "You and Hound are like, together-together? I heard Misty talking to your mom, and Em mentioned that you haven't hardly been in your room at home."

My old reaction would've been to tell her to mind her own fucking business, but things have changed since I came home. Delilah, Ivy, and I spent the majority of the Thanksgiving holiday together. We shopped, hung out, and gossiped about everything. I felt closer to them than I have since junior high school.

"I miss him when he's gone. Dad won't let us share a room in his house, but for some reason, he doesn't mind me staying here." I blush but continue with my confession. "The bed smells like him, and I sleep better in his space than my own."

Delilah snorts, and I see Lawson tighten his grip around her shoulders.

"Some things are private," he hisses in her ear loud enough that I can hear him.

She shakes her head and kisses him on the cheek. When a familiar gleam hits her eyes, I know she's going to spill.

"When I went on a girl's trip with Ivy and a few girls from school during Spring break—" She pauses to laugh, and pink marks Lawson's cheeks. "I came home early and found him asleep with a body pillow. He'd put a thong and a bra on it."

Lawson groans, but refuses to make eye contact.

I laugh, low because I don't want to draw any more attention to him, but it's hilarious.

"That's not the best part," Delilah continues.

"I'm going to choke you with my cock later," Lawson warns.

My eyes widen, and now the pink is on Delilah's cheeks because we both know I wasn't supposed to hear *that*.

Jealousy hits me again. I'd give anything to be choked with Jameson's cock tonight.

She looks back over her shoulder at him, longing in her eyes. As if to seal the deal and guarantee the threat is carried through, she turns back in my direction.

She makes a motion toward her chest. "He had stuffed the damn bra cups with socks. I walk in, and he's passed out with this pillow Delilah gripped against his chest."

"I miss her when she's gone," he mutters.

"When's the wedding again?" I say changing the subject, so Lawson is more comfortable and also because I sleep in Jameson's shirts and sometimes his boxers just so I feel closer to him when he's gone.

Delilah beams as Lawson looks down at the sparkle of her engagement ring.

"October," they say in unison.

"That will make almost three years of being engaged. Why not sooner?"

"We want to get married here. That means graduating, and working around getting the new shop setup for Law." She grins in my direction. "We didn't want the stress of planning a wedding."

Lawson sighs. "I told you, planning shouldn't stress you out."

Delilah shakes her head, and I can tell this is an ongoing argument with them. Clearly, he wants her to have his last name now.

"The dress has to be perfect, the menu, the guest list. It's all very stressful when I want it to be perfect, and that's impossible with school."

He turns her face, the rough palm of his hand cupping her cheek with a delicate touch. Fuck, I miss Jameson.

"If it's you and me, beautiful, then it can be nothing but perfect."

I feel the hot tear roll down my cheek, and I attempt to dash it away with my hand before anyone notices.

"See," Delilah says. "You're so mushy, you're making her upset."

She winks at me, and I can't help but laugh. She knows better. She knows all about my intense feelings for Jameson. I've had several lengthy conversations with both her and Ivy about how much I care for him and how terrified I am that if I tell him exactly how I feel that our entire world will shift and change. Things are good right now. Well, when he's here they're good, and I'm not going to risk upsetting our new normal.

My phone rings, and I scramble to get it off of the table. The bump I'm sporting these days is small, smaller than it should be according to the doctor, but it still gets in the way.

I activate the call, but frown when Facetime doesn't activate fully.

"Hey, gorgeous."

I nearly cry when I hear his voice.

"I can't see you," I complain.

I walk out of the living room without a backward glance. I only feel rude for the briefest of seconds, because this man has all of my attention.

"You know how it is. Technology doesn't always work, but I can see you." I smile not giving a damn that my hair is a mess. "Now show me my little boy."

This happens every time he video calls. I tilt my phone and lift my shirt so he can see the evidence of his child.

"He's getting big." There's pride in his voice, but also an unexplained strain.

"You haven't called." God, I sound like a controlling bitch. I shake my head and try to keep the tears at bay. I'm overcome with relief and if I'm being honest, anger at his silence for the last several days.

"We…" He pauses and clears his throat. "It's been a mess over here."

Over here. That's where he always is. I never know if he's even in the US. Most trips, I know, take him out of America, but he never tells me, never gives me details, never talks about what he's done once he returns.

"I can't wait to hold you in my arms." Tears fall silently at his words. It's Christmas Eve. He was only planning on being gone two weeks. He was supposed to be here with me.

"Wh-when do you think that will be?" I'm needy, desperate to lay my eyes on him, feel his skin against mine, have him hold me through the night.

"Is now soon enough?"

By the time the words leave his mouth, the bedroom door swings open and he's there. He's standing in front of me, looking exhausted and sad, but he's still the most handsome man I've ever laid eyes on.

"Hi," I say suddenly shy as I swipe at my eyes with the sleeve of my sweatshirt.

He doesn't say a word as he crosses the room and wraps me in his arms. I don't care about a single thing other than this moment. My ears register the soft thud of my phone as it hits the carpet at our feet, but I can't be bothered to let go of him and find it.

"Fuck, I missed you."

I sob against his shoulder, feeling silly for the tears now that he's here. I don't usually cry in front of him, and when I do, I blame it on hormones. I haven't sobbed like this since the night he found me in Vegas, and I was struggling with the decision I had to make.

"I hate it when you're gone," I confess and hold him tighter.

"I know." He consoles me with the warm rub of his palms over my back before dropping to his knees, raising my sweatshirt, and pressing his warm lips to my stomach.

My fingers tangle in his hair, but he doesn't look up at me. His forehead is pressed against our growing child, and at first, I find it endearing, loving that he missed both of us, but then his shoulders shudder with his own sob.

He's never gotten emotional like this in front of me. I've seen irritated, lustful, angry, but I've never heard the wretched sound that just escaped his lips.

"Hey." I drop to my knees as well and wrap him in my arms.

"The girl." He shakes his head. "We couldn't save her."

I feel his warm palms flat against my stomach.

"We couldn't save the baby." Another sob, one that matches mine at this exact moment. "We were too late."

I hold him as he cries, as he tries to put himself back together. I hold him when he grows exhausted, and I don't even let him go when he gets heavy and pulls me against his chest on the hard floor.

Chapter 35
Hound

"Shhh," I whisper when Gigi mumbles something unintelligible as I scoop her off of the floor. "I got you."

I tug off her jeans, barely resisting the urge to slide her silk panties down her legs along with them. The sweatshirt, t-shirt, and bra come off next. Resisting the furl of her pink nipples is an exercise in fortitude that I nearly fail. One finger, one sweep of my skin against her delicate flesh is all I allow myself. I know I should at least pull a t-shirt over her head, but I leave her bare, needing the feel of her skin against mine. I cover her quickly knowing she'll be chilled without her clothes.

I want to wake her, to say things to her I've only said once before, but say them knowing I mean them this time. I know, without a doubt, that how I thought I felt for Gabby is nothing compared to the burn I have deep in my soul for Georgia Anderson.

I don't, however. I crawl into bed and pull her back against my naked front. I palm her growing belly and count my lucky fucking stars that they're both safe and in my arms.

***

The familiar tingle in my nuts forces me into semi-consciousness. I do my best to ignore it. Waking with a throbbing erection seems to be part of my daily schedule since Gigi started sleeping in my bed, and it's ten times worse when I'm away from her.

It's the chuckle that makes my eyes snap open, and the firm suction along my shaft that has me nearly coming off the bed.

Looking down, I find the most amazing woman curled over herself between my splayed thighs. She gives me her best attempt at a smile, but the thickness of the cock in her mouth impedes it.

"Eager this morning?" The darkness in the room means it's either earlier than morning or she finally got someone to put the blackout curtains up she was complaining about several days ago.

She releases me with a pop, her tongue tracing the veins along my shaft. "I heard Lawson threaten to choke Delilah with his dick. It made me crave your dick in my mouth."

I frown down at her. "He shouldn't be saying things like that loud enough for you to hear."

She shrugs, tongue never taking a break as it toys with each one of my barbells and flicks the ring in the head.

I cup her cheek, my emotions barely in check after my breakdown yesterday. It took a full day and a half before I could get my shit together to call her after we found Marisol dead, her unborn child brutally cut out of her and also dead by her side. I'd spoken with Kincaid. I knew she was fine, but I knew I had to be close to her, knew I had to be in this house, in this room, when I heard her voice again.

"I love you," I whisper. Her head begins to shake back and forth, throat bobbing up and down. "So fucking much."

Tears spring to her eyes. "Really? Me?"

"You."

"I love you, too," she says back after an agonizingly long minute.

There's too much distance between us, too much space and time. Three weeks is a long ass time to be so far away from a piece of your very own heart. I sit up, and in the next second she's on her back, and my mouth is covering hers.

We don't say another word. We let the room fill with our love as I fill her with my cock. Slight whimpers and an occasional grunt are the only sounds we make, but we never lose eye contact. I'm reluctant to even pull out of her after we climax together, but I'm exhausted, and the last thing I need is my arms giving out and falling on her.

She traces the back of my hand as it tickles over her stomach.

"Mom felt the baby kick yesterday."

My heart breaks a little. She's been feeling the movement for weeks, assuring me it would be soon that I would be able to feel it too. I'm almost bitter at the knowledge that someone else got to do that first.

"Another thing I've missed." She presses her palm against mine until my hand is flat against her skin. "I'm missing everything again."

"I'll talk to Dad. Ask him to keep you home."

"I have to work, Gigi." I fucking hate more than anything that I have to. "I can't get preferential treatment."

"He can find something for you to do here. I know you're good with computers," she bargains.

"I'm better in the field." I know it, and she knows it. Plus, Blade has the computer skills covered, except for the field stuff, which I'm already doing.

"I need you here," she mutters, her breath ghosting over my chest.

I squeeze her tighter and decide to change the subject.

"How did the doctor's visit go? How is my boy doing?"

I feel her tense, and an eerie chill settles over me.

"We did the sonogram." There's something off about her voice, and I know she's fixing to confirm some of the nightmares I've had over the last seventy-two hours.

"What else?" I hate the strain in my voice, but I'm already preparing myself for the worst.

The last couple of weeks have made it very apparent that things can go to shit at the drop of a hat, and I know deep down that I'm never supposed to be happy.

"Camryn says that I'm measuring small." I tense. "So she did some kind of special sonogram. The baby is perfectly fine."

I take a few deep breaths, trying to calm the fear that just won't release me.

"Are you sure? Please, tell me the truth."

"I am." She pushes up and looks down at me. "It's just..."

God, I can't take this. "Tell me. What's wrong with my son?"

"That's just it," she says with a twinkle in her eye. "You don't have a son. You're having another daughter."

"Excuse me?"

A wide smile spreads across cheeks still pink from her orgasm. "A girl. We're having a girl."

My throat goes dry, making swallowing difficult. "But she's healthy?"

She nods, searching my eyes and waiting for my reaction. What can I tell her? That I'm terrified? That I have no clue how to raise a daughter? So I opt to just speak the only truth I know. "I can't wait to meet her."

It's then, with the flex of my fingers against her stomach that my daughter decides to introduce herself to me. At first, it's a simple tremble, but then Gigi's tight stomach moves and I feel every bit of it against my hand. I stare down, in awe of it. The gift of life, a woman's ability to grow and nurture something from a handful of cells into a human being is nothing short of miraculous. This baby, this tiny little girl is half of me and half of her. The sting of tears behind my eyes is welcomed, even after my embarrassing breakdown last night.

"I hope she's nothing like me," Gigi confesses as her head lowers to rest on my chest again.

"I hope she's exactly like you." She snorts. "I hope she's fierce, resilient, able to speak her mind, and doesn't let people walk all over her."

"You won't be saying that when she's fourteen and thinking she's grown."

I pull her closer and kiss the top of her head. "There won't be a boy in a hundred-mile radius that will even speak to her."

She huffs.

"What?" I pull my head back and tilt her chin up. "I said I wanted her to be exactly like you. I never said I wasn't going to be ten times worse than your dad."

"I," she begins but pauses for a long minute. "I was so terrible to both my parents. Gave them such a hard time. Made them worry. I understand now because I know I'll do everything in my power to protect this baby, even if that means protecting her from herself."

"And that," I tell her before I brush my lips against hers, "is what parenting is all about."

"How long are you back for?" God, I don't even want to think about leaving her again. "Dad and Shadow were in the conference room all day yesterday, so I already know there's another job lined up. Is it your team? How long do we have?"

Her eyes grow dark and disappointed when she reads the look on my face. "I have to head out on Tuesday."

"Two days?" Tears form in the corners of her eyes. "We only have two days? How long this time."

"I don't know the details yet." I press my mouth to hers. "But let's not waste a second getting upset about it."

I press her to her back and tell her everything I'm feeling. I profess my love, my devotion, and we make plans for the future. Life is perfect for the first time ever. I can't help smile at knowing that there is actually a way for me to be happy. I never imagined I could have this. Never even let myself picture having a woman that loved me, yet here I am.

Chapter 36

Gigi

"Only two weeks left," Camryn says with a smile as she slips her gloves off of her hands.

"I'm not ready," I confess.

I knew Dad shouldn't have sent Jameson on this last mission. Both promised me it was a quick job, and he'd be home before I knew it.

"First-time parents never are," she cajoles. "But you'll know what to do when the time comes."

I've spent the better part of an hour asking her all of the questions I could easily research online, but I wanted to hear them from a professional, not a book or online chat rooms. I mean, I look at those too since I've become obsessed with all things childbirth.

"I want to see you next week," Camryn says before walking to the door. "Make sure you make the appointment before heading out.

I sigh, rolling off of the exam table and get my lower half redressed.

Kid is waiting for me in the parking lot, but the smiling man I've known all of my life is gone, having been replaced with a man filled with anxiety. He won't even look at me as he helps me inside of the SUV.

"We have to head back to the clubhouse," he informs me as he climbs inside and backs out of the parking space.

"I needed to grab a few things from Target," I whine, knowing he's probably in a pissy mood because Khloe is still getting hit on at school. There's been tension between those two since the spring semester started at her school.

"Not today," he says shutting down any rebuttal I might have had planned.

Pissed, I turn my head to look out the window and rub the tightening spot on my stomach.

The clubhouse is frantic by the time we get back there. The guys who didn't head out on the last job are running around. Shadow is barking orders, and there's a tension in the air that makes the hair on the back of my neck stand up. Something's wrong. I can feel it in my bones.

"How the fuck did that happen?" Dad bellows. The anger in his voice travels out of the open door to the conference room. "I won't calm the fuck down! I lost a man today, and you're telling me to calm down?"

No. No. No. No.

I arrow toward the conference room, standing in the doorway. I almost break at the sight of my dad with his head hung low, one hand clutching his cell phone and the other gripping the top of his shaved head.

"Daddy?" The one word is a guttural plea.

I just know my world is going to come crashing down around me by the devastated look on Dad's face.

I shake my head. "No, daddy. Please."

I'm a twenty-one-year-old woman, but I've turned into a child needing her father to make her world make sense again.

"We lost Catfish." He's broken, torn down, but that doesn't stop the relief I feel in my bones.

I'm a horrible person for being thankful that someone else, someone other than Jameson, is dead.

I clench my stomach, the tightness that's been present increasing to the point of excruciating pain.

"And Jameson?" I ask when the pain subsides marginally and look up to see the same wrecked look in Dad's eyes.

"It all went to shit."

The pain is back, and he forgets who's on the phone as he stands from the table and rushes to me.

"Jameson?" I ask again, his name the only word I can manage with the pain in my stomach.

"We need to get to the hospital," he says, the calm I remember from childhood taking over his voice. He does so well in chaotic situations, and today is no different. He places a soothing hand on my back before barking orders through the open door.

My pulse, pounding in my ears like a damn snare drum blocks out the conversation around me. It isn't until I'm scooped up in my dad's arms that I focus again.

"Where's Jameson?" I'm sobbing by this point.

"We need to focus on the baby, Georgia. You're in labor."

I shake my head. "I can't do this without him." I tremble, my hand gripping his t-shirt to the point my knuckles turn white. "He's supposed to be here!"

"Get Camryn Davison on the phone. I want her at the hospital by the time we get there." I hear a 'yes, Sir.' "And make sure they have a room ready for her. We're not spending a damn second in the waiting room."

I fight to get out of the SUV when Dad places me in the back seat and struggles to get the seatbelt around my swollen stomach. The tremble in his hands betrays his distress.

"You'll be fine." I turn to see Mom sliding in beside me. "You get to meet your daughter today."

Her eyes are swollen, and I know she's been crying. They're both lying to me.

"Just tell me," I beg, my own tears renewed as I watch her face.

She shakes her head, tears brimming and threatening to fall. "I don't know anything."

"Please," I beg. "Please don't lie to me."

I don't miss the relief in her eyes when the next contraction begins and demands all of my attention.

The hustle into the hospital is quick and seamless. Dad cradles me in his arms, much like he did when I was a kid and fell asleep on the couch watching TV. He doesn't have to bark orders here in public. The commands he made back at the clubhouse have been carried out perfectly. We go straight to a room, and Camryn is waiting for us.

"My phone," I hiss after I shed my clothes to get into a hospital gown, and she tries to take my clothes away. "The back pocket of my jeans."

I tap out a text, watching the screen with hope. The three little bubbles don't pop up. The device in my hand doesn't buzz or begin to ring.

"What the hell is going on? Where is he?"

My mom clears her throat. "I don't know."

"Where's Dad?" I push past her in the small bathroom and enter the room.

Camryn is there, waiting, but I can tell from the look on her face that she knows something I don't.

"Someone needs to tell me what's going on," I demand.

"You're going to have that baby a little early it seems," Camryn says with the nicest smile she can manage. She closes the distance between us and helps me climb into the bed. "I don't want you to worry. Two weeks early isn't huge, especially for a girl. Their lungs mature quicker than a boy's would."

Once I'm on the bed, nurses are all around me strapping monitors around my stomach.

My dad is gone for what seems like forever, and my mom won't look at me. She types away furiously on her cell phone and checks it every second when her fingers aren't flying over the keypad.

When Dad enters the room, his eyes find mine before they search for my mother. My whole life, he's looked for her first, as it is in his blood to make sure the other half of his soul is safe before worrying about others.

I swallow, shaking my head as he reaches my head. I've been demanding answers, begging everyone to tell me the truth, to tell me something. Now that the moment has come, I can't even look him in the eye.

"Georgia," Dad says softly.

I don't lift my eyes to his. I focus solely on the texture of the faded fuchsia blanket covering me.

"Please don't, Daddy."

The machines by my side beep, alerting me to another contraction. My epidural an hour ago has numbed the pain to the point it's my broken heart that is destroying me and not the child trying to be born while her father is...

I sob, refusing to think in my head what my heart is already feeling.

A gentle knock and Camryn entering the room keeps my dad from ripping my useless muscle from my chest.

"It's time, Gigi." Camryn stands at the end of the bed and pulls a sterile towel from the top of an instrument tray. She dons gloves and looks back at me. "Are you ready?"

I shake my head and earn a small smile from her lips.

"Diego, are you staying?"

It's then that I meet his eyes. They plead with me, much the same way mine did to him when I begged him not to make Jameson go on another mission. The way I looked each and every time he got orders after we started making plans for our future. My dad is the one responsible for the empty life, the single parenting I'll be forced to do. He doesn't get the right to stand there and cheer me on when he's the sole reason my world is crashing down around me.

"He's not welcome in this room." I expect him to argue, to insist that he's there for his little girl as she brings her own daughter into the world. He doesn't. He nods, kisses the back of my hand, and walks out.

"You have about a minute," Camryn says with her eyes on the monitor at my bedside. "Then I need you to push."

I lie back, not acknowledging my mom when she clasps my hand in her own. Normally warm, the coolness of her fingers is a shock to my system, but I don't respond to that either. My eyes trace imaginary patterns on the ceiling. I ignore the pain and Cam's voice instructing me to bear down.

I shake my head. "I won't do this without him."

Mom begs.

Cam rubs my calf giving me encouragement hinted with agitation.

I don't know how long it goes on. Seconds? Days? Years?

"Listen to me," my mother spits, yanking my chin and forcing me to look at her. "You have to push."

"Jameson," I sob. "I need him."

"You have to do this without him." Tears fill her eyes once again. "He'd want you to carry on."

Oh, God. That's as good as confirmation that he's gone.

"I don't want this without him."

"You're killing her, Georgia." I shake my head. I'd never do anything to hurt my daughter. "Her heart rate is all over the place. If you don't push, they're going to take you in for an emergency C-section."

I shake my head. "No."

I don't know what I'm denying. The loss of him, the fact my baby is in danger? Am I still refusing to push? I don't have a damn clue.

"Please turn that damn thing off," my mom snaps, but she's already reaching to my side.

It's only then I hear my cell ringing.

"Oh, thank God," she says as I see the facetime call from Jameson.

"Jameson," I sob when the video connects.

"We're having a baby today," he whispers as if talking too loud will ruin the moment.

"I need you here," I cry. "I can't do this without you."

"I'm here, gorgeous." I nod, conceding that this is the best I can get.

My adrenaline is through the roof, my entire body shaking uncontrollably. I hate myself for losing faith so quickly.

"Focus, Gigi." My eyes snap back to his. "Give Emmalyn the phone, so you can concentrate on getting my baby here."

I nod and do as he says.

"Head's out," Cam says.

She asks me to stop pushing, and it's only when my eyes flutter back to the screen that I take him in fully for the first time. His face is battered, covered in blood, and his voice, although soothing is low and weak. There are people around him, insisting he lie back.

"One more push," Cam urges.

"You can do it, gorgeous." I smile at his encouragement and bear down even though the medicine is strong enough to keep most of the pain away.

"She's here," Cam says.

There's a rush, nurses shuffling around.

The baby cries, the most amazing sound in the world.

"Amelia Kate," Jameson whispers. Her name on his lips is the second most beautiful thing in this world.

And it all shatters again when I hear the long beep of a heart machine. The same one you hear on TV when someone dies. Confused, I look over at my monitors, but nothing seems wrong. Amelia is still wailing, so I know she's fine.

When I look back, I watch Jameson's eyes roll back. There's a shuffle, the phone pointed at nothing.

"He's coding!" I hear before the call is disconnected.

Chapter 37

Kincaid

The look on my wife's face as she exits Georgia's room is one I haven't seen in a long time, so long, in fact, I can't recall if I've ever seen it before. She's sobbing, and her fists meet my chest repeatedly when she's close enough to make contact.

I crush her to my chest. Knowing how upset she must be if violence is her go-to response.

"Why would you do that?" Her voice has a frantic squeal to it, and I want nothing more than to make everything right for her. For Georgia. Hell, even for Hound because his well-being and the love he has for my daughter is what has kept her around so long this time.

"I had no choice," I begin to explain. "He refused to go into surgery before seeing her."

My beautiful wife shakes against my chest, the tremble in her small body almost enough to bring me to my knees.

"He coded just as Amelia cried, Diego. She was so upset they had to sedate her." Sobs wrack her body. "She didn't even get to hold her baby girl first."

I run my hand through her hair and try to soothe her. If I'm being honest, touching her soothes me, and I need it more now than ever before. I knew what was going on because I was on the phone with Rocker while Hound was on the phone with my daughter.

"Do you know anything else?" Em pushes against me until my arms relax and she's looking up in my eyes.

I sigh.

"Don't give me that *club business* bullshit. This is one time I won't back down without answers."

My gorgeous, stubborn queen.

"They were able to get his heart started back, but he's pretty fucked up. He was hit several times, and one round made it through his Kevlar. We won't know more until the surgeon comes out and gives an update."

"And where are they?"

I sigh again, but I won't deny her the information she's demanding. "Brazil."

"Have you made arrangements for Curt's family?" I hang my head at the mention of Catfish. He's been with us for a couple of years, but I didn't know him very well. He did a great job for the club and always gave a hundred percent in the field, but he's kept to himself, preferring to be alone when he was home rather than hang out with the other guys.

I shake my head. "I was so worried about Georgia. I haven't had the chance."

"She's fine," Em assures me. "Amelia is fine."

I clear my throat. Georgia and I have been butting heads since she was old enough to talk back, but the pain and disappointment in her eyes today was something new altogether.

"She hates me for putting him in that situation," I mutter.

"She doesn't hate you."

"If he doesn't make it," I begin but have to pause and release a shuttering breath. "She'll never speak to me again."

I let the heat of my wife's warm hand seep through my shirt over my heart. She's strength and faith where I'm the realist in the family. I know more than her what Hound is facing.

"He'll be fine," she assures me, and the calm in her voice almost makes me believe it, too. "But you have to go."

"Go?" I shake my head. "I'm not going anywhere. My place is here with my family."

"And I want you here, but Georgia needs you in Brazil. Your men need you. They lost a friend today."

"I've made arrangements for Shadow and Dom to head down. Plane leaves in an hour."

She takes a step back, her hand falling from my chest. "Georgia needs you to go to him because she can't. You're the only one she trusts to tell her the truth."

"I can't leave her. Can't leave you."

"I've got everything under control here." Reaching up on her tiptoes, she brushes her lips across my cheek. "Don't miss your plane."

I cling to her, not happy one bit about leaving her and Georgia here, but hating what I'm going to find when I step foot on Brazilian soil.

"I'll call you when we land," I promise, and walk away without looking back.

If I focus on the pain and fear she's trying desperately to hide, I'll never be able to leave her.

***

Thirteen hours later our boots are on the ground. Two hours after that, we're heading into the hospital. I hate the simplicity of the place. The smell, the grime clinging to the corners and along the walls are telling of just how different this place is compared to hospitals in the States.

Scooter is smoking a cigarette, tossing one away and lighting a new one as we approach. The tremble in his hands and the devastated look in his eyes make my gut clench. We spoke when we landed, but haven't had an update since.

"Hey," he says, face ashen and voice rough and filled with emotion. "They've started the paperwork to release Catfish's body."

I nod, fighting the urge to wrap him in a hug. He reminds me of Shadow's son Griffin, so young and having seen so much evil in his short life.

"And Hound?" Last I heard he was out of surgery, but the doctors refused to consider him stable since he coded twice during his operation.

He nods, swallowing thickly and refusing to meet my eyes. "He's hooked up to a vent. The break-through round hit him in his chest. By the time they were able to operate on his stubborn ass, the bullet had moved into his lung. He's holding on, but they won't let us back to see him with our own eyes."

"Fuck that," Shadow growls beside me. "Let them try to tell me I can't see one of my men."

Scooter gives a small smile and flicks his cigarette butt into the grass. "I was hoping one of you would say that."

"Where are the other guys?" I ask.

"Rocker and Grinch are inside." He hitches a thumb over his shoulder. "Davy and Dragon are with local authorities trying to sort this shit out."

All I have to do is look at Dom, and he's headed back to the SUV to help Davy and Dragon with the mess this failed mission has created.

"Let's go talk to the doctor," I urge as I walk past him.

He tosses his newly lit cigarette away.

"How's Gi-Georgia?"

"She's good. The baby is perfect."

"He refused to go into surgery. Refused to let them touch him with anything but monitors until he talked to her."

It may end up costing him his life.

"I would've done the exact same thing if it was Em," I say instead, knowing it's the truth. It's then that I realize Hound is the best thing to happen to my daughter. If he loves her as much as I love Emmalyn, there's no way I can do anything but give them both my blessing. Hell, I know he'd do anything in his power, including fighting with Satan or Saint Peter to get back to her.

Reassured, I slap Scooter on the back as we climb off of the elevator. "Now point me in the direction of this doctor that has no idea who he's refusing."

Chapter 38

Gigi

Trying to roll over only forces a pained gasp from my dry lips.

"Easy," I hear Mom say from beside me.

"I hurt," I grumble, hoping she can take the pain away just as she has all of my life.

"Childbirth is the most beautiful and most painful thing you'll ever go through." Her voice is soft; her hands warm on my shoulder.

"Amelia?" My eyes flutter open but slam shut against the brightness of the room.

"She's perfect," Mom assures me. "Waiting to meet you."

The reminder that I haven't met my daughter yet is like a knife to my heart. Both for the missed opportunity and the realization of what happened right after her birth.

"Jameson," I sob. It's not a question because I can feel in my soul that he's gone. There's an emptiness in my chest that only he was ever able to fill. That spot is now cold and desolate.

"Shh." The calming hand my mother runs in circles along my arm doesn't bring the comfort it did in childhood. This isn't a scraped knee or harsh words spoken on the playground by mean girls who want to hurt my feelings. This pain is real and so acute I can hardly catch my breath.

"Please calm down," my mother begs.

Calm isn't something I can manage, and I grow angrier at the ridiculous request.

"They'll sedate you again."

My breath hitches, head aching with misery I have no idea how I'll ever survive it.

"Please." I don't know what I'm begging for, but I'm certain that if she had the power to take it all away, she'd do it in the blink of an eye.

"Shhh." The hand, the circles, the energy so strong I know it's something only a mother can possess for a hurting child, is almost enough to settle me. Almost enough to make me believe everything will be okay.

Almost.

But, how can it? How can a day so beautiful be endured when it's also filled with tragedy? Filled with such loss that the good, the beautiful is dulled like a consolation prize.

"He promised me forever, but now he's gone."

Saying the words out loud gut me. Acknowledging my truth rips my soul to shreds.

"No, baby girl. He's not gone."

Her assurance does nothing for me. Lying only makes my anguish sharper, like razors on my skin.

"He's out of surgery," she continues. "He's hurt, but he's not gone."

I shake my head, hope the last thing I need. Hope is only going to make things worse, and in this moment I hate her saying the words. I hate my dad for putting us in this situation. I hate the world for taking away the only man I could ever love.

"I know you don't agree," my mother says, and it's only now that I realize she's walked away.

Chills run up my arm where her comforting touch was only seconds ago.

"Wires and a ventilator are better than her being sedated again because she thinks he's dead."

I open my eyes, head tilting to the side to watch my mother as she paces near the door. I've never heard her use that tone with anyone, much less my father who I assume she's speaking with.

"Now, Diego," she snaps before pulling the phone from her ear and hitting the end button.

Her phone chimes and the familiar sound of a Facetime call makes my heart rate spike.

I shake my head as she walks closer. She's holding the phone away from her chest as if it's a bomb she's terrified is going to detonate in her hands.

"They've labeled him critical stable," she warns. "He looks like hell, but he's not gone."

"This is a bad idea," my dad says from the other end of the call.

"Daddy?" I say as I reach for the phone.

When I turn it to face me, I'm met with the warm eyes of my father. His face softens, the angry, agitated look I expected nowhere on his face.

"Hey, baby girl." I'm comforted by the nickname, calmed by the kind baritone of his voice. "I hear I'm a granddad."

I nod, my voice getting stuck in my throat. I'm a mother, one who's not even met her daughter yet. I'm failing as a parent already, which only proves the things I've been telling Jameson for the last several months as reality sets in.

"I want you to know, before I turn the phone around, that it looks worse than it actually is."

I shake my head. "Please don't lie to me."

"He's holding on," Dad assures me.

"I can handle it," I lie. The tight smile I attempt fails as tears roll down my cool cheeks.

"I love you, baby girl."

His words echo in my ears as the phone shifts before landing on a man I hardly recognize. The beard is familiar, but his color is off. His size, once so huge and powerful, is diminished in the hospital bed. The cords and wires connecting to his ashen body are nothing like I imagined while preparing myself for this moment.

I begin to cry, my body shaking so hard I drop the phone. My mother, being the strongest woman I know, grabs the phone and holds it in front of me. I ignore the tremble in her hands that matches mine.

"Listen, Georgia."

I shake my head, unprepared to hear my dad make promises he's unable to keep. I can't bear assurances and empty words.

"Listen," he urges again. "Hear the beep?"

My sobs quieten as I try to focus on what he's referencing.

"That's his heart monitor," he explains as the consistent *beep, beep, beep* is heard through the phone. "It's strong, steady. He's in an induced coma because of the vent. His lung was punctured. He's not dying, baby girl. He's healing."

"H-he's going to live?"

"I have every faith that he will," Dad answers.

"Promise me, daddy." Tears brim my eyes again. "Please."

"Baby girl." I can hear the emotion in his voice, but I don't miss the fact that he never utters the words. He never tells me everything is going to be okay. How can he?

"Have faith," he urges.

"Leave your phone," Mom instructs.

I watch as the phone is propped against something.

"Love you, baby girl," Dad says before I hear the click of a door. Silence, other than the beep of his monitor and the rush of air every time the machine pushes air into my love's lungs, fills the room around me.

"I'm going to have the nurses bring Amelia in," Mom says as she lifts my hand and wraps my fingers around the phone.

"Thank you." I hope she knows the two words are meant for everything she's done.

My eyes close against the warmth I feel on her lips as she brushes them against my forehead, but then they focus back on the man in the hospital bed.

When the door clicks closed as my mother leaves the room, the begging begins. I beg him to live, to fight, to hold on for me, for Amelia. I make promises I'm not even sure I can keep, but have every intention of trying to manage. I promise to let him do dirty things to me. Swear he can punish me for missteps I haven't even committed yet if only he'll wake up.

He doesn't.

I know he's unable. After Dad's explanation, I know he's physically unable to fight against the drugs they have pumped into his body so he can get better, but that doesn't keep me from selfishly hoping he will. It doesn't keep me from watching him so intently that my eyes begin to hurt because blinking means losing a second of time with him.

A whimper from the doorway is the only thing strong enough to make me refocus. A nurse with a smile too bright for the situation pushes a small cart topped with a plastic basket into the room. Pink and wiggly is all I can see until Mom sidesteps the nurse and reaches inside to pull Amelia out.

I smile back at the phone, hoping the noise was enough to make Jameson wakeup.

"You're missing the most precious moment," I chide as if he's aware of his surroundings. "I know you hate missing this."

"Shh-shh-shh," Mom coos as she walks closer.

"I'll hold her twice as tight until you can have her in your arms," I promise.

I whimper right along with Amelia as Mom pulls the phone from my hand and replaces it with the most perfect angel I've seen.

"Don't," I say as I settle the little bundle in my arm and reach for the phone with my free hand.

"I'm just propping it up," she assures me as she rolls the table closer.

I watch the screen of the phone as she settles it against the pink water pitcher. I don't fight the smile that crests my lips when I split my time between watching the screen and looking down at the miracle we made.

"She's perfect," I whisper to Jameson as Amelia calms, her lips jutting out as she falls asleep.

"She's got his eyes," Mom says. "I imagine her chin is his as well, but I've never seen him without a beard."

"She's a mix of everything good from both of us."

Tears fall from my eyes transforming the spots on the blanket from light pink to fuchsia.

"I'll give you guys some time," Mom says after another brush against my head. She repeats the action to Amelia's tiny head before backing away. "I'm going to have to track down an extension cord and have Misty let Shadow know your dad will need to find one also."

"Thank you." I take a few seconds to look up at my mother. She nods, eyes still brimming with tears.

"There is a waiting room full of people waiting to see you and meet Amelia."

"I'm not ready," I tell her with my eyes back on my daughter.

"Let me know when you are." The softness in her voice is unexpected. I anticipated her telling me not to be selfish, to urge me to consider other people's feelings. "Ivy is chomping at the bit to get back here."

"She's here?" How long was I out?

Mom nods. "She jumped on the first plane. Isabella is out there as well."

I begin to tremble. "I want to see them both."

Mom glances back at the phone before her eyes meet mine again. "It will be hard for Isabella to see him like that. Maybe after you end the video?"

I shake my head. "The video stays until he wakes up."

"That could be days, Georgia." It doesn't come out as chastisement, only her acknowledging the length of time in case my hopes were up for immediate gratification.

"I know. You can explain to her, just like Dad did for me. She'll want to see him."

Mom nods even though she seems unsure.

"Give me ten minutes alone, and then you can send them back."

I don't bother to look at the door when it clicks softly behind my mother.

"Your sister and aunt are going to meet you soon," I tell Amelia's sleeping form.

My fingers trace the small pout of her lips, trailing down her tiny chin.

"Everything is going to be just fine."

My eyes sting as I lie to my daughter for the very first time.

Chapter 39

Hound

"Fuck." That's what I try to say, but even to my own ears I know it comes out as nothing but a garble before I start coughing.

My body hurts. Every fucking inch of it, as if I've been set on fire and then pelted with shards of glass.

"It's okay," a deep voice assures me.

I want to grab whoever it is by the throat for spewing shit he has no idea about. The pain radiates from every joint, every muscle. I cough, and the agony increases tenfold.

"Jesus," I hiss.

"You had a punctured lung," an unfamiliar voice says as harsh hands press down on my shoulders. It's only then that I realize I've been fighting. What, I'm not certain, but the only cognizant thought I can manage is to move, to get away from the fire burning over every inch of my skin.

"I'm burning," I scream. "Get me away from the flames."

"It's the morphine burning off."

"Hound." I stiffen at the sound of Kincaid's voice. "Calm the fuck down."

"Hurts," I mutter. "Make it stop."

A deep chuckle meets my ears "Don't be a pussy."

"Daddy!" I freeze at the sound of Gigi's voice.

I try to force my eyes open, but they don't budge, the heaviness of them too much to fight against.

Everything comes rushing back. The pleading in Gigi's eyes as I begged her to push, the first cries of my baby girl as she entered the world. The pain of losing a friend in a shitty country when the mission went to hell. The harsh burn as the bullet penetrated my vest.

"Daddy?" Her voice is pleading this time, her fear enough to calm me even with the scorching heat from my injuries.

"Keep talking to him, Georgia," Kincaid commands.

"Please," I beg as the hands holding me down loosen up.

"Our daughter is beautiful," Gigi assures me with a sob. "She has your gorgeous eyes."

I smile through the pain.

"Mr. Rawley?" It's the unfamiliar voice once again. It's marked with such a heavy accent, I know I'm still in South America. "I'm Dr. Cardoso. I need you to open your eyes."

I nod but wince when fire lights up my chest. Attempting to take a deep breath, an attempt to gain the strength and courage only leads to more coughing, heavier hands against my shoulders.

"I'm here, Jameson. Stay calm. Do it when you're ready." I want her hands on me. I want to spank her ass for traveling to this shitty country with my newborn daughter.

"Take it easy, Dad."

"Izzy?" What the fuck is she doing in Brazil?

I hate the harsh weakness in my voice. I know what I'm trying to say, but my ears only register a gruff jumble of sounds.

"Eyes," the doctor urges again.

I fight the pain. I fight the heaviness until my eyes open to the smallest of slits, only when I shift my head searching for Gigi and Isabella, all I find is Kincaid's smiling mug and the mocha latte skin of a man I've never seen before.

"Where?" I begin before I have to take a shallow breath and swallow past the sandpaper filling my mouth. "Where are my girls?"

"Still in New Mexico," Kincaid says before holding up his phone. "They're safe."

My eyes open wider, taking in the gorgeous site of Gigi, holding our daughter and Izzy sitting beside her, so half of her is in the frame.

"Hey, gorgeous," I whisper, my voice gaining strength at the sight of her.

She smiles wide even though tears mark her cheeks and her shoulders jerk with sobs.

"I've missed you," she finally manages.

"How I—"

"Almost two weeks," Kincaid says.

I look at him over the top of the phone before dropping my eyes back down to the screen. It's then that I notice the background. She's in my room in the clubhouse. Baby things we've collected surround her, lining the walls to the point that moving around in there is an impossibility.

"You deserve a castle, not a tiny room," I muse, more to myself than anyone in particular.

"Yes, she does," Kincaid agrees, but with humor rather than irritation in his voice.

"Why are you here?" I ask him, my eyes fluttering with exhaustion already.

"You've met my daughter, haven't you?" He smiles. "I was on a plane down here before I met my granddaughter. I knew she wouldn't have it any other way."

"Good man," I whisper.

"We've had you on video since the day Amelia was born," Izzy says, playfulness marking her tone.

Gigi smiles, a nod of her head confirming. "Why are you so obsessed with me?"

She laughs, and the sound washes over me, precious enough to make some of the pain in my body dissipate.

"Because I love you. I miss you, and I need you to get better so you can come home and do the nighttime diaper changes like you promised."

"I can't wait," I answer honestly.

"You owe me a million dollars in data usage," Kincaid adds from my bedside.

I smile, wondering if he knows about the bonus Merlin had deposited in my bank account after shit went down in D.C. months ago. I'd offer it gladly if seeing me, even in a comatose state calmed even an ounce of Gigi's fear.

"So sleepy," I pant. "Hurts so badly."

"He needs his rest," the doctor says. "Mr. Rawley, I'm going to give you pain medicine in your IV. You need to rest."

I shake my head. Sleep, although I can tell it's what I need, is the very last thing I want. I know the deed has been done as my pain numbs to something more bearable and my eyes grow even heavier.

"Love you," I whisper before darkness beckons me and I give into the call.

***

"Goddammit," I grumble as Kincaid's strong arms help ease me off of the bed.

It's been days since I first woke, but even with threats of violence, Dr. Cardoso won't release me until I can walk on my own and am able to get the spirometer up to the fucking smiley face and hold it there for five seconds. He's an evil bastard, and I know he's been sent to do nothing but fucking torture me.

"Today's the day," Kincaid says in an unfamiliar timbre.

"Since when did you go all soft and nice," I hiss, but make it to standing.

"I miss my fucking wife," he complains. "And Georgia says I can't leave until we can make that fucking plane ride together."

I chuckle, the pain not as acute in my chest.

"I can ride on a fucking plane. Let's just leave today." I try for conspiratorial, but the words rush out with over-exertion just from fucking standing near my bed.

"And have your lung collapse mid-flight?" he growls. "I promised her I'd deliver you safely, not some fucking corpse, but if you could speed up your recovery, that'd be awesome."

"Doing my best here, Gramps."

His grip tightens on my arms. "I told you not to fucking call me that."

"Make you feel old?"

"Says the guy who can't get up and take a piss without coughing up a lung and taking a two-hour nap afterward."

He's such an asshole, but for some reason, I'm smiling.

"I can't wait to get home. Can't wait to hold my baby girl. Can't wait to press my lips against your baby girl. Feel her skin against my lips."

I wince when his fingers dig into me. "I'll fucking drop you right now," he threatens.

I laugh, not only at getting a rise out of him, but realizing we've already made it to the bathroom. It's taken half the time it did yesterday. The day before that he had to practically carry me in here.

"Wanna give me a hand?" I ask.

"Fuck no," he grumbles, but doesn't back away completely, still afraid I'll fall from the exhaustion I've always felt when I make it this far.

"Gigi would hold my cock if she were here," I tease, but the growl he releases makes me wonder if I took things too far.

"Say one more thing like that about my daughter, and you won't have a cock to hold."

I laugh when I hear him mutter 'asshole' as he closes me in the small bathroom.

Even though I know he's pissed, he's waiting outside of the door when I pull it open.

"I'm ready to go home," I lament as he helps me back into the bed.

He clears his throat, and I expect him to rage on me once I'm settled on the mattress, but I look up to find softness in his eyes I've only ever seen when he looks at Emmalyn.

"I wanted to say thank you."

"For making you feel old?" I smile, trying to lighten the mood.

"For living. For loving my daughter more than I ever could've asked for." Emotion clogs his throat, and he clears it twice before talking again. "Georgia would've never forgiven me if you didn't survive."

"I could never leave her. Couldn't leave Amelia or Izzy either. I had no other choice. Surviving was the only choice I had."

"You have my blessing." He smiles at me. It's weak but not in a bitter way. It's a smile I imagine I'd have when the day comes with either Izzy or Amelia when I have to trust their heart and happiness to another man.

"So I'm getting married now?" I joke, but warmth wraps around me at the thought of his daughter having my last name.

"I don't think Georgia will have it any other way."

I smile, trying to hide the fact that I'd proposed to Gigi shortly after I told her I loved her the first time, but she refused. She slapped me and told me that there was no way she was marrying me when she was a 'fat cow.' Her words, not mine. I spanked her ass until it was bright red for insulting herself while my child grew in her womb. She came four times that night, and I never broached the subject again.

"Well, there's only one way to find out, and it starts with that." I point to the spirometer on the side table.

Kincaid smiles and hands over the device that holds my future in its little plastic grasp.

"Get to work, Hound. I need my wife." I smile at him before my lips hit the mouthpiece. "Say one dirty word about my daughter, and I'm on the next plane out of here without you."

"I wasn't," I argue, but my smile never leaves my mouth.

"You were, too." His words are harsh, but the twitch in his lips tells me he wants to smile. "I can't handle it."

"She's a grown woman," I remind him. "She's a mother."

"I still can't handle it." His head shakes.

I laugh as he backs a few feet away from the bed.

"You have to let her grow up." Getting him worked up over Gigi is the second-best thing to seeing Gigi on video chat.

"Yeah?" His grin grows. "So now would be a good time to tell you about Izzy's boyfriend?"

"Bullshit," I hiss. "She's too fucking young."

"Then I won't tell you that he's been to the clubhouse several times."

I groan when I sit up straight in the bed. My body is so fucking tight from lying here for weeks.

"Or that he stays the night, on the couch of course."

"I'll fucking kill you." The gleam in his eye is unreadable.

"You'll have to catch me first." He angles his head toward the forgotten spirometer in my hands.

His chuckle as he leaves and the little, yellow piece of plastic floating in the spirometer is all I can hear.

Chapter 40

Gigi

"Where have you been!" I snap as soon as Facetime connects.

I frown down at the blacked-out screen and feel bad for waking Amelia with my raised voice. I cradle her, rocking her gently until she sighs and falls back asleep.

"That's a silly question, gorgeous. Where else would I be?"

I love hearing his voice, but hate that I can't see his face. This last week, reception has been spotty at best and more than a few of our video calls have been just a black screen when I wanted nothing more than to see his bearded face.

"You haven't called all day," I grumble. It's now after midnight, but that doesn't matter. He's been upset he's missed so much the last couple of weeks, he has me call when I wake up at night and nurse. He wants me to call when I bathe Amelia, when I miss him. That means I'm constantly calling. Dad warned me that he needs his rest to gain his strength so he can come home, but he insists I call him. Who am I to deny him?

"I've been resting." Only now do I hear the exhaustion in his voice.

"That's it," I say with renewed energy. "I'm coming to Brazil. Amelia is three weeks old now, and I read online about people who travel with newborns all the time. We'll be fine."

He chuckles, the sound warming me and sounding closer than it has in weeks.

"I miss you," I complain.

"Going to Brazil would be a waste, Gigi."

"I need to be with you," I argue. "I need to hold you, kiss your lips, and trim that out of control beard."

He laughs again. "You love my beard."

"I love everything about you. Going to Brazil is what I need." I look down at our sleeping daughter. "Amelia needs to meet her daddy."

"You sure you're willing to put her in my arms?" I nod, a lone tear rolling down my cheek. "I hear you're spoiling her by holding her all the time."

"Babies are supposed to be cuddled." I trace her lips.

"She looks so good in your arms." I smile wide, grateful that even though I can't see him, that he can see us.

"She'd look even better in yours," I counter.

"You sure?"

I jerk my head up at the shuffling sound near the door, and my breathing stops. Worn, a little tattered, but still as handsome as ever, Jameson is watching me from the open doorway.

"You're here?" Sobs wrack my body as I sit, unable to make my body cooperate and go to him.

"I'm here."

He doesn't bother with his phone as it drops to his feet when he closes the distance that's been between us for far too long.

All but collapsing he falls to the bed, back against the headboard.

"You're here," I repeat, stunned but happier than I've ever been.

I turn to him, head resting against his hard chest as I cry. Every second since he's been gone has felt like a million years. It's been a lifetime since I could touch the warmth of his body, feel his heart beating in sync with mine, that I honestly never thought I'd be able to feel those things again.

Amelia wiggles between us before the room fills with her shrill cries. I move back, allowing her room and giving Jameson the chance to see his daughter unaided by technology for the very first time.

I rock her, trying to calm her as his rough finger trails softly down her tiny cheek.

"She's beautiful." I nod in agreement. "She looks like you."

Fingers trace over her full head of hair, and my tears are renewed as she blinks up at him, instinctively knowing that her family is together and safe.

"You should've told me you were coming home," I complain. "I would've cleaned up. Would've bathed."

Personal hygiene and trying to impress people with my looks hasn't even been a consideration since being discharged from the hospital. At first, I was exhausted, from childbirth and wondering if Jameson was going to survive. After he woke up, I focused on him and taking care of Amelia. I'm exhausted, and even though I've had multiple offers of help from others, I've refused every one, knowing this is something I had to do on my own, if only to keep my mind and my hands busy.

His fingers tilt my chin up, bright green eyes finding mine. "You're beautiful." He watches my mouth, and that familiar tingle that's been absent for so long returns with a vengeance. "So beautiful."

A harsh breath rushes through my nose when his lips meet mine. Everything is apparent in his kiss. Love, lust, and a longing I'm suffering right along with him is evident in the grip of his fingers when his arm wraps around my back.

"Don't cry, gorgeous." His fingers sweep my cheeks, but they're only replaced by new ones.

"I've missed you so much." I've said it so many times in the past weeks, but it's only now, confessing it against his lips that the words aren't accompanied by a pain in my chest.

Amelia wiggles again, getting upset that she doesn't have his undivided attention.

"You're as needy as your momma," he coos down at her.

I laugh, a genuine laugh that fills the room for the first time since I came home. "You have no idea."

"You're here." We both look up to see Izzy standing in the doorway.

He opens his arms to her, and she runs right into them, apologizing when he winces.

With eyes squeezed tight, he holds her, rocking her back and forth in his embrace as she sobs into his neck. I look down at Amelia, giving them a moment when I see a tear break free from the corner of his eye.

"All of my girls are here." He clears his throat, but the emotion doesn't leave his face when Izzy pulls back and sits near his feet on the bed. He glances at all of us, spending long moments looking all of us in the eye before he focuses on Izzy. "Tell me about this boy that's been hanging around?"

"Huh?" Izzy looks as confused as I feel.

"The boy that followed you here from Arizona." She tilts her head to the side before her brows furrow, and she glances over at me.

"There's no boy, dad."

"Kincaid said—" He sighs before turning his eyes up to the ceiling. "I'm going to kill him."

"I'm so confused," I mutter.

His laugh fills the room even though it's not as strong as I remember. "Don't worry about it, gorgeous."

He presses a soft kiss to my forehead.

"I'm going to go back to sleep," Izzy says giving us each a hug and planting a soft kiss on Amelia's head. "I'll see you in the morning."

She lingers near the door, never taking her eyes off of her dad as if she's afraid he's going to be gone by the time she wakes.

"Get some rest, Iz. We'll see you in the morning."

She nods, trusting him and closes the door on the way out.

"I can't believe her mother let her come."

I don't respond, but it doesn't take long before I have to face the hot glare I feel on the side of my face.

"Don't look at me like that," I mutter when I face him. "She's eighteen now. She completed her last classes online. Passed every test. I urged her to go back home, but she refused."

"Gabby knows where she's at?"

I remain silent.

"Gigi?" I remain silent. "You may still be healing, but I will pink your ass."

At just the suggestion, my skin warms as if he's already taken his large hand to my ass. I bite my lip as I look up at him, and almost smile when his eyes heat.

"We'll get to that later," he promises. "Does Gabby know where she's at?"

"She knows that she's safe, but Izzy has been worried that they would come get her, so she turned off her cell phone and refused to give them the information."

He growls, but the warning doesn't do what he hopes because I'm not chastised, merely turned on with the anticipation of his wrath.

"She's still going to college in the fall," I say to appease him. "She just wants to spend the summer here."

"Damn right she's going to college," he mutters.

His irritated voice startles Amelia causing her to begin to cry.

"Oh, baby girl," he coos. "Don't cry."

"I imagine she's hungry," I explain when his soothing words don't calm her.

He watches with rapt attention as I lower the neck of my nightgown and raise her to my breast.

"So beautiful," he praises as his fingers toy with the curly hair at the nape of her neck.

I smile up at him, his eyes switching between the two of us like he can't go a second without seeing either of us.

"Marry me," he whispers.

"You ask now?" I try for irritated, but the light reflecting in his bright eyes makes it impossible. "While your daughter is nursing and my legs haven't seen a razor for the better part of a month?"

He smiles. "Marry me, and I'll shave you tomorrow so you can thank me."

"Thank you?" I squeak. "Thank you for what?"

He's given me everything, including the precious life that's suckling at my breast, but petulant has always been my thing, and I don't intend to change now.

"Thank me for the life I'm going to provide for you. Thank me for the orgasms I may allow you to have."

I narrow my eyes. "May allow?"

He smiles wide. "And I'll thank you in return." He kisses my lips, but it's only a sweeping brush. "I'll thank you for all the babies you're going to give me. Thank you for making the house I'll build a home. I'll thank you every day for loving me, for making me the happiest man in the world. Marry me."

"On one condition," I barter. I smile when his eyebrow rises. The look he's giving me says he's left no room for compromise. "You can't deny my orgasms."

His head shakes back and forth. "Everything I just said, and that's what you focus on?"

Cupping his cheek with my free hand, I focus on his lips for a long minute before looking up in his eyes. "You'll love me, provide for me, and give me more babies even if I don't marry you. I'll make our house a home, and I'll love you until the day I die even if we don't marry, but orgasm denial is brutal, and I won't sign on the dotted line unless you promise."

"How about," he says inching his mouth closer to mine. "How about, I promise not to let you go to bed at night without letting you come?"

I tilt my head, already knowing he can tease me all day long, torture me, tie me up so I can't finish myself off. Hell, he's done it before. But the one time, he put me to bed with my body on fire and my orgasm just out of reach, was one of the most brutal things I ever suffered. Waking up to his mouth and soul-clenching orgasm made it worth it, but it's not something I want to ever happen again.

"Deal," I breathe.

He kisses me again, tongue searching and sweeping against mine until I'm breathless when he pulls away. "I'm still going to pink your ass for taking so long to answer."

"I can't wait," I whisper against his lips.

We both look down at our beautiful daughter, and for the first time in my entire life, I feel complete.

***

I scrunch my eyes against the noise.

"Baby girl," the hiss from the door way echoes around the room again. "Psssst."

I roll my head, face rubbing on Jameson's chest hair. Snuggling deeper, I didn't realize how much I missed his touch and the warmth of him in my arms. I missed all of him. I smile, running my hand down his abs to the thickness of his cock. Even in his sleep he's virile and ready for me.

"Georgia Leigh!"

My head snaps to the door as I jerk my hand away and Jameson jolts under me. Amelia begins to whimper in her bassinet.

My dad, brow furrowed stands in the open doorway, but there's a soft smile playing at his lips.

"I haven't had the chance to hold her yet." He tilts his head in Amelia's direction. "It's almost noon. I've been waiting for you to wake up."

I clear my throat, embarrassed that my dad caught me touching Jameson's cock. "Give me ten minutes and I'll bring her out to you."

Still asleep, Jameson flexes his hips, no doubt searching for the warmth of my palm.

Dad's smile fades away completely. "I'll give you five."

The door closes softly behind him, and my body shakes from a chuckle coming from Jameson's chest. "So I guess a blow job is out of the question."

I swat at his stomach. "Maybe later."

Pulling me closer with his lips against my temple, I allow a few more seconds in his embrace.

"I bet just the feel of your lips wrapped around me would be enough," he bargains.

My hand wanders from the crisp hairs on his chest, past his navel to the thickness straining against the cool sheets. "Maybe the first time," I coo. "But I'm going to take my time with you. Remind you why you love me."

He groans when my soft fingers trace the throbbing vein along his erection.

"I don't need a reminder for that."

Pouting when I get out of the bed, he watches with hooded eyes as I tug off my nightgown and get dressed. By the time I'm out of the bathroom, he's already changed Amelia's diaper and redressed her.

"You're a natural," I tell him, running my hand down his cheek.

"She's perfect." He holds her close, kissing her forehead and sniffing the top of her head.

"Dad's waiting," I remind him. "Why don't you jump in the shower? I may be able to get him to watch her for an hour or so while I take care of that tent in your pants."

Laughing, he hands her over, but doesn't move away until I'm thoroughly kissed and breathless.

"Can't wait," he whispers in my ear, slapping my ass as I walk away.

I find Dad sitting at one of the kitchen tables drinking a cup of coffee. The second I cross the threshold his hands are out, fingers flexing in a demanding action for me to turn her over.

I watch, unshed tears brimming my eyes as my father does exactly what Jameson did just moments ago. He kisses her and breathes in her scent right from that delicate spot on the top of her head.

"I didn't understand my childhood and why you and Mom were so protective of us until her," I confess. "I want to wrap her in bubble wrap and hide her from the world."

"I still want to wrap you in bubble wrap," he says without taking his eyes off of Amelia. "And I want to do the same for her."

"I was horrible growing up. I fought you at every turn. Did things just to upset you, when all you were trying to do was make sure I was safe." I lean my head on his shoulder and look down at my amazing little girl. "I pray she's less like me and more like Ivy."

He turns, kissing the crown of my head. "You turned out just fine."

I swallow thickly, the emotions that I've been bombarded with in the weeks since giving birth are right on the edge, the slightest things making me tear up. Today is no different.

"I got lucky. Jameson and Amelia are the best things that could've happened for me."

He shifts, holding Amelia close to his chest and wrapping his arm around my shoulder. "I feel the same about you girls and your mom. Now I have this precious little one to protect, and I couldn't be happier. It gives me purpose."

"I'll take all the help I can get." My life has made a complete one-eighty in the last year. The old Georgia Leigh Anderson would've told him to fuck off and let me raise my daughter how I see fit. Now, as a mother, I know that there isn't a thing I wouldn't do keep my family safe. Motherhood doesn't allow for stubbornness and digging your feet in just to spite others.

"She looks tiny compared to you, grandpa."

I look up, smiling as Jameson makes his way into the kitchen.

"Can't believe your ugly ass made such a cute little girl, Hound," Dad teases back. "Good thing Amelia looks like her mother."

I expect Jameson to argue, but instead he leans in kissing my lips and looks over at my dad. "I couldn't agree more."

I breathe in the familiar smell of his skin straight from the shower. He didn't towel off completely and there are still droplets of water clinging to the tips of his hair and the back of his neck.

"Think you can keep an eye on her for an hour or so?" Jameson must be more eager than I am if he's asking this of my father.

My dad looks between us before narrowing his eyes at the man by my side.

"No." I pull my head back, shocked at his answer.

Jameson chuckles beside me. "Cockblocker," he mutters but there's laughter in the word.

Something in their relationship has changed over the weeks they were in Brazil together. The tension that existed before is no longer around.

"Come on," Jameson whispers in my ear before tugging on my hand to help me stand.

"He said no," I hiss at him as we get closer to the doorway.

"He wouldn't let go of her right now if I had a gun to his head," he assures me.

Looking over my shoulder at my dad, I find him smiling and looking down at Amelia as if nothing else in the world matters. His phone rings. It startles me to the point of jumping, but he, calm as ever, just shifts so he can pull the ringing device from his jeans.

"Kincaid," he snaps when the call connects.

I watch as his brow furrows with whatever news he's receiving on the other end. The set of his shoulders goes from relaxed to rigid.

"He did what?" His jaw ticks, and before I can go to them, Jameson is already pulling Amelia from his arms. He releases her immediately before standing from the table.

"I appreciate your discretion in the matter." He nods, even though the guy on the other line can't see him. "I'll let Morrison know."

Shadow?

My dad ends the call.

"Oh God," I whisper. "Has something happened to Griffin?"

My heart is thudding, crashing against my ribs so fast my hands are already trembling.

"Tell me he's not dead," I beg, unable to respond to Jameson's around my shoulder.

"He's not dead," Dad answers as he storms toward the back door leading to the houses. "But he may be after Shadow is done with his ass."

I hear him mutter something about selling drugs on base before the door snaps shut with a bang. Amelia begins to cry hysterically, and as much as I want to follow him to get the details, my duties and responsibilities rest solely on the little girl currently throwing a fit in my arms.

What do you think?
Join my group and let's talk about it!!
Marie James Stalkers

More From Marie James
Marie James Facebook: Marie James
Author Group: Author Marie James' Stalkers
Twitter: @AuthrMarieJame
Instagram: author_marie_james
Newsletter SignUp: HERE
Reader Email Share: HERE

Crowd Pleaser
Spring 2018

You know those love stories you read about? The ones where the heroine remains untouched, virgin-like, until she meets the man of her dreams? The stories where she's always in the shadows, always on the outside, no one knowing her name until she meets her one and only? A shy glance across the room at her first ever college party captivates the man she'll soon fall in love with?

This story isn't that.

In my story, everyone who's anyone has seen the heaviness of my tits. They've all heard the soft moan I make when a man slides inside. They've all heard my whimpers, heard me begging for more.

My name is Randi Simms.

And I'm a Crowd Pleaser.

Macon

Tossing a middle finger to Macon, Georgia as I made my way to Nashville was always the dream. Sing country music, go on tour, top the charts—with my popularity growing every day, I was on my way.

But then a gust of wind blew up your skirt, and those white cotton panties had me hooked. I didn't know your name, and you turned down every attempt I tried to throw your way. But I knew you were different, even though you told me I was the same.

"Friends" is what you offered, and I played by your rules, but, Adelaide Hatfield, you have to know, from that day, it was only you.

I just hope I can make you see how much you mean to me before we both drown in the sorrow of what heartbreak can truly be.

We Said Forever

Rock bottom.

They say the only way to go from there is up, but what is "up" when you're born into someone else's rock bottom?

At ten, football became my first love. It's what got me out of the house away from my self-destructive family. My love for football landed me at Las Vegas University with a full ride scholarship, and the orange on my jersey was my favorite color...until my eyes landed on the red dress Fallyn wore the night we met.

At twenty-one, I jumped off the cliff into the unknown the second Fallyn McIntyre danced in my arms at a party. I had the greatest girl in the world and the opportunity to play college ball every Saturday. My rock bottom was looking up, thanks to my two first loves.

Parties, sex, and football—life was perfect. But one drink too many, and my world came crashing down. When I chose pills over my second love, my head told me it was the best decision I ever made. The pills keep me warm and protect me from the distance Fallyn created. Percs don't judge me. They make me feel alive.

Threes.

They say the best things come in threes, but one leads to a stable future, one is my salvation, and the other drags me to hell—a hell I'd willingly burn in for eternity...if it weren't for my second love.

More Than a Memory

"You're gorgeous. Even better looking than the day I fell in love with you."

The words are a constant reminder of what true love is. Olivia Dawson's alarm goes off at the same time every day and she disappears into her room to hear Duncan's voice, see his face, miss him even more for being untouchable. Olivia loves with her entire heart, and her love for Duncan is unmatched, but there's something about her new roommate she just can't seem to ignore—no matter how hard she tries.

"I miss you so much."
"Can't be more than I miss you."

The words are a constant reminder of how unavailable Olivia is, and Bryson Daniels isn't one for competition off the baseball field, but since the moment he knocked on the door to his new apartment and his roommate "Ollie" wasn't who he expected, he can't help but consider bending a few of his rules—even if it means heeding to Olivia's.

"I love you, sweet cheeks. Chat with you later?"

Bryson hears the conversations through the paper thin walls, but there's a pain inside Olivia he can't seem to walk away from. He vows to be there for her when the voice on the other side of the computer inevitably breaks her heart, but will he ever be able to compete with someone who's more than a memory?

Hale Series
Coming to Hale

The only time she trusted someone with her heart, she was just a girl; he betrayed her and left her humiliated. Since then, Lorali Bennett has let that moment in time dictate her life.

Ian Hale, sexy as sin business mogul, has never had more than a passing interest in any particular woman, until a chance encounter with Lorali, leaves a lasting mark on him.

Their fast-paced romance is one for the record books, but what will happen when Ian's secrets come to light? Especially when those secrets will cost her everything she spent years trying to rebuild.

Begging for Hale

Alexa Warner, an easy going, free spirit, has never had a problem with jumping from one man to the next. She likes to party and have a good time; if the night ends in steamy sex that's a bonus. She's always sought pleasure first and never found a man that turned her down; until Garrett Hale. Never in her life was she forced to pursue a man, but his rejection doesn't sit well with her. Alexa aches for Garrett, his rejection festering in her gut. The yearning for him escalating until she is able to seduce him, taste him.

Garrett Hale, a private man with muted emotions, has no interest in serious relationships. Having his heart ripped out by his first love, he now leaves a trail of one night stands in his wake. Mutually satisfying sex without commitment is his newly adopted lifestyle. Alexa's constant temptation has his restraint wavering. The aftermath of giving into her would be messy; she is after all the best friend of his cousin's girlfriend, which guarantees future run-ins, not something that's supposed to happen with a one night stand.

Yet, the allure of having his mouth on her is almost more than he can bear. With hearts on the line, and ever increasing desire burning through them both, will one night be enough for either of them?

Hot as Hale

Innocent Joselyne Bennett loves her quiet life. As an elementary teacher, her days include teaching kids then going home to research fun science projects to add to her lesson plan. Her only excitement is living vicariously through her sister Lorali and friend Alexa Warner.

Incredibly gorgeous police detective Kaleb Perez was going through the motions of life. His position on the force as a narcotics detective forced him to cross paths with Josie after a shooting involving her friend. On more than one occasion Kaleb discretely tried to catch Josie's eye. On every occasion, he was ignored but when her hand is forced after a break-in at her apartment Josie and Kaleb are on a collision course with each other.

Formerly timid Josie is coaxed out of her shell by the sexy-as-sin Kaleb, who nurtures her inner sex-kitten in the most seductive ways, and replaces her inexperience with passionate need. The small group has overcome so much in such a short period of time, and just when they think they can settle back into their lives, they are forced back into the unknown.

Can Kaleb protect Josie from further tragedy? Can she let him go once the threat of danger is gone?

To Hale and Back

Just when things seem like they're getting back to normal and everyone is safe, drugs, money, and vengeance lead a rogue group into action, culminating in a series of events that leave one man dead and another in jail for a wide range of crimes, none of which he is guilty of.

This incredibly strong and close-knit group of six will be pushed to their limits when they are thrown into adversity. But can they come out unscathed? The situation turns dire when friendships and bonds are tested past the breaking point. Allegiances are questioned, and relationships may crumble.

Hale Series Box Set

Love Me Like That

Two strangers trapped together in a blizzard. One running from the past; one with no future. Two destinies collide.

London Sykes is on her own for the first time in her life after a sequence of betrayal and abuse. One man rescues her only to destroy her himself. An unfortunate accident lands her in a ditch only to be rescued by the most closed-off man she's ever met, albeit undeniably handsome.

Kadin Cole is at the cabin in the woods for the very first and the very last time. Since his grief doesn't allow for him to return home to a life he's no longer able to live alone, he's finally made what has been the hardest decision of his life. His plans change drastically when a beautiful woman in a little red car crashes into his life.

How can she trust another man? How could he ever love again? Will happenstance and ensuing sexual attraction be enough to heal two hearts enough that they can see in themselves what the other sees?

Teach Me Like That

Thirty-three, single, and loving life.

Construction worker by day and playboy by night. Kegan Cole has what many men can only dream about. A great job, incredible family, and more women fawning over him than he can count. What more could he ask for?

Lexi Carter spends her days teaching at a private school. Struggling to rebuild her life after tragedy nearly destroyed her, she doesn't have the time or energy to invest in any arrangement that could lead to heartbreak. That includes the enigmatic Kegan Cole whose arrogance and sex appeal arrive long before he enters a room.

It doesn't matter how witty, charming, and incredibly sexy he is. She plays games all day with her students and has no room in her life for games when it comes to men, and Kegan Cole has *'love them and leave them'* written all over his handsome bearded face.

When Lexi doesn't fall at his feet like every other woman before her, Kegan is forced off-script to pursue her because not convincing her to give in isn't an option.

How can a man who hates lies be compatible with a woman who has more secrets than she can count?

Can a man set in his playboy ways become the man Lexi needs? More importantly, does he even want to?

This is a full-length novel that has adult language and descriptive sex scenes. It is NOT a student/teacher book. Both main characters are consenting adults.

Cerberus MC
Kincaid Book 1

I am Emmalyn Mikaelson.

My husband, in a rage, hit me in front of the wrong person. Diego, or Kincaid to most, beat the hell out of him for it. I left with Diego anyway. Even though he could turn on me just like my husband did, I knew I had a better chance of survival with Diego. That was until I realized Kincaid could hurt me so much worse than my husband ever could. Physical pain pales in comparison to troubles of the heart.

I am Diego "Kincaid" Anderson.

She was a waitress at a bar in a bad situation. I brought her to my clubhouse because I knew her husband would kill her if I didn't. Now she has my protection and that of the Cerberus MC. I never expected her to become something more to me. I was in more trouble than I've ever been in before, and that's saying a lot considering I served eight years in the Marine Corps with Special Forces.

Kid: Cerberus MC Book 2

Khloe When Khloe Devaro's best friend and fiancé is lost to the war in Iraq, she's beyond distraught. Her intentions of joining him in the afterlife are thwarted by a Cerberus Motorcycle club member. Too young to do anything on her own, the only alternative she has now is to take Kid up on his offer to stay at the MC Clubhouse. As if that's not a disaster waiting to happen, but anything is better than returning to the foster home she's been forced to live in the last three years.

"Kid" Dustin "Kid" Andrews spent four years as a Marine; training, fighting, and learning how to survive the most horrendous of conditions. He never imagined that holding a BBQ fundraiser for a local fallen soldier would end up as the catalyst that turns his world upside down. Resisting his attraction for a girl he's not even certain is of legal age was easy, until he's forced to intervene when her intentions become clear. All his training is wasted as far as he's concerned, since none of that will help him when it comes to Khloe.

Will the self-proclaimed man-whore sleep with a woman in every country he visits as planned, or will the beautiful, yet feisty girl living down the hall throw a wrench in his plan?

Shadow: Cerberus MC Book 3

Morrison "Shadow" Griggs, VP of the Cerberus MC, is a force to be reckoned with. Women fall at his feet, willing to do almost anything for a night with him.

Misty Bowen is the exception. She's young and impressionable, but with her religious upbringing, she's able to resist Shadow's advances... for a while at least.

Never one to look back on past conquests, Shadow is surprised that he's intrigued by Misty, which only grows more when she seems to be done with him without a word.

Being ghosted by a twenty-one-year-old is not the norm where he's concerned, and the rejection doesn't sit right with him.

Life goes on, however, until Misty shows up on the doorstep of the Cerberus MC clubhouse with a surprise that rocks his entire world off of its axis.

With only the clothes on her back and the consequences of her lies and deceit, Misty needs help now more than she ever has. Alone in the world and desperate for help, she turns to the one man she thought she'd never see again.

Shadow would never turn his back on a woman in need, but his inability to forgive has always been his main character flaw. Unintended circumstances have cast Misty into his life, but will he have the ability to keep his distance when her situation necessitates a closeness he's never dreamed of having with a woman?

Dominic: Cerberus MC Book 4

Dominic Anderson knows exactly what he wants in life: simplicity, safety, and solidarity with his brothers. He's vowed to spend each day living his life exactly how he chooses since the day his wife betrayed him and his four year military career turned into twenty.

Returning home after retirement from the Marines, he's traded the sand in the Middle East for that of the New Mexico desert, Humvees for a motorcycle, and the comradery of men in uniform for the occasional woman at his feet.

Life was perfect until Makayla "Poison" Evans, Renegade MC Princess, knocked on his door, bruises on her face, neck, and arms, and no money to pay the cab driver. Pink hair, perfect body, and a mouth that Dom yearned to teach a million lessons, Mak asks more from him than he's conceded to a woman in decades.

She needs his help, his protection, and against his better judgment, she expects him to keep her secrets. Only her secrets are deadly, dangerous, and have the potential to start a war between two MCs.

At what point does safeguarding a woman become a betrayal to the men Dominic calls his family? More importantly, can he get back the sanctity of his home once Makayla is no longer in the picture, or will he be forever tainted by her poison?

Snatch: Cerberus MC Book 5

I've been Jaxon Donovan since the day I was born, obviously. My road name, Snatch, came years later due to my ability to literally snatch up any woman I set my sights on. I've always been a connoisseur of the opposite sex. Tall, short, thin, thick and juicy, my tastes knew no limitations.

I didn't think there was a limitation to my sexuality, and I found out just how true that actually was the night my best friend took it upon himself to take me in his mouth. Sure, there'd been close calls before, the slip of a hand or misplaced lips. With our propensity to share women, it's bound to happen. That fateful night, I was met with pure intention and an experience I never want to forget.

How do you explain to your friends, your brother's in arms, that your extremely active sexuality has led you to your best friend's doorstep? How do you admit, after twenty-six years of heterosexuality, that you're into something else?

I'll soon find out that what happens in the dark will always come to light.

Lawson: Cerberus 2.0 Book 1

My plan was as simple as they come... in theory. Show up at the Cerberus clubhouse and give dear old Dad a piece of my mind. What I didn't expect was being welcomed by the open arms of a father who had no idea I existed.

More importantly, I didn't anticipate HER. Delilah Donovan was a breath of fresh air. She would soon become my reason for wanting to become a better man, my reason for getting out of bed with a smile on my normally sneering face. But no matter how much I changed, she'd always be too good for a man like me.

It was over before it could even begin.

61245558R00128

Made in the USA
Columbia, SC
24 June 2019